Vintage Magic

Sally Anne Morris

HEADLINE PUBLISHING GROUP
An Hachette Livre UK Company
338 Euston Road
London NW1 3BH

www.littleblackdressbooks.com
www.headline.co.uk
www.hachettelivre.co.uk

First published in Great Britain in 2010 by
LITTLE BLACK DRESS
An imprint of HEADLINE PUBLISHING GROUP

A LITTLE BLACK DRESS paperback

1

Cataloguing in Publication Data is available from the British Library

ISBN 978 0 7553 5441 2

Typeset in Transit511BT by Avon DataSet Ltd,
Bidford-on-Avon, Warwickshire

Printed and bound in Great Britain by
Clays Ltd, St Ives plc

Headline's policy is to use papers that are natural, renewable and
recyclable products and made from wood grown in sustainable forests.
The logging and manufacturing processes are expected to conform to the
environmental regulations of the country of origin.

Here's to the Foxes for our adventures in vintage
and to Bob, Martin and all of the wonderful vixens
who shared the journey with MG X

As ever – many thanks to the ever-patient Claire B.

London. Capital of England. Style capital of the world. Birthplace of the Swinging Sixties and spiritual home of punk. A catwalk of fashion landmarks – Carnaby Street, Camden Market and Oxford Street, to name but a few. Host city for Harrods, Selfridges and Liberty's – iconic shopping emporiums housing quintessential British fashion labels such as Burberry, Vivienne Westwood, Lulu Guinness and Paul Smith; names as synonymous with red buses, beefeaters and tea at the Ritz as they are with impeccable styling, luxury, quality and timeless design.

But Rose Taylor does not live in London. Not any more. There were far too many bad associations with high rents and low-life cheating boyfriends. Well, just the one cheating husband-to-be, to be precise, and that was exactly why Rose swapped the nightlife of Soho and the native wildlife of Gorillaz, Monkeys (Arctic) and Peaches (Geldolf) for a place – to the left and down a bit on the AA map – best described as a World Heritage Site in south-west England.

This is why Rose left.

She had arrived home early, one grim, dreary February afternoon, having opted to 'work from home' (which everyone knows is a euphemism for turning on your computer but spending the afternoon surfing the far reaches of cable television and finding channels entirely devoted to fly-fishing) by feigning 'women's trouble' (which you can only really use on a male boss whose upper lip breaks into a sweat at the mention of anything vaguely gynaecological). She had been feeling that feeling that comes on dull days, when the summer feels a long way off and she could not pretend for another single minute that ISAs, balance transfers and tracker mortgages really did excite and interest her.

Even interesting, creative people (people like Rose), people who do amazing degree courses (like Rose) that involve blowing glass, making beautiful delicate models from paper and sculpting in felt – even they end up having to pay their way by doing jobs so far removed from being either interesting or creative that they should come with a government mental-health warning.

Just as Rose had been about to sling her bag into the coat cupboard, a noise – something like a furtive rifling – drew her attention to the bedroom. Armed only with an umberella (a retractable one at that), she had advanced cautiously forward, expecting to find a young hoody burglar ransacking her dressing-table only to find her fiancé Carl, in the flat they shared, in the bed they shared, with the friend they shared.

The very friend who would have been – had the bought, paid and planned-for June wedding gone ahead – her Chief Maid of (now indescribable dis-) Honour.

'It's not what it looks like,' he, the Potential Husband, had said. As if his rhythmic push-ups between the cellulite-dappled thighs of her once best, now worst friend ever, could, even in a parallel universe, be construed as anything else.

Had they somehow fallen? Tripped accidently as they were trying on their wedding outfits in the British tradition of Oh Vicar! Carry-on movie farce? Were they practising for the local am-dram version of *Eyes Wide Shut – the Musical* and were only going to tell her on the opening night as a big surprise? Maybe they were doing yoga or practising an obscure martial art?

Many times Rose wished that it could have been explained some other way. All the while, in fact, that she was packing away her belongings – the big-eye crying children pictures that he loathed, the collection of burlesque fliers and the dirty secret that was her entire collection of Danielle Steeles. Then began the mammoth task of clearing all of her clothes from the closet (the very one that her fiancé had obviously been hiding skeletons in for quite some time) before she then had to cancel all the wedding invitations.

'Weren't you just in the slightest bit tempted to join in?' asked Mimi in her Queen's English husky smoker's rasp between deep drags on her ubiquitous cigarette. Not the best role model, as mothers go. Even if she did believe in *Rule Britannia* and the enduring quality of a Jaeger suit.

The Potential Husband had planned to tell Rose some other way, he explained. Gently, kindly, over an extravagantly prepared meal, perhaps a James Martin recipe (squeaky clean and affable, unlike that shouty, sweary Ramsay chap), and he would have set the table using the Sophie Conran dinner service that they had been collecting from John Lewis piece by piece. Though even that would have been a slightly thought-less gesture, salt in the wound, as it were, since the remainder of it had been itemised on their wedding list.

What had made it worse for Rose was her standing there, bag still slung over her shoulder, still wearing the navy nylon trouser/patterned polyester blouse ensemble of building society uniform, gazing on her so-called friend's self-tanned/hooker-heeled bedroom wear and realising that the contrast between their appearances – dowdy, slightly plump (in Rose's opinion) worker attire vs up-for-it, slutty lingerie get-up – could not have been more marked.

Rose's self-esteem, fragile at the best of times, had splintered into a million shards at that point.

And boy, it hurt, really hurt, but Rose had to admit that they – the Maid of Honour (M'o'Ho) and the Ex – did seem happy and somehow right for each other.

But it was stomach-churningly awful to bump into them on the high street walking arm-in-arm together and gazing at each other like an advert for a Sandals resort. Completely vomit-inducing when, especially when, with unwashed hair, you've nipped to the shop for milk and cat food wearing an old man's tweed overcoat over your pyjamas, which are tucked into a down-at-heel pair of imitation Uggs, and driving another nail into the coffin of Ever Standing a Chance of Winning Him Back.

That was the point at which Rose, feeling she had to be mature (she – just shy of hitting thirty), had decided that enough was enough. That she would leave the City, the Big Smoke that she loved. Leave its history, its art, and its exhibitions. Leave its boutiques and markets, its global food and its Cutting Edge of everything. Leave her job, (not really a career), her friends (that included cheating, lying, man-stealing ones). And, as she countered to anyone who thought she was making An Error of Judgement, it's not so bad when you were moving to a city celebrated for its nightlife, its sophistication and frivolity.

'Yeah but that was in the 1700s,' snapped older (just the other side of thirty), gorgeous sister Lily, crushed that she was losing her crash-pad in the capital when the need arose for 'jollies' and 'benders' away from the more sedate life of Bath, though secretly delighted that her sister would be on the doorstep – quite literally, as it happened, for the first six months.

Lily had been the first to leave London, heavily pregnant and following her heart (and the fashionable exodus of celebrities such as Kate Moss, Pearl Lowe and

Liz Hurley) to a simpler life in the country, but with a lingering envy of her sister still living it large with the Tower, Bridge and Eye all just a Tube ride away. But, as Rose said, what was there to keep her in London, anyway, when you can get sushi in a Sainsbury's anywhere?

Rose and Lily. Two sisters. Named – in an uncharacteristic fit of hormone-induced whimsy – for Mimi's favourite flowers. One light and one dark. One curvy, the other willowy. At first glance it would be hard to believe they were sisters at all. Until they laugh together and their noses wrinkle identically, or their mouths set exactly the same in a grim, hard line when they are stressed. And their hands, of course. All of the Taylor women have good hands, Mimi included. Anyone of them could have had a career as a hand model advertising creams, washing-up liquids and doubling up for gnarly handed celebrities – if only they had been discovered.

Daddy had been tall and dark. Not a fleck of grey showing – even right at the end – although Grecian 2000 and Just for Men may have helped. Mimi – small and fair; hair still worn in the puffed-up bob of her prime time and the rest of her preserved by the skills of her plastic surgeon (though her daughters questioned the ethics of a man who would allow a pensioner to have breast implants).

Genetics are rather like a lottery or some sort of bad cosmic joke when it comes out in the mix. So Rose thought, anyway, since she had inherited her father's Mediterranean colouring (and tendency to being a little hirsute), her mother's stature and an unknown grandma's child-bearing hips. Lily, tall and pale as her namesake, had Daddy's height, Mimi's hair – which she left long and untamed – and the snake-hips, even after child-bearing, of a pubescent boy.

Rose, being the younger sibling, had suffered the indignity of people's thoughtless looking up and down and 'Oh, you're nothing like your sister' comments and had taken them to be expressions of disappointment, of her failing in some way. Coupled with her exaggerated fear that without waxing or threading she would continually sport a five o'clock shadow on her upper lip, it was no wonder that she had grown up feeling somewhat in Lily's shadow. Quite literally at times, depending on the position of the sun, what with Lily being so tall and having all that hair.

So there was Rose, with the curves of an acoustic guitar and her sleek, shiny jet-black hair hanging just past her shoulders, her love of fifties tailoring that suited her shape and her home-making tendencies; and then there was Lily as loyal, bouncy and enthusiastic as a retriever puppy with the blond, curly mane and big brown eyes to match, making her favoured jeans and sweatshirts look like a key-style statement. Each envying the good points of the other and each blind to the merits of themselves: Lily wishing she had Rose's bust; Rose wishing she had Lily's endless legs. Such is the way with sisters. Or best friends. Or women in general, in fact.

As for the men who passed them by, it's not true to say that Gentlemen Prefer Blondes. Most men are fairly democratic when it comes to a choice between blondes and brunettes. They'll have either if there is something in the package that pleases the eye but, in reality, would rather have both. At the same time. Preferably in the land of fantasy where all sexy grown-up sisters wear baby-doll nighties and have pillow fights before debagging the plumber.

Life was looking up. What had seemed totally unbearable only months before had now become, almost, a normality. Rose barely thought of her ex-nearly-a-husband's bare arse bobbing away in the red-nail clutches of her ex-best friend at all. Whole half-hours passed by before the image of his back reappeared in her mind's eye. Even with her contact lenses in, had she really been that short-sighted to have not seen it – or rather him – coming? At least he had bought her out of the shared tangled web of their finances with a generous, pre-credit crunch Guilt Money cash settlement, though he had insisted that he keep custody of the cat.

Bought Rose out and moved the M'o'Ho in.

But life with Lily in Bath was OK. There is nothing like the company of good women to mend a heart that is broken and bleeding from being jilted so close to the altar. For a start, there was her giving-Suri-Cruise-a-run-for-her-money little niece Leia (as in Princess), named for Lily's obsession with the iconic seventies sci-fi epic. When Rose first met Leia's father – all hair and beard – she suddenly recalled Lily's strange pre-teen crush on Chewbacca.

Not that Lily and Matt were together any more. Not that Rose could ever understand why they had split up in the first place because they were forever in each other's homes or taking three-year-old Leia to the park together. Always laughing. Still friends.

Just like Rose and the Ex and the M'o'Ho were trying to be. All pretending to be so terribly grown-up and civil and middle class about it all. How she wanted to scream like a (benefits-claiming) fish-wife at them on the *Jeremy Kyle Show* and hear the audience baying for blood!

And underneath a cloud of smoke, in a small, fashionable, iron-railing Bath town house bedecked with a single circular ball of dangly greenery, there was Mimi ('Don't call me Mummy, darling – it's soooo ageing') clutching a cigarette and inhaling from it, as if, ironically, it were the sustenance of life itself. Feigning disinterest in her grandchild, she had settled in Bath coincidentally soon after Leia's birth, bringing to an end a lifetime of following her now-deceased diplomat husband around the globe, painting the town red in the key capitals of Cold War Europe and living the expat lifestyle of sun-downers and 'It's six o'clock somewhere in the Empire'.

And occasionally, when the mood took them, adding their keys to the bowl. Mimi and Daddy had not had a conventional marriage.

So, for the first time since the girls had been packed off to school in England when they turned eleven, they were all together again. A little depleted in one way – Daddy gone for two years now and how they all missed his big laugh, his extravagant suppers and his always picking up the bill. It was only in the aftermath of sorting out his estate – and his debts – that they realised they'd been blessed with all the advantages of class but none of the money.

But they were a little bigger in another way; Leia being the apple of all their eyes, even if Mimi tried to deny it. A little bruised and battered from the fall-out of break-ups – Rose, boring them senseless, talking about her Ex all the time and trying to make sense of it being Over – and Lily, fixed and firm, saying nothing and refusing all attempts to say why it was Over for her and Matt.

How many ways are there to get over broken love affairs? There are the ice cream and chick-flick DVD cures; some turn to drink and emerge months later happier but can't remember how they got there; acting from anger can be a quick release; ties, shirts, shoes shredded; cars scratched or kippers left to rot under floorboards but lengthy court cases can follow; or prison sentences, if the urge to mow him down in a car was acted on.

There are stages which the magazine articles say are like grieving. And Mimi knew all about working through it to the Recovery stage. She'd been making whoopee as a Merry Widow ever since.

'It's what Daddy would have wanted,' she told her girls when they looked at her disapprovingly. Daddy and Mimi had put the swing into the sixties quite literally.

Therapists advise on giving in to the stages of Denial, Rage and Letting go. But Mimi had her own version for her daughters.

'You've got to get Dirty, Slutty and then you Re-virginise,' she said between puffs. The vaguely rude-sounding words seeming incongruous with her tones of BBC newsreader circa 1968.

'Dirty: the stop washing/tidying-up phase when you let yourself go. Slutty: you're ready to get back in the saddle, as it were. Sleep with the first person who smiles at you to re-upholster your self-esteem and then when you've got it out of your system you can become a bit more picky and are ready to start afresh – Virginal, as it were.'

Neither Rose nor Lily tended to follow their mother's advice.

Some people buy new clothes, reinvent or redis-cover themselves. Lose a ton of weight or hit the gym sending a two-fingered see-what-you're-missing salute back at their ex. Some flaunt a new lover who is better-looking/younger/looks slightly like they might smash the ex's face in, just to reaffirm that yep, they've still got It. Or they travel the world, go on yogic retreats or get a tattoo. Or remove one, if it happens to say, 'I love Dave' and now Dave is gone. With Trevor.

For Rose and her Ex and for Lily and Matt it was Over. The sisters needed to do something. Something life affirming in the tradition of 'I Will Survive'. Something that made a statement, to mark the end of an old chapter and the start of a new. Lily cut her wild, long blond hair into a sleek, needing-straighteners (rather like her mother's but nobody dared tell her) bob. Rose Taylor opened a shop.

2

How had it gone so wrong when he had seemed so right?

'So right into your friend,' reminded Lily with a caustic honesty only a sister or exceptionally good girl-pal can deliver. And more than a little bitterness. She had never quite recovered from the thought of she and Leia sharing the bridesmaid slot with someone else. Especially someone who self-tanned to the point of basted turkey.

It was one of those nights in when the food was cholesterol-raising but comforting and the grape in the wine is counted as one of the five-a-day. Lily hadn't yet got bored of being hostess in the flat that Matt had rented for her when she had told him that she needed to leave. Mimi was round, ignoring the food and claiming she'd already eaten. Rose was well on her way to being round as she devoured her fifth slice of pizza whilst she went over the same old ground again. The more she drank, and it only took a glass or two to loosen her tongue, the more she reminisced and the more maudlin she became.

He had been quite perfectly right for her, Rose explained. Again. And she began to list all his commendable attributes. He was tall but not freakishly so. (Her friend Penny was happily married to an Official Giant – he was six foot eight and a professional rugby player. Penny was a hobbity five foot three. Together they looked like Gandalf and Frodo.)

He was good-looking enough to make Mimi curl an eyebrow on first sight but not pretty-boy/boy-band gorgeous or shaving-ad, square-jawed alpha male attractive. Just easy on the eye. Just enough to keep your interest. And looks are important, for all Wayne Rooney's wealth when procreation is in the picture you wouldn't want your sweet baby daughter to inherit those looks.

He had a build best described as 'athletic', not 'pumped' or 'ripped' or 'tonk'. Not Peter Andre in his Mysterious Girl days. Just normally fit obtained from normal amounts of exercise a few times a week that did not involve grunting every night in a gym, slicking all the machines in a sweaty frenzy of 'roid rage'.

He had a job with prospects. An old-fashioned concept in these uncertain modern times but a worthy one in an age where even school careers advisers give advice about getting on reality TV or pole-dancing as a career move. So there he was with his GCSEs, his A levels, his degree and already a grasp on the slippery pole of Law. When Rose's future fantasies pictured a nice house of a comfortable size and being at least a partial stay-at-home mum, then a man of reasonable income is a very good catch for someone who wishes to be a wife.

He had good dress sense, too. He knew when it was appropriate to 'scrub up good' and knew his way around a good quality suit. He knew how to look funky in a seventies shirt. He even looked good in hats – spaniel-eared fur-lined hats in winter, stylishly edgy pork pie hats for the summer. He could do Sunday morning casual and, whilst Rose would never have asked him to carry off white linen trousers and bare feet as she'd seen Daniel O'Donnell and Cliff Richard do on office calendars, Rose was quite sure he could even pull that off with aplomb.

He loved their fickle cat, scratching its chin for as long as it was required and when he'd held Leia soon after the birth, cradling her, gently sniffing and kissing at her downy head – after they'd raced from London to Somerset as soon as Lily's waters had broken – well, Rose thought her ovaries would burst from sheer desire. Not since George Clooney as caring, sexy paediatrician in *ER* had there been such a collective sigh of worship from nursing staff.

So many boxes ticked. So many hero qualities. So seemingly in line with everything you should look for in a man. He had got on well with her sister but was not so attentive as to make Rose feel neglected – or so she thought. He had managed a blokey bonhomie with new dad Matt; not easy since their tastes in music were at opposite ends of the spectrum (he preferred James Blunt; Matt professed it was rhyming slang), as were their politics and views on football. 'It's too easy, too *poncey* to support Manchester United. You don't even come from there!' Matt had screamed – yes, screamed to his shame – when he discovered who Rose's fiancé supported.

And he had flirted gently with Mimi, lighting her cigarettes with the flair of a hard-boiled detective from film noir. It had seemed that he had been given the Lily and Mimi stamp of approval with very few reservations. OK, his hair style verged on dodgy with the swept-back flicky-wing thing that he had going on, a little too Kevin Costner in *Robin Hood*, one inch shy of a mullet, but hair can be fixed, changed or fall out and his forehead did seem to be getting higher.

But he had seemed reliable, he had appeared dependable, he had never given her a moment's doubt, but then Rose had not exactly been raised by Mimi to be jealous in relationships. Three years was such a long time to merge your life and plan your future with someone else.

She missed him. And she would tell any old lady who stood long enough at the bus stop all about it. She missed having dinner with him, taking it in turns to find a foodie recipe like spinach purée, which really did look like baby food when it was done, or shopping in out-of-the-way delicatessens for obscure ingredients like lupa clams which sounded more like a skin complaint in need of ointment than something edible. ('Ooh! I've got terrible lupa clams at the moment. I'm red raw!')

She missed trolling around IKEA (he didn't) and reading the papers over his shoulder whilst dunking her biscuit in his tea. She missed watching a film on Saturday night and putting up with the lasers, gun shots and car chases when he got to choose. She even missed picking up the socks, pants and damp towels that he left littering the floor.

'*That* would've soon paled,' snorted Mimi, forcing the smoke out of her nostrils like some disbelieving dragon. But the pain was throat-catching so that she could not even say his name aloud. Not even to herself. It lodged there, the ache extending all the way down through her chest, and she could only say 'him' or 'he' or in an attempt to pretend it really didn't hurt as much as all that – The One that Got Away.

'Was it me? Was it my fault?' Rose asked Lily for the thousandth time. 'Did I nag him? Was I no fun any more? I knew that preparing the wedding was taking a lot of time and stressing me out. Was it just pre-wedding nerves? Had I bored him?'

Lily thought for a moment about the concertina box file with the sections labelled amongst others 'Cake Ideas', 'Dress Designs' and 'Suggested Readings'. She considered the frenzied sewing of the mile of bunting from vintage scraps. She recalled the Post-it note-marked knee-high stack of wedding magazines and the year-long marathon of weekend viewings of venues, wedding fairs and the sampling of cheeseboards. She remembered hour-long phone conversations when Rose would ask Lily's opinion on what was the ideal toilet-to-guest ratio.

'No,' she lied. 'You weren't boring. I thought he was excited about the wedding.' And he had been, to start with. He had, after all, asked Rose to be his wife, completely out of the blue. He had stooped on bended knee at the feet of Anteros the symbol of mature, reflective, selfless love in Piccadilly, correcting Rose gently that it was not, as some mistakenly think, Eros, who is more associated with carnal lust and unrequited affection. He had chosen his spot carefully even if he hadn't factored in the traffic volume at the time which meant that he had to shout. He had carefully considered all the reasons he was asking for her hand in marriage.

'I know I'd put on a bit of weight and we'd stopped going out so much *and* cancelled that skiing trip, but we had agreed that we were saving for the wedding. I know that . . . well, this isn't easy to say but . . . you know . . . the sex had got a bit samey. A bit like a well-rehearsed dance. Boobs first, downstairs next. Foreplay done in five minutes. Hop up and ride the pony and then . . . but everyone goes through patches like that, don't they? Don't they?' she repeated when neither Mimi nor her sister took the bait to validate her comment. Mimi had never known a dry spell in that department, even after the menopause. Lily just avoided eye contact.

'No comment,' was all she would respond.

'It's that trollop of a so-called friend,' Mimi consoled. 'Men are simple creatures. So simple that most of them are borderline retarded – especially when it comes to social skills and sex. They can't help it. It's in their genes. They are handicapped by evolution. They need variety. Your weight has nothing to do with it. There is nothing you could have done short of wearing a Cheryl Cole mask to bed and perhaps a little role playing where you agree to meet up as strangers and have sex in the back of a taxi. That might have kept him interested.'

Both of Mimi's daughters feigned vomiting to try to get her to stop. She continued anyway, raising her voice above the retching and sounding imperious.

'I know that there are men *and* women who claim to be faithful but, really, how boring! Rose, you love Chinese food but you wouldn't want to eat it every night, would you? The pleasure would soon all be gone. Your friend – what's her name?'

'Isabelle.'

'Mmm – Jezebel would be more appropriate! You could see her ambition, she wore it like a cloak – or, rather, she hid it under those layers of fake smiles and false eyelashes. She was in Sales, wasn't she?' Mimi uttered the word 'sales' as if she was saying 'slave trade'. 'They are a glib sort, all easy patter armed with their "How to Win Friends and Influence People" manipulation psychology. She was all smoke and glamour. Once her relationship was off with that chap in the bank – what was his role again?'

'Head of Strategy and Marketing.'

'Yes, a jumped-up Jonny sort of job. They were perfectly matched. Anyway, once that was over, she was looking for the next catch. Your ex-husband-to-be just happened to fall in her line of sight, that's all. He was like the hapless mongoose charmed by a snake that Daddy and I saw in India.' This was pronounced as the old colonial 'Inja'. 'He has been bedazzled, that's all.'

' "Women, beware women",' quoted Lily wiping Leia's face who had just come back in the room having devoured a chocolate chip cookie – most of which she wore on her cheeks and in her hair. 'Mimi and I saw straight through her. We never liked her. Not really. We've been saying it for years. I know you've worked together since, I don't know, *for ever*, but she always wanted what you'd got. She'll probably get bored of him before long. It's like owning that handbag you dream about; once you've had it awhile you set your sights on the next thing . . . then the next. She got that promotion that should have been yours—'

'I didn't really want it—'

'But she didn't know that! She went all guns-out to get it. God knows how she put you down in order to secure that step up the ladder. You're too loyal, Rose – it's your failing. Next, you'll be saying that she didn't really mean to steal your fiancé!'

'Well, I don't think she did. I mean people can't help where they fall in love, can they?'

'Nonsense!' cut in Mimi, opening and shutting her

cigarette box in such agitation that the lid snapped off in her hand. 'That sounds like sales department brainwashing to me! There is never any need for lies. And to hell with this "being friends" nonsense! When Daddy and I were in the Middle East, that slut would have been stoned to death for her treachery and the crowd would have cheered.'

'I think there are a lot of double standards for men and women in the occasionally polygamous Middle East, don't you?' Lily was warming up for a political debate.

Mimi wasn't. 'It's one thing to have a fling with someone, but to lie about it? The sex is immaterial, but the lies! Daddy and I supped at the Horn of Plenty but we were totally honest with each other and totally sure of our love for each other—'

'Here we go again!' muttered Lily. 'Leia, will you go fetch your plate and cup? *Grandma*' – said with extra emphasis to wind Mimi up – 'is going to talk about grown-up things. Again!'

Mimi continued: 'I am utterly convinced that it's nothing but a *Nine-and-a-Half-Weeks* thing.' Then, as an aside, 'Although she's no Kim Basinger. In another six months it'll all be over – eight at the most – and he'll probably be back asking to eat you – his favourite dinner – all over again. Mark my words! And this time, throw it in his face and shut the door!'

'Amen!' said Lily. 'Now can we *please* stop talking about it? Leia will pick up on all the discussion about break-ups and all I've said is that her daddy is busy working right now. She's already asking questions, and Matt is in the other room!'

They had all forgotten. For a heterosexual man he had achieved the almost unattainable status of Honorary Girl. He was busy in the lounge sticking together a model of a *Lord of the Rings* castle that he had been collecting piece by piece in weekly instalments since Leia was born. 'It will be an heirloom,' he'd assured Lily. It had cost him several hundred pounds more to buy than if they had approached Peter Jackson and asked to buy the real one from the movies.

Lily raised her hand. 'And don't go there! I don't want to talk about it! The break-up, I mean, not the fort made from matchsticks, or whatever he's doing in there, and I think Rose is doing enough talking for the two of us. Her constant warts-and-all examination of this is like listening to previews of the next Katie Price autobiography!'

But Rose was in a bad way, Lily and Mimi knew that. That's why they listened when they'd heard it all before. That's why they sided with her, exaggerating all the bad points of Isabelle and the Ex. That's why they bolstered her ego with emphasising all the great things she had going for her. And they worried that even after all these months she wasn't letting go and moving on. Lily dwelt more on Rose's situation than she did her own.

No matter that she had moved town, he'd moved her friend in and that the wedding was off, Rose seemed to be in denial that it really had finished. After all, hadn't they mapped out their futures together? The years of travelling, followed by children and a move outside of the city? Rose had pictured it all in her head so many times.

Was it just a fling? Rose wondered again. A six-month wonder? There were signs that he wasn't letting go either. For a start, there were the phone calls, the emails and the texts – not all instigated by her. All part of the 'being friends' post-break-up manifesto, checking in to see if each other was OK. He asking how things were, telling Rose it was important that she held it all together and all the time, saying he was sorry.

Each phone call, each text – even if it was a round-robin forwarded sexist joke – was a glimmer of hope, confirmation that though he might be bouncing off the walls with the French-manicured Isabelle, their connection was still there. He still wanted to know what she thought about the headlines or about the in-house politics at his law firm.

'Isabelle doesn't really understand the dynamics, the history of it, like you do. Are you sure that you don't mind me bending your ear about it all?' And the answer was, of course, she didn't. Rose would have taped the phone to her head 24/7 if it meant she kept him talking about things that Isabelle and her Brazilian wax couldn't possibly understand.

Rose had taken to reading the 'We overcame the adultery/I forgive his affair'-type articles in the magazines favoured by ladies hurtling towards the menopause with children and large mortages in tow. *Glamour* and *Cosmo* held no truck with forgiveness and forbearance. 'Kick that Cheat to the Kerb in Killer Heels!' they crowed. 'One Hundred Ways to Keep Your Man Faithful' came too late. Number 67 had seemed eerily familiar with its advice about stranger role play and the back of taxis. Number 69 was entirely predictable.

But Rose had understood from reading the columns of the heavy-spectacled agony aunts that if she waited it out, listened understandingly and didn't make judgements, time would be a healer. Even Mimi, with her extensive and varied experience of men, her open marriage and recent hot-tub parties, had said as much, hadn't she? Rose had stopped listening at the point when the advice had been to slam the door in his face when he did return. Her mind had fixed on the part that said he'll be back to eat his favourite dinner. He'll be back. She played it on a loop in her mind but without the sinister Arnie-Terminator overtones.

Particular conversations she recalled and examined over and over again.

'I think this separation could be good for both of us.' Not 'split'. Not 'break-up'. Separation. Rose felt that was significant. It wasn't. They were just words. Carefully chosen to soften the blow words, but she couldn't see it.

'The job was stifling you. You just weren't the person I'd met and fallen in love with any more. You'd got so serious. You were only concerned with the wedding.' These, Rose felt, were clues about where she had gone wrong, about what she could do to make it right. She did not see it for what they were – excuses for his being stupid enough to get caught.

'I want us to stay friends. I still want you in my life.' These were the words that bound Rose to him and stopped her moving onwards and away. They rooted her to the spot at the side of their almost-marital bed. The point at which she had been coitus interruptus to him and her friend.

Mimi still had more to say. For the sort of mummy who believed in the parenting school of benign neglect, who had employed nannies, asked for the children to be sent for, for one hour only, after their supper, and who had dispatched them off to boarding school before all the money ran out, she really was very fond of her girls and the pain she saw in Rose was unbearable.

'You need to move forwards, darling. Put it behind you,' she said, stroking the hair from the side of Rose's taut, anguished face. 'A year from now it won't matter, you'll see. In a month you'll feel differently. You need to seek out opportunities. Do something new, something different. Take me as a role model, for example. I could sit at home every night and knit in front of soap operas or I can get out there, play bridge, do a little dancing and meet a Mr X or two—'

'Mr Triple-X, knowing you,' interrupted Lily, trying desperately to lighten the mood and to avoid another night of tears as she saw Rose's eyes beginning to fill. 'Mother' – guaranteed to make Mimi irritable – 'do you realise that STDs are increasing significantly in your age group? I blame the rise – pardon the pun – of Internet sales of Viagra.'

Rose snorted a big snot bubble through her laughter, making her sister scream at the sight as Rose scrabbled around for tissues. Both girls were united in their condemnation of Mimi's nocturnal activities.

'Not so much a Milf – that's me, by the way!' chortled Lily, egged on by her sister's laughter, 'as a Gilf.' Rose was crying now – with laughter.

'Granny I'd like to . . .'

'Yes, I know what it means,' defended Mimi. 'I read in *Saga* magazine that I should be called a Cougar.'

'No, that's women in their fifties or sixties who date much younger men,' Lily corrected. Mimi was older than that, having had her girls at an age when the hospital referred to her as a 'geriatric pregnancy'. 'I think your age group are called Sabre-toothed Tigers!'

Rose's phone burst into a trill rendition of the 'Mexican Hat Dance', cutting through all their hilarity. She checked the caller.

'It's Carl!' she cheeped, her heart fluttering as, unconsciously, she rearranged her hair with one hand and accepted the call with the other, running from the kitchen to speak alone with him in another room.

'Now she can say his name!' Mimi shook her head as she locked eyes with Lily. 'The name of a Nazi villain!

I'm going for a cigarette.' Indeed, she did feel like a sabre-toothed tiger when it came to her daughters and their broken hearts. She slid off the bar stool, banging the balcony door shut behind her.

Once the 'How's things? Fine/OK' bits of the conversation were over and Carl had given her the latest Machiavellian office goings on and Rose had listened and advised and sympathised and asked after the cat and even asked after Isabelle, he asked after her life.

'How's the job hunting?'

'It's not. I've been thinking about what you said, I mean, you know me so well. You're right. I do need to do something that's more . . . I don't know . . . me, I guess. Jobs aren't that easy to come by, especially in the banking world, and was it ever really what I wanted to do? So I was thinking about what you said to me the day I packed up my stuff and moved out—'

'What? What did I say?' His tone was suddenly sharp and defensive. Carl felt panicked, cornered. Hadn't he bought her out with a king's ransom? Why did she always make him feel so bloody guilty? It was not that he'd stopped loving her. Not really. She had been his best friend. Rose was the right side of good-looking and good company but Isabelle . . . Isabelle was *Nuts*, *Zoo* and *Loaded*. Isabelle was his Wag, his Trophy Wife. Had he made some rash promise? Said something, anything, to stop her guilt-inducing tears that she'd now hold him to task over?

Rose's talking cut off his train of thought. 'You laughed that I had so many things to pack. The books, the pictures – you said that you weren't sorry to see those go. All of those clothes I'd kept when you couldn't understand why I didn't throw them away if they didn't fit or needed mending. As I folded up every garment you said that it was like I was carefully packing away old friends.'

Had he really said that? Quite eloquent, given the circumstances. 'You said that you liked how my wardrobe was like a history tour through the decades of fashion.' She tried to ignore the nagging thought that a wardrobe tour of Isabelle's would be like roaming around Ann Summers with a Next power-suit thrown in for good measure. 'All those clothes I've collected but don't wear. Well – it's given me an idea for a business. I haven't told anyone else about it yet.' See how special to me you still are? underscored those words. So special she'd not even told her sister yet. Her sister, who was her rock through moving schools and changing countries. 'I wanted to run it past you first.'

'Atta girl!' Carl enthused more than was necessary. 'That's my Rosie. The girl I used to know.' Rose would store these words away to revisit later. 'Creative! Go-getting! What'll it be? Clothes design? Making hats? Reupholstery? One of those things you've talked about doing for years? You could do any of them!'

'I've seen some premises. Sure, they're a little old, and they've been empty a while. I was out walking with

Lily and she started to chase a pigeon—'

'Where are they?' He hadn't got time to listen to some how-fate-intervened story.

'Between the Roman Baths and the Fashion Museum. Perfect for what I have in mind. The offered lease is a little shorter than I would like, but there's living accommodation and I can't stay with Lily and Leia for ever. If there was a reason why I worked for the building society for all those years, then this is it. I understand about cash flow and capital, tax returns and risk. Plus I understand the market and the merchandise. You could say I have a passion for it.'

'So tell me! Don't keep me in suspenders!' Carl always did have this annoying tendency for altering sayings to what he thought was comic effect. Saying 'destructions' instead of 'instructions' was another that she generally overlooked but which, Rose had to admit, did put her teeth on edge.

'Vintage clothes,' Rose announced. Carl reacted as though she had suggested something seedy, as if she'd said that she was going to sell her used undergarments to Japanese business men on-line. She was confused. She couldn't understand his reticence, his disapproving tones. This was meant to be Phase One of earning his approval, of getting him back. It was not like it was entirely out of the blue either. She'd always favoured a retro look. If not wearing the real thing, then buying replicas. Rose's Unique Style, he used to call it. Now he just condemned the whole idea.

'Bath isn't exactly Student Central, is it? I mean, how many charity shops can one town hold? It's what I'd call a niche market. I wouldn't advise one of my clients to go ahead with a project like this in the current climate.'

'I'm not one of your clients, Carl, and it's not going to be a charity shop.' Now there was a sting of hurt in her voice and something else – anger. He had taken so much from her, stamped all over her plans for the future and her perception of what life was. Could he not give her this? Could he not support her in this dream that had arrived like a life raft when he had left her drifting? 'There *is* a market for the right sort of vintage clothes. I'm exactly the sort of person who is always buying them. You always said I've got enough clothes to start a shop. And people are always telling me that I have a good eye for putting things together. So, that's what I'm going to do. Vintage clothes, maybe a few home wares. Why don't you come and see it first and then tell me what you think?' Phase Two. The shop'll look great. She'll look great.

Carl thought for a moment. It was good to hear her excited and motivated again instead of that dreadful tremble in her voice that made him feel guiltier than if he'd kicked a fluffy kitten to death in front of a nursery school. At last, she was moving forward, getting occupied by her new life. Soon there would be fewer phone calls and the relationship would die of natural causes. There might only be the odd email or Christmas card. By then she would be able to cope with hearing that he and Isabelle had set a date, that there would be a wedding after all. Isabelle was pushing that he should tell Rose. That he should cut off all contact. You've got to be cruel to be kind, Isabelle believed.

He should be all enthusiasm for this scheme of Rose's but then a cold terror struck. Who would she cry to when it all went wrong and she was penniless? These were hardly the times for setting up a business. How much money can there be in second-hand clothes? Hadn't he and Isabelle been more than generous with helping her to move out and move on? Would she be knocking on their door with more tears, wanting more handouts? After all, Mimi couldn't help her out, anything resembling a family fortune had gone years ago, blown on funding a lifestyle of casinos and renting yachts as Rose's daddy pretended at being a playboy.

He could feel Rose now, breathing into the telephone, needing his support and approval for this business that would be the salve to heal the wounds, the hurts that he had inflicted. Rose was a good person. He hadn't meant for all this to crush her like it had. Well, he hadn't really been thinking at all. It was difficult to think clearly when Isabelle was in the picture, especially when Isabelle was wearing that lacy bodystocking thing with all the strategic bits cut out.

Carl suddenly felt irritated. He had a new life now. Rose should just get over it and stop making him feel like the Bad Person in all of this. So instead of offering kind encouragement, in the end, all he could say in a voice that was like a teacher admonishing a reckless teenager was: 'I think you're making a big mistake. Second-hand clothes, really? Hardly a big profit to be made, is there? All those savings gone in a flash. Shouldn't you be buying a property? Thinking about your future? I don't think you know what you're doing, Rose. Have you thought this through?'

'Why vintage? *Why?* Why is he even asking me that question? Doesn't he know me? Doesn't he know me at all? A second-hand clothes shop, he called it! Can you believe it? I won't be selling "hand-me-downs"! It's not "used" clothing! Yes, of course, mostly, vintage clothes have been worn but that's not to say they're worn out! It's not "nearly new" either! He's trying to make me sound like a used-car salesman! My shop will only sell the pieces that have been cherished. The well-made items saved for high days and holidays. Clothes heavy with memories. But only the good ones!' Rose Taylor was slurring and very, very drunk. She'd had a few. One too many, as it were. She was blotto, trolleyed, pickled, absolutely steaming. It hadn't taken many drinks at all because Rose – unlike her mother – was a total lightweight in the *Lambrini* stakes. She'd never really cut it as a Ladette; unlike Lily, who could down pints in one go, had a fondness for real ale and could keep up with Matt's rugby club mates. No, Rose Taylor had obviously lucked out on the booze gene, too.

Red wine was too 'heady', lagers too 'gassy' and she couldn't mix her drinks either. Not quite true – Rose could actually mix drinks expertly, Mimi having trained her and Lily from the cradle on how to fix a Tom Collins or a Dirty Martini, but if Rose drank Hop and Grape in one evening then disaster followed. It was one of those nights and a three-day hangover was to follow.

Oh – and a minor incident in front of a CCTV camera which would lead to Rose's television debut in reality show *Boozed-up Britain*. Local paper headlines would scream: 'Bath's Boozed-up Britain Binge-Drinking Shame' and carry a grainy still of Rose in action, mouth wide open. It could happen to anyone.

Lily had been determined that Rose wouldn't sit around feeling sorry for herself on the day of her should-have-been Big Day. Matt babysat; Mimi didn't. She was having a friend round for supper. 'So don't call in!' she'd warned. That could only mean that she was planning for some action with the coffee and the After Eight mints. Rose had tried to resist going out but Lily would hear nothing of it. They were now in a chilled-out bar of soft velvet banquette seats and grown-up indie sounds.

Some drunks are giggly or cackly – as in the case of many Girls' Nights Out. Some are affable, friends with everyone, giving away all of their taxi money to the homeless or telling their mates that they love them, they really, really do. Others like a fight, sparking off if a stranger so much as glances their way in a Whatchu looking at, Pal? tradition. Others succumb to an insatiable libido that overlooks physical defects and obvious incompatibility, and shrugs off the need to know names or past police records until the Morning After. Then is the time for regrets.

Alcohol enhances all those emotions, base feelings and more, that lie dormant or repressed until they spill out like a shaken bottle of Grand-Prix champagne. Anger, despair and hurt were all in the cocktail of Rose's emotions tonight. It was like any other night lately with Rose, thought Lily, only times ten. Had they been at a house party, Rose would have been the guest who sat on the stairs and cried. There's always one.

As it was, this evening, she alternated between ranting and crying until the mascara ran down her face. She should have bought the super-lash extending, growth-enhancing volumiser, non-clumping waterproof one that Isabelle (traitorous ex-best friend) always wore. With the teary-eyed Gothic look, there was no chance of Rose and Lily pulling that night, even though they'd started off the evening looking fly. Lily in jeans and loose kaftan, which highlighted just how slender she was, and Rose in a late-fifties black satin fit 'n' flare dress that was now hanging off one shoulder and riding higher up her thighs every time she sat down. It was definitely time to take her home.

'And you know that Isabelle . . .' – pronounced Ishabill with a definite slur – 'Isabelle said to him, "Well, she always did like old-fashioned clothes." Old-fashioned! As though I'm a twee OAP surrounded by lace doilies and horse brasses. Just because I don't care about what's "in" or "out" from fashion magazines, or this month's "must haves".' She seemed to be addressing the whole bar at this point. Her arms waving around far too much for reason. 'I don't dance to the beat of that drum; what might be right for her may not be right for some . . . I prefer different strokes.'

Oh no, thought Lily, we're on to TV references now. Next she'll be singing the theme tune from *Friends* or *The Golden Girls*. It was just a matter of time.

'I don't care about "last season". It's not like my clothes are borderline socially unacceptable, is it? You've never seen me in a shell-suit or a furry jacket with husky dogs on it anywhere. But you see, people like Ishabill – they don't get it.' Rose was swaying and doing that beckoning thing that drunks do when they have the secrets of the universe to impart. 'Isabelle' said very precisely and slowly to correct mumbled pronunciation. 'She thinks wearing anything other than brand-new clothing stinks of poverty, jumble sales and charity shops, but she's wrong.' Rose pointed a finger very emphatically and leaned back on her heels with an air of smug self-satisfaction.

'Girls like her. Girls whose only talent is wobbling about in high heels. Girls who can make a five-hundred-pound dress look cheap.' She was no longer the staunch friend. The claws were out. 'They don't get the magic of vintage. They don't get it at all. You see, vintage is not Victoria Beckham but it's . . . Daisy Lowe. That's what it is! Vintage is Notting Hill and Shoreditch but not Alderley Edge. But I'll tell you what the secret is –' Rose was whispering. Loudly. 'Clothes make you behave a certain way. Holding an old granny bag makes you demand good service and respect, just like its first owner would have done. A forties tea dress got me through my final exams because I felt stoic like all those women who coped with blackouts and air raids.' She saluted with the wrong hand. 'Give me an ethnic maxi-dress – well, not me, I'd look like a dwarf stuck in a two-man tent, but put you in one' – Rose jabbed her finger into her sister's sternum – 'you'd be Marianne Faithful! Your inhibitions would melt – just like the infamous Mars bar of Rolling Stone legend and you'd be seeking satisfaction, baby, yeah!' Rose clapped her hands together and started to dance a little Jaggeresque jig.

'Let's get our coats,' Lily suggested and started to manoeuvre Rose towards the cloakroom – it was like a *Strictly Come Dancing* waltz with John Sergeant.

'Vintage changes a personality, don't you see?' Rose was imploring with all the exaggerated feeling of a religious fanatic at Speaker's Corner. They were drawing the attention of other people. 'What are you like whenever you try to wear grey knitwear? Lumpy, washed-out and irritable. You're a picture of PMT without the painters ever visiting.'

'Yeah, thanks for that, Rose.' Lily was smiling and eye-rolling in an 'Oh Dear, I've got a Drunk on my Hands' appeal to their audience.

'A dress from the start of the fifties can unleash the inner ingénue, put a spring in your step with circular skirts and petticoats' – Rose did a little Sandy-from-*Grease*-before-the-slutty-makeover skip – 'but by the end of that decade, get yourself a fitted wool-mix sheath dress with cap sleeves and I promise you'll be channelling Mad Men's Joan Holloway. You'll be everyman's Queen of Sexy Secretaries,' she said to a passing girl who was not, in fact, a girl; just a very pretty boy with a long fringe. He didn't look offended.

'Here, put your arm in.' Lily was dressing Rose who had all the motor co-ordination of an oversized toddler.

'It is an unleashing of the inner actress; wear it and you'll be it.' An arm was flung to the left. 'It's a disguise. Vintage is playing dress-up as a grown-up. It's waking up and saying Who shall I be today? Audrey/Dita/a kid from *Fame*?' Another arm flung to the right and she hit a man waiting with his cloakroom ticket in the chest.

'Sorry,' mouthed Lily with a pleading look. Rose continued her speech unchecked.

'You don't have to stick to one era. You don't have to only wear clothes from the fifties – though some do and that's my thing, you know that. Why not be a Style Slut? Take your fashion from where it takes your fancy. It's becoming the person you want to be, and you can be anyone you want. It's finding a part of yourself unknown or lost from all the constraints, drudgery and dullness of our modern lives. I was lost when Carl left me . . .' They were outside now and waiting for a taxi. It had been a struggle getting Rose up the stairs. Lily winced, the tears were coming again. There was just one other person in the queue, the man from the cloakroom whom Rose had smacked in the pectorals. 'Out there is the One. We spend our lives looking for the One.' Rose was talking through the tears and a runny nose.

'Carl wasn't the One,' soothed Lily. There was a taxi pulling up at the kerb.

'Do you want to go first?' Cloakroom Man was asking, eyeing Rose with a mixed look of wariness and pity.

'Thanks.' Lily really meant it. 'Thank you very much.' It was getting hard to hold Rose up – her legs appeared to have gone all rubbery. Cloakroom Man advanced to help.

'We're in an endless pursuit for the One and it's nothing to do with men.' Rose pointed accusingly at the helpful stranger and then hiccupped, belching out nacho fumes from their earlier bar snacks. 'We – we vintage fans – we live in nameless fear that someone else will find it before we do. It's ever elusive. It is our Scarlet Pimpernel, staying just out of reach and around the next corner.'

The taxi driver was looking doubtful about whether he wanted to take them at all. Lily started to bargain after propping Rose against the stranger, who was struggling like a man trying to hold a roll of carpet vertical.

'It's all in the chase. We're like pigs snouting for

truffles through the rails.' And Rose made a very unattractive porcine snuffling face. 'It is our Mission Impossible . . .' She was feeling a bit queasy but what she had to say was important. She was earnest. She was totally sincere. Since Lily was occupied, she directed her speech to Cloakroom Man now and he nodded along, humouring her. '. . . and it's all a little bit different but what we seek is essentially the same.' Her voice went all high-pitched and wheedly. 'It could be a dress, it could be a handbag or a pair of gloves. But out there, somewhere, is the One.' She held her finger up into his face. 'The Numero Uno.' She paused then. A dramatic pause, drunken and more than a bit wobbly, and when she spoke it was with almost religious reverence. 'It is The One Vintage Piece that we know will change our lives for ever.'

Her speech might have been coming from the heart but what Rose deposited all over the stranger's shoes came straight from her stomach. She didn't offer to pay for them to be cleaned, but she did promise through the medium of song that she'd be there for him when the rain started to pour and when it hadn't been his day, his week, his month or even his year. No one, it seemed, had told her that life was gonna be this way.

V intage Magic opened one Saturday in late
September. Unfortunately, unlike Rose's behaviour
on her Non-Wedding Day, it did not make headlines but
there were balloons, fresh flowers and cupcakes. A
tower of cupcakes – like the ones Rose had wanted for
her wedding. Only instead of iced words spelling 'love',
'happiness' and the overly optimistic 'fidelity', there
were simply sprinkles, sugar hearts and flowers. The
fated marriage bunting had been put to good use
creating a fête atmosphere hung at the front of the shop
and ironically retro Babycham was served in mismatched vintage teacups. Old 78s crackled from a
Dansette record player and the weather had stayed fair
so that beaded cardigans were all that were required to
enjoy sitting on painted chairs at the front of the shop
while nursing a cup and saucer of something fizzy and
looking out on to the Square. Leia and her nursery
friends ran in and out of the shop, changing hats, beads
and scarves at a big old dressing-up chest with pieces
deemed too battered or unsaleable but perfect for play.

Leia was dancing a wild Charleston with a little boy wearing evening gloves and a pair of high wedge heels.

'Ahhh bless!' said indulgent daddy Matt. *'Will and Grace – the Prequel.'*

All day, people came and saw and bought this and that: a vintage string of pearls here, a frothy prom dress there. Lily had recruited nursery school parents, Matt had rang around all his old school pals and handed out fliers for three consecutive weeks, but Mimi had shocked them all by siding with Evil Carl, as she called him, out of Rose's earshot.

'Rose. A junk shop? Really! And my other daughter can barely read! Why did I let you both study art? All that education wasted!'

'Like our inheritance!' scolded Lily leaping to her sister's defence.

'And Lily can read!' Rose was also her sister's staunchest supporter. 'How many times do we have to tell you? She's dyslexic! You just don't get it, do you, Mimi? People pay good money to wear beautiful old clothes. Like the stuff in the back of your wardrobe!'

'But what will I say to my friends? I can't invite them to this . . . this jumble sale! Old clothes can harbour pests, you know – fleas, lice – you'll be crawling with them! I could never understand why you girls insisted on wearing others' cast-offs! Oh, I can just imagine the smell.' And she pressed a handkerchief to her nose in horror.

But presiding over events like a sepia Coco Chanel,

Mimi was there at the grand opening, although, conspicuously, her friends from Bridge Night were not. She was charming, bringing a blush to the cheeks of young girls as they emerged from the changing room – 'Oh, you sweet creature. That's a darling little dress!' – and thereby securing her daughter a sale. She entertained the lost-looking men as their ladies shopped, making a bee-line for the best-looking ones and boosting their self-esteem with her hungry, appraising look like a poshed-up Dorian from *Birds of a Feather*: 'You're in Sales? Oh, that sounds riveting. Join me outside, let's smoke and you can tell me all about it . . .'

From the front the little row of timbered terraced shops that leaned slightly to the left resembled something from a Harry Potter film. Vintage Magic sat in the middle. Rose could not believe after all the months of painting, hammering, dusting, cleaning and pressing of stock that it had all finally come together.

Matt, using all the skills acquired on his parents' farm where he and Lily had lived until their separation, had thrown himself into the task of renovating the antiquated bookshop into a house of style.

'That's what families are for!' he'd said when Rose had thanked him and they had caught each other's eye and both looked embarrassed.

'If it's any consolation, I don't know what's going on in Lily's head either.' Rose felt that she had to say something.

'It's no consolation at all, but you know . . . thanks,' he said before returning to fashioning dress rails from reclaimed scaffolding poles, and looking, in his woollen beanie, old combats and football shirt, not so much Badly Drawn Boy as just plain Badly Dressed.

Why oh why has my sister left you? thought Rose. Why had she chosen to hurt this man who had fitted so seamlessly into their lives like a trusty pair of weekday knickers? And why, when they were so close, had Lily shut her out completely over this decision?

The whitewashing of old dark wood furniture and the running up of curtains on Rose's ancient hand-propelled Singer had the sisters in an old-school *Changing Rooms* fever. The air sang with makeover programme cliches: 'But with just one day to go, disaster strikes', 'We have transformed their living space', 'But the rebuild will take us way over budget.' They vied to be Lawrence Llewelyn-Bowen until after rifling through a bin bag of clothes waiting to be sorted, Matt donned an old frilly Laura Ashley blouse and declared himself The Fop.

This led to a spot of Phil/Kirsty *Location, Location, Location* speculation. Had they or hadn't they? Were they mates who got the sex out of the way early, as Lily suggested? Or were they still harbouring unrequited lusts that would one day explode into a sexual frenzy over in an en-suite bathroom, as Matt hoped? Rose felt that they had a relationship that could have worked in the right circumstances but they had decided to remain loyal and faithful to their respective partners (unlike some other people she could name). Mimi wasn't there to suggest that Phil and Kirsty probably swapped partners on Bank Holidays as she surely would have done – she had given the whole messy project a wide berth.

And in amongst the chaos of Rose's furniture fresh out of storage, new central heating being installed and a lavatory spouting backed-up sewage (not their own; Rose never used pink toilet paper for fear of urinary infections from the dye) strolled Mooch. Rose had not only acquired a new home and a business, but it seemed that she had also acquired a black cat. He had walked through the back door, mooched about – hence his name – and decided he wasn't going to leave and Rose had little choice about it. With Beast of Bodmin proportions, the expression 'feline grace' did not apply to him. He moved with a sort of lope, as though about to spring into action and take down a gazelle or an unguarded small toddler. He had no patience with Leia at all and kept tantalisingly just out of her chubby-fisted reach, but eyed her, as if waiting for his moment, with a tail-twitching hypnotic stare that unnerved Lily.

To demonstrate his usefulness to Rose and secure his right to live there, Mooch began to lay fresh kill routinely on the back doorstep as though it were a sacrificial altar.

'No need to worry about the rodent issue in the cellar,' cheered Matt. Farm boys are rarely sentimental about animals and he shared a manly pride in each pink-tailed corpse that was found and the blood lust that Mooch displayed. He charted each success *Apocalypse Now*-style with a small notch carved into the back door frame each time he was needed for body disposal.

'We are hunters!' he declared, fluffing at Mooch's head and pushing out his chest like Tarzan. 'They are mere women and should serve us.' He dodged the platform shoe thrown at his head.

Rose displayed a 'Found' sign in the shop window for weeks before Vintage Magic opened but it seemed that nobody knew where Mooch had come from, not even her neighbours.

Neighbours. Everybody needs good neighbours. And these were something Rose had not even considered as she signed her name on the dotted line that spelt the end of any savings, nest egg or high-interest account that she might have held.

On one side, an old bow-fronted shop announced itself as Ye Olde Coffee House though a lesser sign painted and peeling on weathered wood swinging below it promised 'Tea and Sympathy'. Old newspaper cuttings blu-tacked and yellowing in the window detailed infamous celebrities and famous dignitaries of byegone eras who had patronised the café. Amongst them, Danny la Rue and that chap who used to operate the glove puppet Spit the Dog. But in its heyday – some three centuries before – it had been a meeting place for prime ministers, idle dandies and ladies of questionable repute.

'Mimi will feel right at home then,' laughed the sisters.

When Rose had been in possession of the keys to the property for less than two hours and was giving Lily, Leia and Matt a guided tour, two ladies had appeared on the back step. Mimi was absent, saying that there were finer ruins to visit in Bath. Still reeling from her daughter's decision to become 'trade'.

'She clearly has no idea what that means in today's terms,' observed Matt to Rose. 'Let's hope she doesn't use that expression to describe you at the Townswomen Guild.'

'Coooeee!' Voices had called out and any hint that it might be an unwelcome intrusion was swept away as they offered a cake stand of French Fancies, Maderia and chunky, rough-cut lemon drizzle slices as a welcome gift. Both women were like Mimi, well past their sell-by-date – unlike their cakes – but were not quite as well preserved. Grey hair was curled and permed, faces wrinkled but warm and homely contrasted with Mimi's streaked, frosted coiffure and plumped, tightened cheeks. They were all smiles, finishing each other's sentences in their sing-song West Country accents and giggly as school girls. They gave Rose the potted history and menu – which included potted meat – of Ye Olde Coffee House.

'We do teacakes, light snacks –'
'Cheese on toast –'
'Soup of the day –'

'And a roll, if you need one,' they directed to Matt with a saucy wink and elbow to the ribs and away they tittered.

When Leia refused a slice of Manor House because of her dislike of dried fruit, they cajoled her into trying it.

'Those aren't raisins, Little One. They are ginger-bread men's eyes!'

Leia, intrigued and with quite a macabre streak, ate the lot.

They introduced themselves as Mrs Waters – 'Everyone travels to Bath to take the Waters!' they said, curling into balls of hysteria – and Mrs Bridges. 'What's this? What's this?' they choroused as Mrs Waters stooped to touch her toes with a face of pantomime tragedy and Mrs Bridges loomed over her, forming an arch.

'Bridges over Troubled Waters!' And they roared anew, pushing shoulders and back-slapping as if it was the most hilarious joke they had ever heard and they'd only just heard it for the first time.

'What about "Still waters run deep"?' Rose tried to get in on the joke but the laughter stopped and they looked at her as though she were quite mad. They described their little coffee shop as a Home for Lost Crockery, explaining that whenever they saw odd cups and saucers in the windows of the Cancer Research shop that they bought them up – 'They look so lonely, poor things!' – and later they lent Rose the mismatched china for the opening day of Vintage Magic. It was obvious that the shop was not just their job but was also their hobby and their reason for being. They took great pride in serving traditional, home-cooked snacks of Welsh rarebit and boiled egg and soldiers, and were adamant about the No Pasta policy.

'No! No pasta! Absolutely not!' they asserted without ever explaining their aversion.

They were excited by Rose's plans but warned her that Bath was no sleepy town when it came to thieves, shoplifters and pick pockets.

'We can always spot a runner, can't we, Mrs Bridges?'

'That's right, Mrs Waters. We can.' And they described a routine that involved Mrs Waters barring the door with broom, mop or cooking implement whilst Mrs Bridges, the one with the build of a seaside postcard mother-in-law, would persuade the miscreant to either pay up or get to it over a pile of dirty dishes. Very few refused.

'But you'll not get any trouble from our tenants!' twinkled Mrs Waters.

'No, they are no trouble at all!' They nearly burst with the laughter they were trying to contain.

'Do they rent the rooms upstairs?' queried Rose, and Mrs Bridges and Waters began their double act.

'No, no, no! That's our stockroom –'

'They're not there all year round –'

'Only when needs must –'

'In the back room, down the steps, not quite the cellar –'

'In the cold room, that was once a dairy –'

'Very hush, hush!' And they tapped their noses and went off bubbling into near hysteria.

'Over the way' – they pointed through the back door – 'there's a funeral directors –'

'Been there for centuries. In the old days, they would get very busy and –'

'– Run out of space. So they had a few extra hidey holes, as it were, for their clients.'

'The sign – Tea and Sympathy – it's our little code for those who wish to visit their loved ones.'

'It was built into our lease. We get a few paying guests once or twice a year, but –'

'– They never complain!' the two chorused together.

'Oh my God! You live next door to a morgue!' Lily hissed after they were gone, hairs raised on her arms she was so spooked. Luckily the whole exchange had passed by Leia, who had not passed up the opportunity of her mother being occupied by conversation. She had eaten the icing off as many French Fancies as she could in the given time and replaced the stripped sponges all very neatly back on the cake stand.

'This is an antique shop, not a museum!' The words had caused Rose to jump sharply, nearly knocking over a small glass dome containing a stuffed baby owl that she had been holding. 'If you're not interested in buying the merchandise you're handling, you can put it down and get out!'

After meeting one side of her adjoining neighbours, Rose had soon decided it would be a good idea to make the acquaintance of the other. Birdcage Antiques had a painted sign of curling script and a rusting version of its name swinging from a bracket level with its first-floor window. The Victorian cage contained a single, metal bird clinging to its perch. As the wind moved across the square, the cage swung, squeaking out its melancholic birdsong. Rose was determined to get Matt up there with some WD 40 as soon as the coast was clear.

Jam-packed with antique ephemera – military jackets, marble washstands, antlers, beetles and butter-flies pinned into cases – little light came from the crowded display window at the front. Each surface and every inch of wall space was crowded with piles of leatherbound books on which balanced delicate figurines, while crystal necklaces draped from gilded wall sconces and umbrellas, shooting sticks and parasols jutted from large vases like haphazard floral displays. Cluttered stairs curving to the floor above suggested that the shop's stock had overflowed to another level.

Rose was still stammering for words as she approached the crowded counter where a woman of indeterminate age sat knitting, watching a computer screen where a role-playing fantasy game of elves and orcs played out while, simultaneously, an open book lay in her lap. Rose had not seen her there in amongst the taxidermy, ancient library and kitchenalia. As she approached to make her introductions, the woman watched her steadily over her reading glasses, her ash-blond hair with silver threads of grey piled loosely at her neck. It was impossible to judge her size or stature as she was sitting surrounded by the chaotic piling of her shop's merchandise.

'I'm Rose Taylor. I'm the new—'

'I know who you are,' the woman said coolly, cutting her off. 'What sort of place are you thinking of opening up, then?' she asked, getting straight down to business.

'Vintage clothes.'

'Mmmmm,' was the woman's non-committal reply, but it seemed to Rose that she had confirmed something for the woman, earned brownie points, somehow. There was a mild softening of the features. A small thawing of the ice cap.

The woman made no attempt to give her own name or initiate conversation. She made no effort to disguise that she was scrutinising Rose from head to toe.

'And you are?' Rose kept smiling, though her face was aching with the effort.

There was a brief pause in the knitting as the woman stared straight at Rose and, after a very uncomfortable pause, said: 'Cynthia.'

'Cynthia, I'm really pleased to meet you. I'm sure I'll be round asking for all sorts of advice about the water rates or the bin men.' Rose babbled almost incoherently but started backing away towards the door. The introductions were over. 'Well, there might be a bit of noise as we get the place up to scratch and all that, but we'll try to work outside of shop hours so that your customers aren't disturbed—'

'He went mad you know,' Cynthia said without emotion but with the same steady gaze fixed on Rose.

'Who?'

'Brown – who had the shop before you. The bookseller.'

'Oh,' was all that Rose could think of to say.

'Said he could hear voices. That they came for him at night. It's been empty for at least twenty years now. No one would touch it. Not anyone local, anyhow.'

'Oh,' repeated Rose, but inwardly thought: *Thanks a friggin' bunch. I'll sleep well tonight, won't I?* Nevertheless, she tried to keep the mood light and the Mimi-taught stiff upper lip for Blighty.

'I was hoping that when I do my window display I might take some items on a sale-or-return basis with a credit in the window for you as a supplier because I think it would really set off some of my pieces,' Rose rushed on, and the energy of her speech seemed to disturb the dust of ages in the room. Her mouth was becoming tickled and dry as she spoke. 'Like the old gramophone, for example, or one of the domed stuffed birds. I think they'd look great alongside some of the more kitsch items I've collected.'

All the while the woman click-clacked at her knitting. Again there was that awful pause where Rose felt compelled to fill the gaping silence with inane chatter.

'I'll think about it.' The words came finally and Cynthia looked down at the book in her lap. The meeting was over.

Rose turned to leave and as she did so the skirt of her fifties shirt-waister caught on the corner of a barley-twist gate table leg. As she tugged to free it the entire table leaf began to wobble and Rose just managed to catch a very, very expensive-looking pale porcelain shepherd and shepherdess as they tumbled sideways as the whole side panel gave way.

Rose tried a 'Phew, gosh, that was close!', grimacing as she placed them back into a safer position to try and win round Cynthia who was looking at her with a face of thunder.

She then resorted to flattery, not entirely ingenuine, as she made her retreat.

'I love the things in here. You have a good . . . a good eye.' Rose used the very phrase that made her glow with pride. There was no pause this time, no hesitation. No invitation for discussion or acceptance of praise given.

'Yes, well, I charge for any breakages and those are not for sale. Goodbye!'

Rose was to discover that she had clearly made an impression of some sort because the Dansette record player and 78s had come from the Birdcage. As had the little Victorian glass dome that sat on a shelf at the back of the till with the bright black eyes of a baby owl looking quizzically down at the customers. An odd thing, not to everyone's taste. And not to Mimi's, who shuddered every time she looked at it but definitely to Leia's, who asked endless questions about its being dead – how – and then stuffed – why – and what with and by whom?

But with each passing day as Vintage Magic was open for business, Rose knew she had made one of the better decisions of her life – like the one to stop watching *Big Brother* – even celebrity versions.

When a teenager skipped out clutching a pink bri-nylon slip that Rose had worn in her grunge years under a plaid shirt with army boots, it gave Rose a kick to think that a slip she could no longer wear without control underwear would have a new lease of life with someone else. The girl described excitedly how she was going to team it with stacked platforms and rolled hair, forties-style.

Then, a seventies Margot-from-the-*Good Life* chiffon full-length evening gown in neon pink, yellow and green, which Rose had once bought for a fancy dress party, left for a new home with one of the most beautiful women Rose had ever seen in her life.

'You are Elizabeth Taylor in the Richard Burton years,' blurted out Rose when the woman came out of the changing room on tip-toes to check her reflection in a different light.

'I feel it!' laughed the woman without a trace of arrogance. It was simply true and they both knew it. 'I feel like a film star.' And Rose knew that this woman had been infected with the special magic of vintage, that indefinable feeling that only vintage can give, transporting the wearer to another time and another way of being. Rose was just so glad that her shop name was a testimony to it.

Rose enjoyed dressing the window; her plan was to change it each week and Cynthia was letting her have a choice of objects once she realised it brought her more sales. So far, Rose could get away with the vintage pieces she'd saved and others she'd bought from market but soon, very soon, she would have to find a new supplier as the clothes were selling fast.

Rose was even enjoying her new home and there were certain advantages to living alone, she began to realise. No holding in of wind until her stomach cramped with the effort; she could just let it all go and no one could complain. The boring task of bikini-line epilation could be done in front of the TV. She did not find pee splashes on the toilet seat that were not of her own making. But as she arranged her belongings, Rose still found herself wondering would Carl like it? Would he say it was bohemian and craftsy – the look she was going for? Or would he say it was studenty and a *60 Minute Makeover* rush-job?

It was no *Livingetc* magazine interior but it was clean and fresh and liveable in. Rose had painted everything white, even the floorboards, the grotty much-glossed kitchen cupboards and the greying tiles and sludgy grouting in the bathroom.

'It's Narnia!' quipped Matt, his hair and beard speckled white, once they'd finished an evening of rollering, brushing and emulsioning, his eyes wide with wonder or snow-blindness.

She had a new business, a new life. On her mantel-piece was a card of best wishes from Him (and Her – a fact Rose chose to overlook), but Carl had said he'd come soon and when he did, he'd see a house of serenity in contrast to the cluttered home they once shared. He would see a New Rose, confident – no longer needy, lean and healthy from good eating not crash diets, looking gorgeous in something she hadn't quite decided on yet. Carl would look at his life with Isabelle in the little boxy new build they were now buying on some brown-field site that had been declared relatively asbestos-free and wonder if he'd made the right choice.

He would walk in, he would see her smiling and successful, radiant behind her vintage bar shop counter and he would want her back. And when he asked her – it was just, after all, a matter of time – when he came and said he had made a big mistake and would she, could she, ever forgive him? Then Rose Taylor would smile and say yes and they would begin their life, the life they had planned, all over again.

5

Peggy Mountford had lived. Lived in the sense of 'been places' like St Tropez, New York and Monte Carlo. Lived because she'd 'known people' – famous, rich, influential people – like David Niven, one of the girls from the Profumo affair and someone who was rumoured to spy for the Russians. A good-time girl, she had loved fast cars and faster men. She'd been a looker, too, in her day, dating only the wealthiest because she was beautiful enough to choose. There had been millionaire businessmen, an infamous East End gangster and the odd well-known actor – not all of them married.

She had not believed in natural beauty. She believed in putting on her face, keeping on top of roots, plucking, shaving and padding out (boobs) or sticking on (nails or eyelashes), if the God-given ones weren't big enough. She kept her hair titian till the day she died and had never – not once – in her life sun-bathed.

Her obituary read 'beloved aunt' and so she was. Indulging her nephews and nieces with an ear for every problem and a tenner slipped expertly into the hand to help get the sexy new shoes or a round in the pub, whatever it was, parents had forbidden. 'If you can't be good, be careful, and if you haven't been careful, come and see me,' Peggy would say with a wink, but she knew from bleak experience the need for caution and there had been solemn, painful visits to grim terraces in the parts of town she'd sung her heart out to get away from.

'One-time singer'. Three words could not possibly give a true account of this part of her life. She had been a torch singer, the slow and sensual feature of a night of variety. Her signature being smoky-voiced renditions of 'Cry Me a River' that earned her the title of Blackpool's Julie London. She had cut her teeth in the working men's clubs that formed the backbone of the British entertainment industry before an agent, whom she'd only slept with once, secured her the top slots in places that don't sound so glamorous in this modern age – theatres in Morecambe, Brighton and Bournemouth – the holiday hot-spots of their day. Then there were the cruise ships, travel to Europe. Exotic places for a girl whose family worked the docks in Bristol.

She'd kept all her show costumes and the best of her day-wear, even though she had not fitted in them for years. Her devoted grief-stricken niece, now a grown woman, explained all to Rose.

'That's why we called you. We don't know what to do with them and my girls won't wear them.' She gestured to a trilogy of sportswear-clad, Maccy d-complexioned girls and Rose wondered what their great-aunt must have thought of them.

Each piece was zippered into garment bags; boxed shoes, dyed to match, were wrapped in tissue. Barely used handbags were stowed away in covers along with boxes of crystals and paste jewels – the real diamonds long since pawned when times were lean. Peggy would open the wardrobe when they visited as children, the niece recalled, unzipping each bag to reveal the beauty within, recounting stories of where that dress had been, the famous people it had mingled with. The dresses still smelled of her perfume and of the cigarette smoke that would have hung in strata in the nightclub air.

So, childless and forty, she got married to a long-time friend. Years later, the nephews and nieces would learn that she was his 'Beard', his disguise for a sexuality that had been both illegal and a sectionable offence. Peggy knew. Of course she knew. You could not work in show business and not know a 'fruit' when you saw one. But they had the best sham marriage, better than any real marriage would have been had she taken up any of the offers. Thirty-five years they had together before he passed on. Thirty-five years of recreating Fanny and Johnnie Cradocks' dinners for the group of friends that got smaller every year with old age snapping at their heels. Years when he consoled her as she looked in the mirror at a face that was not the one she remembered.

'Worse to have looks like hers taken away. Worse to

age when you've only known beauty.' The niece shook her head at the cruelty of the passing years.

They had their Pekineses and occasionally holidayed at the old remaining haunts in the South of France. Peggy had all the cuddles and kisses and compliments that she could ever wish for and she had her memories of places been to and people seen.

But the nieces and nephews would never know the other stories she could tell; tales of torn stockings, steamy windows and clumsy fiddling at the hooks and eyes of girdles. Of quickies in dressing rooms, desperate, fur-clad fuckings in the backs of old Bentleys whilst the chauffeur stood chain-smoking outside, of hotel rooms where chairs, tables and balconies were not out of bounds. Of sex on the beach as the sun rose over Nice. Of being seduced by an oil-wealthy Saudi Arab with the eyes of Omar Sharif and a voice as smooth as honey-sweetened coffee. Of the aphrodisiac high that comes when a companion wins several thousand pounds at the spin of a roulette wheel. Of diamonds, clasped sensually, to the neck and the zippers of dresses slowly, slowly undone. Oh yes, Peggy Mountford had lived, all right.

The wardrobes – for there was more than one; a whole box room in the semi-detached house had been devoted to the storing of costumes that would never again grace a stage or be discarded in heat to the bedroom floor – were a treasure trove. As the cache in each one was revealed, Rose felt like Carnarvon at Tutankhamen's tomb. There were heavy satins and intricate beading. Floaty chiffon numbers and shantung silks. There was underwear too; bras that looked like miniature works of engineering, girdles that would make the Lady Gaga wannabees who came to the shop very happy indeed. There were negligees and peignoirs in shades of girlish pastel to whorish reds and blacks that made Rose wonder if she and Carl would still be together had she gone to bed in these at night instead of the tartan flannel pyjamas that she favoured.

Day and evening wear dating from the late forties to the end of the sixties had been preserved in sizes that reflected a woman's changing body shape as decades rolled by. Accessories – hats, scarves, belts, shoes, jewellery – all this and a back story. Rose instantly knew which customers she would be on the phone to with news of this haul and who would be beating a path to her door.

As Rose left, her car crammed with booty, the niece presented her with a promotional card, framed and signed. A young and glamorous Peggy, a woman in her prime, in a slashed-to-the-waist satin number, all pointy bosoms and swirly signature stared confidently into the camera with 'I'm Going to Eat You Up' eyes and hands on hips that promised more than one night of entertainment. Rose couldn't wait to get home and hang that picture on the wall, and she would keep it on her wall for ever.

*

She had to get a website. Scratch that, she had to get a computer, but she knew nothing about Intel Pentium Dual Cores, broadband connections or gigabytes of hard drive. Did they do hand-propelled ones like her sewing machine? In her old life, Rose had left all that side of things to Carl and hadn't even thought about a PC's essential place in modern living whilst she had access to Lily's laptop. Even Mimi had surpassed Rose with her computer know-how, having gone on one of the many courses that she liked to attend. 'Cruising grounds for Senior Citizens,' Lily called them.

It wasn't that Rose was a Luddite, it was just that her brain didn't work like a computer. Her mind did not comprise of folders and files stored alphabetically or in date order. Hers was more like a teenager's chest of drawers; overfull, in need of a good dusting, with things – dirty and clean – stuffed in anyhow. She liked computers, loved the web with all its access to obscure sites like babyanimalz.com and bizarre postings of girls in Iceland listing everything they ate; but the whole business of how things popped up on her screen was like some mini jet-haired/orange-skinned David Copperfield trick performed in her living room. And she couldn't cope with the need to keep updating and keeping abreast of blogs and tweets! It was a language she couldn't be bothered to learn governed by laws akin to witchcraft.

But Peggy's wardrobe had been a catalyst. Before

she put all the pieces out for purchase she wanted to catalogue and keep a record of every item in that once-loved wardrobe, plus she needed somewhere to file her clients' names, not just pencil them into her old puppy in a flower-pot-fronted address book. She could send out emails as new stock arrived – cheaper than phone calls – and now that she'd sorted out her supply issue there were a number of clients waiting for old band T-shirts. The popularity of old Rolling Stone tour shirts and kitsch – the more horned helmets the better – heavy metal band tees was something Rose had not anticipated. Plus everyone who came through the door asked her if she had a website.

Ironically, Cynthia's antique shop had the most up-to-date system that kept track of merchandise in the shop or out at storage; it automatically kept an archived record of stock sold and allowed for Internet purchases alerting Cynthia as items were sold by a text to her phone. Short of making the tea and putting the hoover around, there was not a lot that it couldn't do. Rosie had made up her mind to get something similar.

'Aaargh! Mooch, stop it!' The black cat leapt into a box of Peggy's clothes causing a rustle of fabrics that had him spooked and leaping around in both attack and defence. Rose was petrified that he would get his claws out and there would be rips and pulls to repair in clothes that had been pristine for the last forty years. She grabbed Mooch out of the box, almost straining a muscle in the process, and put him to the floor.

He was an odd cat but then, perhaps, no odder than any other. Always lying in strange places, like in the middle of the entrance to the changing room so that customers had to step over him. Always favouring a cardboard box over the fluffy cat igloo bought at great expense. He would choose to slink into the very seat that Rose was about to relax in and hold her in a staring contest until she relented and let him stay there, or he would race around the room as though being chased, or arch his back like a Halloween ornament, fluffing up his tail in a loo-brush style and spitting venom at thin air. The cellar door would only have to open a crack and he'd be down there in the dark for hours – not that it bothered Rose, but she knew he would bring her back a little mauled present with eyes shut tight and pink mousie paws in a pose of begging for life. And occasionally, very occasionally, he would crawl on to her lap for a little fuss and shower her with affectionate purrings and head rubbings. That's when she knew that he needed feeding.

But Rose was very glad of his company. His weight at the foot of the bed was reassuring and comforting on those nights when she began to think about Carl and couldn't sleep, when the squeaking of the bird cage grated on her nerves and her imagination ran riot. When she thought about the life she once had and the future she now wouldn't. When, after the busyness of the day and the absorbing business of the shop, there was that gap in activity where negative thoughts creep in. It was a time when she thought about friends who stole men right from under your nose and of corpses, lying in a cold store, a stone's throw away. Time when her dressing gown on the back of the door looked like a hooded figure in the half-light when her glasses were out of reach and when she heard whispered voices and names called and had to remind herself that they were drunks reeling their way home or lovers who had stopped to kiss out in the square.

On those nights, Rose thought about the mysterious bookseller Mr Brown, driven mad by hushed murmurings, and how if you didn't realise that sound could bounce around the walls of the square you might think that the voices were in the room with you or creeping their way upstairs. It would be easy if you were lonely or lacking in logic to think that someone was just behind the door or muttering at your shoulder.

Mrs Bridges and Mrs Waters, bringing over one of the many snacks Rose now purchased – she had become like Mimi; she rarely cooked in the kitchen, only dusted – spoke sadly of Mr Brown.

'It's a shame, a real shame.'

'A brilliant man.'

'Loved ancient history.'

'There was nothing he didn't know about Bath. Collected artefacts.'

'They either went to Cynthia's or in the bin. No relatives, you see.'

'Still, in the funny farm we've heard—'

'Best place for him. He was *very* troubled of mind.'

'Said the place was haunted, but these old houses, they creak –'

'And groan and shift about on their foundations. But, as we always say, it's not the dead you shared you should be scared of –'

'It's the living!' And they broke off into peals of laughter at their shared in-joke, their eyes glittering, but Rose was still left with an uncomfortable feeling that would not go away, that she couldn't pin down, much as she loved her new home. A feeling of fear, of unease, an angst reminiscent of monsters under the bed and ghosts behind the curtain.

Like now, for example. Eight o'clock in the evening, church bells chiming the hour and all of the tourists and shoppers had left the square. Rose was photographing and hand-writing descriptions of each item in the Peggy Mountford haul with some inane television programme playing quietly in the background. It was something that involved people who were too embarrassed to show their doctor some pustulating sore in the anal region but for some reason were entirely happy to show television cameras that would beam the image out to the nation. In HD. Not exactly riveting, but 'car crash' television; Rose couldn't peel her eyes away. It all should have been enough to distract and absorb her but part of her was stuck on red-alert.

'Rose! Rose!' A gentle sing-songy voice, barely audible, caught her attention. The sort of voice used when somebody is trying to be simultaneously quiet and shout to get attention. Her ears pricked like the cat's. Then she ignored it. She wasn't expecting anybody. It wasn't a voice she recognised, it was just her imagination. She turned the television up but there it was again.

'Rose! Rose!' it repeated several times. Then she checked her mobile phone. Nothing. Matt had once thought he was talking to voices from beyond the grave before realising he had accidently called someone and they were just shouting to get his attention from his coat pocket.

'Rose! Rose! I'm here. I'm heeeeerrrrrre.'

Pure horror movie lines, far too Jack Nicholson at the door swinging an axe, for Rose's liking. She was adrenalised now. Heart pumping, every hair standing up on her body, but not her upper lip, she was pleased to note, her scalp prickled as every nerve strained in attention to detect the location of the sound. *This is ridiculous*, thought Rose. *Haven't I grown out of believing ghost stories? I'm getting too over-dramatic. I've not been sleeping well.*

'Ro-o-o-ose! I'm down heee-rrr-e.'

The voice was there again, the pitch rising and falling like some sinister nursery rhyme. It did sound like it was coming from downstairs, right underneath here. Oh my God! Maybe Mr Brown was right and the place *was* haunted.

'Rose! Rose! I'm heeeerrrre! I'm going to get you –'

Enough, thought Rose there must be someone out there playing tricks and she ran to the window, letting out a primitive roar as she pulled back the curtains and flung open the pane in one, single, deft movement.

There was no one there. The square was completely and utterly empty. Just her shout echoing back off the stone of the tattoo shop on the other side.

'Rose! R-o-o-o-se! Can you hear me, Rose?'

It was in the house. The sinister voices that said they were going to get Mr Brown were right here in the house! And they were going to get her! She grabbed her mobile to dial 999 just in case.

'And ask for what?' Lily sneered when Rose told her about the event later. 'Fire, police, ambulance or exorcist?'

Then Rose looked for something to use as a weapon. There was nothing except a few of her treasured art school pieces so Rose arranged her hands into something resembling a karate chop. Wasn't looking confident half the battle won? She was not yellow! She was no Mr Brown! She would face these voices head-on, relying on nothing but being pure of heart and some basic – very basic – judo lessons. Isn't that how it worked in the movies?

Advancing down the stairs, feeling very Lara Croft all of a sudden, Rose snapped on the light.

'Aaaaaaaahh!' Cynthia screamed, caught in the halogen spotlights.

'Aaaaaarghhhh!' Rose responded.

'I was just on my way home.' The antique shop owner sounded affronted, holding her hand to her heart and steadying her breathing. 'I've been calling for ages. It's no wonder you couldn't hear me with that television blaring out.'

The TV doctor could clearly be heard saying '. . . and this rash extends all the way round to your scrotum, does it?'

'Your bell's not working and you hadn't locked the front door! You should be more careful! You looked like you were going to attack me and I was only going to offer my help!'

'I thought you were a ghost threatening to get me! Or a burglar,' Rose quickly added, feeling stupid as she said it aloud.

'I'm going to get you the card of my web designer!' Cynthia enunciated in clear tones preserved for speaking to the hard of hearing or mentally impaired. 'That's what I was trying to say! You asked me to, remember? I'll put it through your door in the morning, unless you're going to leave it unlocked all night.'

Rose, desperate not to offend her neighbour, who was sounding very prickly indeed, found herself inviting Cynthia in.

'Come up. Come up! Come and see what I've done in here.' It was the first time she had seen Cynthia out from behind her crowded shop counter. Her age was still difficult to determine – older than Rose, certainly, but by how much? Even her build was difficult to define under the layers of jumpers and coats. She was accentless but not *Antique Roadshow*-posh like Mimi. She was just a very regular-looking woman who was not on the breadline but who could be a millionaire who chose not to show it. She didn't wear labels or easily definable status symbols that might give clues to quantities of cash or job done. She was like anyone you could work with or somebody's mum. Cynthia was quiet, looking around Vintage Magic and then the flat with the same unhidden scrutiny with which she had assessed Rose. 'I've been thinking about Mr Brown and the voices,' Rose said meekly, trying to explain her neurotic approach as she led her neighbour back up to her living room.

'What for?' Cynthia said after her usual pause. 'It's over. Gone. In the past. You can't change it.' Cynthia was abrupt and matter of fact, refusing the offered drink and, considering it was she who had spooked Rose with the story in the first place, she was now acting like it was No Big Deal.

'Even so. It's so sad—'

Cynthia cut her off. 'People go mad all the time for all sorts of reasons. It's not worth thinking about. The trouble with Bath is that there is too much history, too many legends. He let himself get carried away by them.'

'But you said he heard voices—'

'He did. It was just a comment. That's what he claimed, anyhow; but you're here now and you're not hearing voices, are you?' There was more of that

Cynthia scrutiny – the peering, the reading for a response.

Rose, speaking aloud but more to herself and lying, said, 'No, but it keeps preying on my mind. I might burn a bit of sage or sprinkle some holy water or something. It's meant to be helpful, isn't it? To get rid of bad vibes.'

'You can't do that.'

'Why not?'

'No exorcisms. It's in your lease. Check it.' And then suddenly, 'Well, I can't stay! I'll bring you the card tomorrow.' And she was retreating back down the steps and gone before Rose could detain her with a cup of tea.

No exorcisms?! Maybe she should have got Carl to check over all the legalities after all because those funny old bye-laws existed. Hadn't Matt's parent's got some ancient stipulation hanging over their farmhouse that anyone could ride a horse through the kitchen on Christmas Eve if they so requested? But Rose burnt some essential oils and lit a candle anyhow and hoped that no one would find out to tell.

That was the first inkling that all was not right. That things in and around Vintage Magic were at odds, a mix of dichotomies. To feel so strangely at home and yet scared was an odd combination. So there were eccentric neighbours, so what? But sometimes there were dead bodies in the old dairy. All quite normal . . . but also abnormal. And Mr Brown, Rose reasoned, had been – and still was – mentally ill; that's not sorcery, that's one in three of the population at some point in their lives.

But it was an old, old building built on older foundations and history does tend to leave its mark, breathing its happiness and sorrows into the atoms of a place. Like castle dungeons that resonate with horrors once seen or warm parlours where the laughter and love of happy families tumble from the walls.

Rose, who understood very little about cyberspace, knew absolutely nothing about time and space. She might have had her suspicions based on almost mute instinct and forays into the sci-fi channel, but knowledge about how the fabric works that keeps everything as it should be, Rose had none. Gauzy and flimsy as voile, the web at the intervals of time can wear very thin indeed. In places it can be weakened by a combination of energies beyond the knowledge of your average physics teacher but somewhere in the grasp of fans of *Dr Who*. It can be torn open, ripped like a frayed seam and a fissure appear, meaning that the past can slip into the present or other worlds leak into this. It can happen in places least expected.

In Rose's cellar there was one such spot. Behind the boxes of books stacked by Mr Brown as a primitive form of protection before they took him away, boxes that Matt, that very weekend, was planning to remove. Behind the crumbling, patched plaster that had cracked to the vibrations of the drilling, sawing and hammering of the Vintage Magic preparations. Beyond the broken plasterwork, layers of wattle and daub and crude clay bricks were now revealed. Here, the strands of time and place were tissue-paper thin and little breaths from other realms evanesced into the air like warm vapours on a cold morning.

Mooch had sensed it and watched, green eyes unblinking, catching mice to pass the time as he waited to see what would unfold. Rose had only that faint discomfort to warn her but she could not have prevented all that would happen even had she known. Some clumsy, accidental repair work may have held it back for a time but would just have delayed the inevitable. She could not have foreseen that her funky little shop with its fairy lights and Meatloaf 'Dead Ringer for Love' pinball machine would become a portal for an unstoppable, uncontrollable energy capable of wonder and terror, life and cataclysmic destruction, if it so wished. And down in her cellar it was building its energies like a fizzy bottle of pop on a cycle ride home.

She had no idea of what was to come. She thought she had created a good atmosphere for happy customers to enjoy adventures in vintage. It was beyond Rose Taylor's imaginings that powers, unexplained by science and the industrial age, were amassing beneath her feet, altering subtly the laws of how things are and should be. And Rose could not have conceived that Vintage Magic, beyond its advertised promise with its cheesecake shots of Diana Dors, would really, absolutely, quite literally release the glamorous goddess within.

Rose found it endlessly fascinating what customers chose to buy and she played a little game to see if she could guess what would appeal. The choice of a vintage district nurse's uniform – did it belie a quirky sense of style, sexual fetish or sense of the historic? Often she could not predict what someone would buy but sometimes she was right, completely spot-on.

A rockabilly girl, with hair quiffed, falling on a rail of circular skirts and vintage baseball jackets was hardly surprising. Which coat for the wannabe jazz-baby with Velma Kelly bob? (A look that had failed for Rose; more Velma from *Scooby Doo* once her glasses were on.) The astrakhan cocoon coat? Too easy! Indie students in coloured tights with skinny, leather-jacketed boyfriends in tow tended to be attracted by the man-made fibres of the sixties and seventies. Maybe because they were too young to recall the sweaty, static cling of wearing them as hand-me-downs first time around. But there were times when Rose was way off target.

She was not a customer Rose recalled seeing before:

a young woman in her mid-twenties, her clothes were Gap-safe and supermarket staples, worn for practicality and purpose. In muted shades of beige and grey intended to camouflage, the utilitarian fabrics washed well and tumble dried even better. Even her footwear – loafers, in the driving shoe sense of the phrase – screamed comfort, easi-clean and light for packing. Nothing – from the hair cut that would never require product to the bag that was actually a compartmental-ised satchel – nothing was frivolous or worn for pure adornment or sensual pleasure.

She looked nervous, nervous as hell. She stared at a few rails, moving the clothes but not really seeing them. There was no eager pulling from the pack or holding garments to the light. She did not dive to the rummage bargain box, reaching straight to the depths for a grown-up game of Lucky Dip. Instead, frowning, she looked around the shop, biting her lip and looking a little like she might just rush back out the door.

Then it struck Rose. She was a Vintage Virgin. Not as common as they used to be, and Rose, filled with an evangelical zeal to convert (or deflower) her, approached all smiles, trying not to rub her hands together in pantomime glee.

The girl blurted out, 'I'm looking for a dress to wear on a night out.' A simple request, and Rose, with her rails upon rails hidden in her spare room/secret stock cupboard, could certainly help. But what the girl didn't say but meant was 'a dress to make me feel special. A dress that stands out but doesn't make me feel stupid. A beautiful dress but one that doesn't itch or scratch or make me walk like a builder in heels. A dress that is me. A dress that means he will know I exist.'

Not a feminist sentiment or a sophisticated one; quite primitive and not in keeping with the intelligent woman that she was. But clothes and the changes they wrought are embodied in the oldest of folk tales. Fairy stories of glass slippers, girls disguised as boys leading conquering armies, paupers, princes, poisoned girdles and red cloaks fill children's heads at bedtime. No one is immune from this early socialisation. The power of dress to transform lives and to find the perfect match.

'Fantastic! Let's see if we can find what you're looking for,' enthused Rose. 'Is it a special night?'

The girl nodded mutely.

'Is it formal or casual?'

'It's a meal with work.' She named a restaurant where somebody trained with somebody who once trained with a celebrity chef. The portions were expensive and small but it was a place to be seen and the food was first class. This was not the Harvester or eat-all-you-can Chinese buffet that was Rose's experience of work outings.

'So do you have anything in mind?'

'That one!' She pointed with sudden decisive intention to an emerald green satin sheath with small sequin and beaded flowers straight from the Peggy Mountford Collection. It had been in the window for over a week, drawing many glances from passers-by and Rose had cleaned the window more than once from all the pressed noses and drooling chins. She had set up, with loans from Cynthia, a scene of cocktail shakers, Martini glasses, vintage nudey-girl playing cards and original Rat Pack records.

'Wow! A bold choice, but' – Rose hoped she hadn't made it sound like I could never have imagined *you* choosing that – 'it's had a lot of interest. It's certainly a stunning piece.' Rose pulled it from the rail and held it against her customer. It highlighted the subtle red tones of her hair and pale skin. 'With your colouring I think you're going to pull it off.'

There was much scuffling behind the changing room curtain and Rose had to retrieve Mooch twice as he started heading with a purposeful stride to investigate. Vintage fit is always hit and miss. Body shape then is not body shape now. Fitted bodices were intended to be worn with two-way stretch 'lift and separate' corsetry. Bosoms were higher, elevated and offered as if being served on a tea-tray. Shoulders were narrower in times past and quite often the last two inches of zip are the ones that lead to defeat.

Rose waited, busying herself with straightening and folding chores. She wanted it to fit. Clearly this young woman had spotted the dress and decided it was the one. It could be the start of a lifetime of vintage love.

Eventually, the curtain swept back and Rose's

customer emerged walking, bare feet and flat footed, towards the mirror, and as she did so running her hands on hips, up and down her newly discovered waist, enjoying the sensation of smooth satin and the cool, rough texture of the beading.

She had new added colour, maybe from the exertion of pulling the zipper up alone, but there was a flush to her cheeks as if she were suddenly filmed in Technicolor. But there was more. As she walked towards the long swivel mirror, she raised herself slowly up on tiptoe as if in heels. Suddenly her hips had a certain fluidity, swaying in Monroe rhythm so that by the time she stopped at her reflection her stance was pure Peggy not-so-pure Mountford.

Another customer let out a long low whistle. 'That is so you!' and the girl blushed and basked under the compliment. Rose was nodding in appreciation.

'Mmmm . . . shoes.' the girl said to herself. 'Hair . . .' She was piling it up on her head, tousling it, testing it first in a French pleat – not quite long enough – then behind the ears, then nape of the neck. 'Lipstick . . .' She was testing ideas in her head, posing this way and that, pouting a little. Any shred of self consciousness was stripped away. Rose loved this part of her work, running ideas past her customers as she ran to get accessories. Jewellery? Too much. The dress was embellished enough. Shoes? She had some just the right height but . . . shame . . . the wrong fit. Coat? A black A-line opera coat in a light wool? Perfect! Just enough to keep out the chill but the dress could still be glimpsed with each step.

By the time dress and coat were being folded in tissue and placed carefully in the paper carrier bags made from recycled copies of *Jackie* and *Judy* magazines, Rose had told the complete story as she knew it of Peggy Mountford, the portrait had been shown and her customer had left still with a blush to her face, a dream of a dress in her possession and hope for a promising night out in her heart. So simple. Job done. Another happy, satisfied customer taking away a little Vintage Magic. It was like putting a loaded gun in the hands of a baby.

'Lily, why are they staring at us?' Rose hissed.

'They are staring because we are girls and this is Nerdy-Boy-Central. Very few will ever have had girlfriends and even if they have, they will all still be virgins,' Lily whispered back whilst retaining a wide grin and nodding at each blank, staring face as they passed. 'It wouldn't matter if we had three breasts or no head. They would still find us devastatingly attractive because we are female. End of.'

They were in the offices of Hands Solo Web Design, home of Cynthia's website designers and, other than the Buffy the Vampire Slayer posters, they were the only female presence in the room. Lily had wanted to come because the company name had more than a nod to her favourite film of all-time-ever. Rose had misgivings; she felt the name sounded like a massage parlour and not one that did good things to muscles or your lymphatic system at that. The looks being given were not lecherous or leering but it was as if Lily and Rose represented a new species that had just happened to walk into the room. The sisters half expected one of them to leap up and start sniffing at their hair, all the while murmuring, 'Pretty. Pretty.'

The office team were a mixture of odd shapes, heights and facial hair combinations. One had nails that were creepily too long and another had piercings, but they all had tell-tale monitor tans from sitting in front of a computer screen for too many hours a day. Real sunlight and fresh air had not touched their skin for a very long time.

Rose and Lily were being led to a waiting area next to a water cooler, where they were told by a pale youth in a Slayer T-shirt to take a seat, which they did so uncomfortably on the bean bags and the banana gaming chairs provided. There was a notice board of unread fire exit direction and spoof health and safety directives about how an increased incidence of haemorrhoids correlates with sitting at computers for too long. There were office calendars but not the sort found usually in an all-male environment, say a garage or a building yard. They were of all the *Star-Trek* spacecraft that ever were or *X-Men*.

Lily's eyes were wide open. There were shelves of *Star Wars* merchandise, an R2-D2 phone, a Lego Death

Star and, sitting in imperial isolation, spot-lit and gleaming in a dedicated position, was the life-sized head of a Storm-trooper. Disbelieving, Lily reached out to touch it.

'Please don't touch my helmet!' came a curt voice. 'It is the genuine one as worn by the trooper-extra on the right of the screen that bashes his head as he enters the control room where C3-PO and R2-D2 are hiding out. The scene is so popular that entirely due to fan request it has remained in the digitalised HD version of the film.' A film so famous it does not need naming. 'Do come through.' Lily came over a little giddy at being so close to a genuine Lucas *objet d'art*.

Except for the odd introduction, bordering on OCD in the full weight of its obsession and attention to detail, he was quite, quite conventional-looking. OK-looking, in fact. He was a nerd in normal clothing. Jeans, check shirt, V-neck; business-casual and inoffensive. Average height and build, he had the sort of stubble that suggested you could watch his beard grow in one night on the town. A twice-a-day shaver, definitely. Been there, done that, thought Rose empathetically. He was talking now, all business-like and professional and shaking hands. Nice hands, oddly, girlishly smooth compared to Matt's, which were callused from practical outdoor labour or even Carl's, which had palm callouses from exercising on his bike. ('Bike? Is that his new pet name for Isabelle?' Lily had once commented.) Yes, he had smooth hands but they were nice hands, none the less. He was eerily familiar.

'You're Vintage Magic, right? Richard Clarke. Call me Rich. Pleased to meet you. I'm afraid my partner John can't be with us today – he's undertaking some advanced training on the latest updates to Dreamweaver. But we set Cynthia up a while ago and she's never looked back. We can develop an easily maintained package at the minimum of cost to you and your business, all off-set against tax, of course. I think for this first phase, a face-to-face to meeting works best and, of course, we'll come out to your premises . . .'

Rose was only half listening. She was suddenly sweaty and distracted. Pinned to a noticeboard to her left was the front page of a local newspaper, screaming headlines about boozy Britain and supported by the legendary still of Rose Taylor in mid-purge, vomit cascading on to her companion's shoes. Thank God you couldn't really tell that it was her from the photograph but the man in the picture attempting to hold her upright and having his shoes doused with regurgitated Mexican snacks could be identified clearly. His portrait had been circled. Fame at Last! was the marker-penned picture title. *Oh no it isn't*. Rose thought, her stomach cramping. *Oh yes, it is*, came the pantomime audience reply in her head. Rich of Hands Solo Design was He of the Ruined Suede Shoes. He, sitting on the other side of the desk, was Cloakroom Man.

Rose lolled over the desk, leaning her head on her

hand and hoped she was obliterating the newspaper cutting before Lily could spot it. Lily, unable to stop herself, was asking about the business name now and he was explaining that it was part homage to *Star Wars* but was also so-named because he and his partner had set up their business alone and without any backing from the banks and very little know-how. They were the only 'hands on deck' and had spent their first few years winging it as best they could.

And still Rich's face was instantly familiar. And it was nothing to do with having vomited on his shoes – those brogues Rose would have been able to pick out in a line-up. Rose searched amongst the moving, changing features, trying to decide who he looked like and why she felt she knew him and then the penny dropped. Then it was clear. He was part Face from the *A-Team*, maybe around the eyes, with an indefinable touch of Christopher Plummer as Captain von Trapp in *The Sound of Music* in the almost aquiline nose and then there was, yes, it was there, just a hint, a shadow on the chin and jaw-line of *Magnum PI* himself – Tom Selleck. If he grew that moustache unchecked, most definitely. It was like looking into all of her childhood crushes in one strangely blended package. And somehow it worked.

He was still talking business but Rose had not been listening. 'I'll introduce you to the team and then you'll know who's who and we'll talk you through the full range of what we can do. We'll give you a variety of quotes for you to consider according to your financial situation and we'll take it from there. Once we're past the initial set-up phase we can exchange most of our information on-line and there won't be any need to come into the office again unless you'd like to—'

'Oh yes, I'd love to! I mean I'd like to . . . I'd like to do that.' Rose's enthusiasm was a little uncalled for in that situation. He looked at her quizzically. So did Lily.

Rose thought that she was just trying to bluff out any comparisons between herself and the drunken, ranting, singing harpy of their first meeting. She was not self-aware enough to recognise that this man had piqued her interest. Her pain at losing Carl was so all-consuming and habitual that it had left her numb, unable to register clearly any other reaction. But Lily was aware. She'd noticed as soon as she saw the glazed look enter Rose's eye when he walked in the room, her vagueness so unlike her sister's usual sharp responses. A little smile played at the corner of Lily's mouth. This was a Good Thing. Rose might be on the road to recovery after all.

'So, is your PC in the shop?' Pen poised, Rich was ready to take notes.

'Yes. I always strive to be politically correct, equal opportunities and all that.'

'No, *your* PC. Dumb Ass!' Lily elbowed Rose. Good Thing or no – Rose was being embarrassing. 'She hasn't got one at the moment. She's not long moved into the area.' Lily spoke for her as if she was very slow or elderly.

Then it was as if he was seeing Lily for the first time.

'You're not Mimi Taylor's daughter, are you?' he said frowning incredulously when Lily nodded agreement. 'We've got the contract for the college and I do some teaching on the University of the Third Age computer courses. She said she had two daughters and you are the image of her!'

Rose wanted to get off this conversation about looks and who had met who before – the newspaper article seemed to be magnified in her peripheral vision, calling out to her, mocking her, but Lily was already making the introduction about them being sisters.

'And you're Mimi's other daughter? Oh!' No comment, then; clearly he was wondering how a short, hirsute and vomity dwarf could be related to Lily and Mimi. He was still looking at her and he held her gaze for a long time. 'I'm sure I know you from somewhere . . .'

'Oh no – I've lived in London for a very long time,' Rose mumbled.

'So did I for a while . . . what a woman!' he said suddenly, breaking off. 'Mimi, I mean. We had a terrific time!' and he chuckled to himself at some memory of good times shared.

The sisters shuddered involuntarily and then caught each other's eye when they realised that they had both done the same thing. Both of them could picture her flirting shamelessly and worse . . .

'Maybe we can fix you up,' he mused and opened up the door to speak to the office floor. It took a second for both sisters to realise that he didn't mean on a date.

'Did you hear that?' Lily nudged Rose. 'He said I'm turning into Mother!'

'Well, he didn't say that exactly,' cajoled Rose whilst her eye roved over Lily's Mimi-copied hairdo. And then she pointed to the newspaper cutting on the wall. Lily nearly choked. 'Don't you dare say a word! I mean it! I will scalp you as you sleep. I will . . . I will . . . I don't know what else I'll do, but you won't like it! Don't you dare say a thing!' Lily swore Scout's Honour but since neither of them had been so much as a Girl Guide it didn't stand for much.

There was lots of excited discussion out on the office floor about the best computer for Rose to purchase and, judging by the heated shouts, it was the best fun the team had had in years. Words like processor power, Quad-core, memory and hard drive were banded about as if each really understood what the others were saying.

Rich was asking her if she used Powerpoint, Excel, Photoshop. Rose wanted to put her hands over her ears and spin in a circle shouting, 'Too much talking! Too many words!'

By the time the meeting was over, the team of geeks had been introduced to them by name, Rose had agreed to purchase a computer that was to be built to exact specifications of – she wasn't sure what, a website was being designed that allowed for safe on-line purchasing and they would be delivering the whole lot with a basic site, up and running, by the end of the month.

'I think you would have bought second-hand clothes off him if he'd offered,' Lily said on the way home, trying to goad Rose into a 'You fancy him, you do!' conversation.

'What do you mean?'

'You know exactly what I mean. You practically had your mouth open all the while you were talking to him.'

'Only because I was terrified that he'd put two and two together.' Rose was protesting rather too much. 'I ruined his shoes with vomit, Lily! I *sang* the theme tune from *Friends* to him, remember? But I don't think he twigged, do you?'

'Not with you lying over the desk like you were trying to seduce him! Poor man looked frightened for his life . . . But I know that look when it comes into your eyes!'

Rose didn't respond to that comment. She was too busy reading a text and waving her phone at Lily triumphantly. Carl was coming! To Bath! Coming to see Vintage Magic! . . . and oh! What a shame, ha!ha!ha! Isabelle couldn't make it.

'What perfect timing!' said Lily sarcastically. Rose was already texting a reply. Just as things might have started to look interesting, thought Lily, and she cast a glance back at the offices of Hands Solo Design.

7

What a night! The emerald beaded shift lay carelessly thrown on to an armchair. Shoes lay discarded at the front door, stockings next, dress in the living room, underwear somewhere near the top of the stairs and why was she sleeping naked? Kerry Brinton never slept naked; after all, what if there was a fire in the middle of the night? But last night she had slept like a baby. A big naked baby. Now, she found herself thinking deliciously devilish thoughts about firemen and wondering whether being naked would mean being rescued first and rescued faster. Was there a fine for ringing 999 needlessly?

Then she shook the thoughts from her head. Fantasising about fireman, wasn't that a bit *Loose Women*? Having now woken with a dull headache, she found it impossible to piece the evening's events together without thinking drink had been involved and lots of it. But barely a drop had passed her lips *and* she'd been driving, ferrying the party diehards from the restaurant to the karaoke bar and then on to the club.

Karaoke bar? She groaned as the memories came flooding back. 'You Gimme Fever' had been a hit with her work colleagues, couldn't she have stopped there? Why did she let them egg her on to sing 'Candy Shop'? And why did she have to go and dance along to it too?

The dancing . . . Kerry put the pillow over her head, trying to blot out all remembrance. She didn't dance. She couldn't dance. Her dad – and he was a geography teacher and wore socks with his sandals – had better rhythm than she did, but last night she'd danced – and danced and danced – until her feet were sore. Then she'd kicked off her shoes and danced some more.

But the music had pulsed through her, thumping in her chest like a heartbeat and spreading out to every limb where she had found this new animal way of moving, surrendering herself to the bass notes and electric guitars like a being possessed. She hadn't been herself.

Something had shifted in her, knocking her off axis and altering her core. What, exactly, Kerry could not say. It was indefinable, intangible. A sea change. A metamorphosis of her very being. As if she had been sleepwalking through her life until now; emerging like a glorious drag-queen butterfly version of her former self. Shy Kerry always apologising for being in the way and worried that people were looking at her had been devoured, engulfed by a life force she could not explain. She was reminded of stories from the shock-horror revelations of Sunday supplements. People who'd had transplants of some kind taking on characteristics from their donors; waking up and being able to draw when previously they had no artistic talent or desperate to eat lobster when they loathed shellfish. Now she was aware that she had such an appetite for things she had never before tasted.

The dress. It can only be the dress. Its previous 'one lady owner' liked to have a good time and it had been wishful thinking on Kerry's behalf to copy it a little, to sample a little of what life might be like if you have the guts to wear a cocktail dress of green satin. That was it. A bit of self-fulfilling prophecy. I have the dress, therefore I am.

Padding down stairs, she picked up the dress, with the intention of straightening out the creases and hanging it away but found herself holding it against her naked skin and the cold satin sent a shiver through her.

He had hardly left her side all evening, said he couldn't believe that he hadn't ever noticed her before. Kerry hugged the dress to her in recollection. She had made some flirty remark like 'But now you'd like to see more of me or all of me?' and followed it up with a saucy wink. What was she thinking? She was no vamp. Twenty-five and still a . . . well, there had never been anyone special enough, but the kisses . . . kisses where she had found a power she didn't know she had in the look of helplessness in his eyes as she left him at the kerb side, hungry for more. He was sending her texts before Kerry even had her key in the door.

It felt as though there was different blood running through her veins. Energies she could not name were surging through her chakra points then exploding out into little rivulets of electrically charged current so that she tingled from scalp to toe. Was it desire, lust? Excitement, love, passion? Whatever it was, it was heady stuff. Addictive. Kerry felt as though she had been born again. And she was hungry for everything. She had lived in the shadows, now she wanted to stand in the spotlight.

As she dressed to meet him for lunch – his texts had been persistent, how could she refuse? – her own clothes felt coarse and leaden after the smooth satin of the night before. Something about the fit was wrong. She filled them differently. They seemed to choke the life from her, this new way of being that resonated with vitality and crackled with no longer repressed desire. Staring at her reflection in the mirror, Kerry shook her head with disappointment. She needed to do some serious shopping but the clothes would have to do for now. She would make some pun to him about her clothes being worse for wear but she was oblivious to how they really sat on her now and the effect they would have on him.

Never had chinos, deck shoes and a simple white shirt looked so sinful.

Rose couldn't place the customer at first. She was familiar and she walked into the shop with all the confidence of having been there before, of knowing her way around the rails and, with her casual 'Can I try this on?' the changing room too.

Rose knew her customers by, at the very least, their purchases, if not by their real names. There was Crocheted Waistcoat Girl who bought every home-knit, sleeveless garment that came into the shop and Croc Bag who had paid the full asking-price for a vintage piece of reptile skin with a cracked handle that Rose thought no one would ever buy. But this girl she couldn't immediately recall.

Her hair was dyed a vibrant red and pinned casually up with a slightly back-combed crown. Her eyebrows were plucked into a high pencil-filled arch. She clacked in on mid-high pointed sling-back shoes worn with a belted trench. A retro look but timeless and classic too, sexy but understated, smart but casual as if there were two different, warring sides battling for supremacy.

Rose talked to Lily about it later; the change was so marked, so complete a transformation, you would think fairy godmother Gok Wan had had a hand in it. The penny hadn't dropped for Rose about the source of this revolution, not immediately. Not until the girl had lunged for the rail of Peggy Mountford show costumes with a frantic 'Do you have any more cocktail dresses like this one?' did Rose recognise her customer.

Rose prickled with a hunch, an instinctive nagging that wasn't going away, that, irrationally, there was more to this girl's transformation. Why did she feel that things were, somehow, not quite as they ought to be? Like one of those movies where only one person gets a hunch that things are wrong – she could only think of *Groundhog Day*, which was a lousy example, or the narrator of Daphne Du Maurier's *Rebecca*, whose name is never learned – it was an unsettling disquiet that would not go away.

How could a mousy-haired Gap girl in BHS basics, wallflower-quiet and as bland as a beige anorak now appear only a few weeks later oozing sex like a pizza dripping cheese? The change was as drastic as Susan Sarandon in *The Witches of Eastwick* mutated from frumpy school teacher to passionate muse. Was all this Vintage Magic's doing? Could one dress really change a personality that much? Totally alter the direction of a life path?

Peggy Mountford had worn it, worn it well, but the dress was, after all, just a dress that was just fabric, stitching and a few plastic beads, right? Or wrong?

What if the essence of Peggy remained? A trace of her life, seen and lived? Something in the fabric, the silk or the satin, something indefinable from the very stitching that holds the garment together? Is it possible for it – whatever it may be – to seep into the skin of its wearer and infect them with a memory, a feeling, almost a déjà vu of the life it once had, of times had by those who wore it before? What if the heart of Peggy, that vivacious, all-feminine, positive, bon-viveur spirit, had somehow left an imprint that the girl had picked up on, allowing a strong psyche to invade a weaker one? Was it ridiculous to think that the girl had become a retro-styled sex bomb overnight all because of an emerald green satin dress?

But the girl seemed happy and so did Rose's other customers, or they wouldn't keep coming back for more, would they? She hadn't had a single return or complaint about the merchandise. No reports of any person developing Multiple Personality Disorder on account of a pussy-cat bow blouse. This customer didn't seem unduly bothered by the change and, after all, hadn't she swept into the store with a new-found ass-kicking confidence? That had to be good. She was in the changing room now trying on everything remotely Peggy-related; daywear, evening wear, underwear.

'Sorry, did you say something?' The voice was muffled behind the curtain as the girl swopped a Susie Wong dress for Capri pants and shell top.

'No,' called back Rose from the other side of the shop. 'Not unless I've started talking to myself!' and they both laughed. Polite-strangers-sharing-a-not-really-hilarious-joke sort of laugh.

Then the girl said, 'That's funny. I could have sworn you were right here, whispering through the curtain of the changing room!'

An innocuous comment, a thought spoken aloud without editing. Meaningless when taken in isolation. Nonsensical, really, to people who never lay awake at night, trying not to listen to a rusty birdcage moving in the wind and thinking about the swings moving all by themselves in that scene from *The Shining*. Not designed to unsettle and upset. Surely not enough to make the hairs rise up on arms and pulses to quicken. Certainly not to be taken as evidence that the building pulses with unseen forces. A totally innocent, off-the-cuff remark. Totally harmless.

Unless you are Rose Taylor. And you have tried everything logical to explain the murmurings that come in snatches like an untuned radio flicking from station to station. It's kids hanging in the square, skateboarding over roughened concrete. It's a cistern filling overhead. It's a television reverberating through the walls. It's a transistor turned to Talk FM to keep the budgie company whilst somebody goes out. It's centuries-old pipes swelling like arthritic joints. It's ancient timbers hewn from forests long-gone, groaning with the effort of sustaining heavy walls.

But it is none of those things and Rose worries that she is being sent slowly mad by the hushed voices that seem to come, only in the dark when you are alone, from the very walls of Vintage Magic.

Weddings bring out the worst in people. Not a popular sentiment, but one that Rose now firmly believed. She had seen many sane friends with professional careers at all levels of management turn into tulle-wearing, frothing-at-the-mouth harpies, speaking in tongues about almonds in netting and how ivory does not match cream!! Embarrassing to say, but that is exactly what Rose had let herself become and, looking back, it was hard to believe it was her. She had mutated into the stereotypical Bridezilla, obsessed with stage managing the day that all the advertisers kept saying was going to be the Best Day of Your Life. So no pressure there, girls! Presumably, it was all downhill from then on, so little wonder that such hysteria surrounded the day.

It certainly would have been a good day – a marquee wedding on the green of Carl's parents' village in Oxfordshire adorned with Rose's homemade bunting; a small fleet of Morris Minors would have transported the bride and groom and attendants from church (Church?

Rose Taylor? Really?); her hair would have been worn up with a homage-to-Hepburn fringe; and she would have worn a vintage-inspired dress, ballerina-length skirt, tight bodice and sweetheart neckline to show off her best assets – the Puppies, as Lily referred to them. Play to your strengths, Mimi had told her girls, and Rose's strengths lay in her slightly freakishly sized, creamy full 32FFs. ('That's not a bra!' Lily had protested when Rose returned with her new size after a fitting. 'That's a corrective orthopaedic garment. Your boobs have Special Needs!')

The wine would have flowed, tears of happiness would have been shed and, as the summer sun went down, the band would have played easy listening numbers to appeal to all age groups. That had been the fantasy, anyway. So why, if weddings were about love, togetherness and strengthening bonds, did they cause so many arguments and resentments?

Rose heard it all in Vintage Magic. Girls complaining as they hunted for outfits about too much money spent on extravagantly arranged hen nights – when, one customer complained, had a drunken night in the pub wearing a hat decorated in L-plates and water-filled condoms become a weekend in a five-star spa in Tuscany? She overheard people moaning about who else was invited and how it was likely to end in a fist-fight, who wasn't invited, which drunk they were likely to be sitting with, who would guzzle all the table wine, what monstrosities they were being made to wear in bridesmaid colours of bad-school-uniform burgundy or bottle-green, and what they weren't allowed to wear (no legs or cleavage in case the bride was upstaged), and Rose marvelled at the tyrannical powers of the brides – and, even worse, their mothers.

Then she overheard post-wedding analyses; tales of fighting off lecherous best-men, of bridesmaids knowing that the bridegroom had slept with the stripper from the night before and of cringe-worthy buffets where Wotsits had been skewered on to cocktail sticks as a touch of class.

What would people have said of her wedding? Rose wondered. Mimi would have complained about the lack of provision for smokers or how they were slow at opening up the port.

'A June wedding?' Lily thought for a moment. 'In Britain? The green would have flooded and the marquee collapsed under gale-force winds. Oh, and everyone would have said that there was something definitely going on with Carl and the orange-coloured bridesmaid.'

Considering how she had been obsessed by her own wedding, and was someone who was now working with clothes, it was possible to think that Rose would have an interest in other people's weddings or their dresses. She didn't. Post-her own disastrous non-wedding, any glimpse of a white dress made her skin crawl. They were as ghoulish to Rose now as the lifelike Reborn Baby dolls with their real eyelashes, heartbeat and mottled, painted skin.

Maybe it was the Miss Haversham factor that meant white lace and veils had connotations of insanity and, whilst Shakespeare had felt love was a temporary madness, it wasn't. It was planning a wedding that drove people loopy. Still, catching your husband-to-be in bed with someone whom you had planned would catch the bouquet was enough to create a wedding-dress phobia in anyone.

But Rose knew customers who loved vintage would get married in vintage and that meant she had to keep a stock of wedding dresses at all times, but she could not bear to be surrounded by them. She especially wanted them to be shut away when Carl came to visit. So, a big sign in the window declared 'Weddings dresses on request', and at the back of the shop near to the cellar, an old pantry became a perfect store. Decorated in iridescent wallpaper of Japanese blossoms and housing a three-sided gilt-edged silver-spotted mirror, it contained at least one dress from every decade of the last century. Though pre-war brides were so tiny unless the wedding was planned for an under-sixteen, they were unlikely to fit a girl of today but frequently they were bought for fabric to be refashioned or lace to be plundered.

Rose was surprised by the requests for eighties Lady Di replicas – more than odd, considering how that marriage had ended, but for the children of the eighties, somehow she was still symbolic of a fairytale dream.

Where Inuit Eskimos have a hundred words for

snow; wedding-dress designers have twice as many to describe white. So, in hues of – amongst others – ivory, cream, champagne and the oddly named 'button mushroom' (Rose imagined it should still have bits of soil clinging to it), they hung there, symbols of purity, loaded with promise of Happy Ever After and Rose, steeped in bitterness, very much doubted if a single virgin ever wore one.

But when a customer asked for a wedding dress, Rose gritted her teeth and smiled and cooed and oohed and aahed and asked about the day and the groom and marvelled at the planned menu, swooned at the proposed flowers and, even if they didn't find the dress of their dreams in her cupboard, wished them all the luck in the world. Although often they would just alight on a regular dress from the rack that bucked all Victorian conventions of marrying in white; like the redhead who found a perfect scarlet satin and dazzled all on her Big Day. In fact, she'd liked it so much she got married twice – to the same man, it must be stressed. But why not? If it's worth doing, why not do it well and more than once and enjoy every minute.

But one day, with a particular client, the conflict was just beginning. She could hear tension in the bride-to-be's voice as though she was having to talk through gritted teeth. Instead of Mum, she was now saying 'Mother'. Always a sign. She kept asserting, 'I know what I want', but Mother seemed to know best. There were lots of mentions by Mummy of other people's extremely successful weddings where the bride wore Pronuptia ('and she married a solicitor!') and 'helpful' suggestions such as 'What about a nice wash-n-wear suit that you could use for work afterwards?' or 'The function room is still free at the Golf Club for a sit-down carvery, you know.'

Whilst the bride-to-be took some dresses to try on, Rose offered tea and cakes to the bride-to-be's mother.

'She's very excited about the day,' Rose said by way of small talk and was taken off guard by the next comment.

'I don't know why! It's not as if it's a real marriage, is it?'

Rose struggled to find something to say but she didn't have to; she realised, swiftly, that she had removed her finger from the dyke, as it were, and the banks were now bursting. A torrent of pent-up venom about the forthcoming nuptials flowed out.

'It'll be a fiasco and I don't know why she is going to go to the bother of a big white dress, do you? Will they both wear a dress? That's what I want to know!'

Visions of a transvestite husband, all platform heels and Widow Twankey make-up, came to mind.

The bride's mother continued: 'It's just a civil partnership. Not the same as the real thing—'

'I think it is, in the eyes of the law—' Rose began.

'It's not like she even gave boyfriends a proper try. If only she'd met the right fella . . .'

He would have to have been a girl. Rose added her own comments to the conversation in her head.

'I think she's just jumping on to a very fashionable bandwagon.'

Or Gay Pride float.

'She was always trying to shock us, first it was the pierced nose, the funny-coloured hair and going on protests – Ban the Bomb, Save the Sealion . . . she went on them all. She went off to university, gave up all her sports, met Charlie, and we all waited to meet this nice boy she was bringing home. Her father thought Charlie was a lad when he first saw her, all shaved head like that Sinead O'Connor, and that was that. The trouble with my daughter is that she is just too easily influenced, but not by me! When she came home and said she was lesbian, her father wasn't a bit surprised. He said to me, he did, he said "Sheila – nothing that girl does would surprise me." Lesbian or single mother, we knew she'd be one or the other.'

Rose was speechless. She felt like she'd just taken part in the lancing of a large boil and been sprayed by the contents. She felt soiled listening to the complaints about this woman's daughter as it became a rant of homophobia. Although this lady probably thought that meant not liking Colin and Justin's house makeover.

Luckily, Mimi was there to move the conversation along. She came through the back door, having been smoking out in the yard. Even the slight whiff of tobacco over the layers of Youth Dew did not detract from the vision in Hobbs and MaxMara separates that was Mimi. The Littlewoods-dressed Hyacinth Bucket of a Bride's mother was instantly impressed. She knew Posh when she saw it. She had Taste.

'Did I hear somebody say lesbian?' Mimi's accent so belied everything about her class and education that she could never go undercover in a bingo hall. 'I tried that once, around 1966, with that Prendergast woman – you remember, darling – you boarded with her daughter for a couple of terms. They bred horses somewhere in Surrey. Apparently, it was all the rage in her lacrosse team before they all got married off.' She pronounced it 'orf'. 'Give it a try,' she spoke directly to the Bride's mother. 'You might like it! Good luck to you and each to their own and all that. It just wasn't my cup of tea.' And she floated off up to the flat above.

To this aspirational, anxious Mother of the Civil Partner-to-be this was as close to Lesbianism by Royal Approval as one could get. If it was good enough for the classes whose children boarded, owned horses and played lacrosse – then it was good enough for her and she made sure all her friends knew about it.

'Hello – yes, it is the lady of the house . . . chortle! chortle! . . . that's right, it will be a Civil Partnership of the Sapphic order. I know . . . very Radclyffe Hall! Well, what can you do when you move in those circles? When in Rome . . .! Who disapproves? Oh them! How very *bourgeois*! What a very narrow-minded, *uneducated* – and I wouldn't be one to say it, but others might –

working-class way of thinking . . . and tell them, if they must know, they're ten a penny at the Young Conservatives, you can't move for lesbians . . .'

Rose later pinned to her wall the photo of a happy couple both in white, giggling in their sixties minis, with cropped hair like two twin Mia Farrows in the *Rosemary's Baby* years, being showered in confetti by a mother who, judging by her big, broad smile, had come round to thinking that Wearing a Sensible Shoe was all right after all.

So a transformation was brought about without the supernatural or *The Unexplained*, just a little Mimi interference, which could be construed as the meddling of an old witch but there would be no need to drag Derek Acorah and the team around to determine what spirit forces were at work in Vintage Magic. Not yet, anyway.

The news of Carl's visit had pretty much obliterated every other thought from Rose's mind as she worked frantically on the preparations. Maybe all her imaginings had been down to stress; overworking and overthinking. She had been sleeping better on account of the small sips of brandy taken at night to calm her nerves (Mimi's recommendation – 'It's medicinal, darling. Just don't overdo it – you know what you're like.'), but Rose's mind still raced around all the things yet to perfect about both the shop and herself. The cellar had been emptied, old books passed over to Cynthia to see if there were any of worth, and Matt was busy creating a 'laundry', feeding into Rose's Domestic Goddess fantasies by making a room devoted to ironing, laundering and repair in what was the old ground-floor kitchen.

The more industrial of the machines were being hidden behind the sort of vintage fabric that had inspired Cath Kidston and he was busy installing shelves, racks and two large Victorian airers. She wanted it all done for Carl's visit and was exploiting Matt's desire to be near to her sister by getting him to do the work. She was paying him but it was hardly what could be called a Living Wage and it was lucky his parents could spare him from the farm.

Lily had arrived at the shop, as usual, and was helping Rose to fold washing and press clothes. Leia moved between them, helping Matt one minute, emptying pegs on to the floor the next.

The door opened and a customer Rose recognised came in clutching a Vintage Magic bag. Rose recalled how she was usually escorted by her partner.

There were men who came shopping with their partners who sat in Rose's man-crèche area reading retro copies of *Shoot!*, waiting until it was time for them to answer the question all men dreaded: 'What do you think?' or, even worse, 'Does it make me look fat?' The hunted look in their eyes, of being cornered with no place to turn, was comical.

But there were some men (discounting the ones who would encourage their fag-hags to choose Alexis

Carrington shoulder-padded power suits) who really took an almost creepy interest in what the women in their life were wearing to the point of choosing every garment and passing damning judgement on any choice they made for themselves.

'No, that does nothing for you.' Ouch!

'Well, you say yourself that you should cover your arms . . .' Double ouch!

'You need to stand up straight if you want to wear that. You do have a tendency to slump.' Whammy!

The woman holding out the seventies safari dress, asking Rose if she would very much mind if it could be swapped, was immediately recognisable as someone who had been on the receiving end of those sorts of 'I only want what's best for you' statements. Rose also recalled how, whilst she had been wrapping up the items and chatting, the telephone had interrupted them and, soon after, she had found that the debit card was still in the chip-and-pin machine but they had gone.

Within half an hour they had returned. He was furious, his jaw tightened in rage.

'She's an idiot. I've told her about this before.'

'I'm so sorry. I'm such a klutz.' The poor thing had been wringing her hands around in anxiety and Rose had felt responsible at the time for causing their row.

'No, no, no! I was distracted. It wasn't your fault. I would have contacted your bank if you hadn't returned.' Rose had tried to calm the situation and then made a little joke to lighten the mood. 'I worry that if I had a child I'd forget where I left it.' And though the girl had managed a weak smile, he had not and Rose could hear his bullying and criticisms from across the square after they had left.

Now she was back holding out the safari dress for Rose to see.

'I don't know if you remember, but I bought this a little while ago and though I sort of like it, a very odd thing happened to me when I wore it out.' Rose assured her that she remembered and would be happy to exchange it. The girl went on, 'It became more and more uncomfortable. You see' – the girl began unbuttoning her coat, removing her layers – 'I think whoever made it must have left some pins in . . .' she lifted her sweater to reveal strange scratches at her sides and waist exactly like little pin scores criss-crossing this way and that. As she turned, she revealed how it travelled the full circumference of her waist.

Rose's hand flung to her mouth. 'Oh my God! That is absolutely awful. I can't believe that one of my garments did that to you!'

'I tried to bear it,' the young woman went on to explain sweetly – she didn't seem to bear a grudge – 'because we were out and I wasn't going to return it, but—'

'I don't understand how those pins could have passed me by.' Rose was appalled and bracing herself for a law suit. Good job Carl was coming.

'But that's the weird thing. I've looked and I've felt

and I've gone over it with a magnet, but I just can't see any . . .'

Rose was going all over the garment now, stripping it of its lining and searching for pins or uneven fabric, promising a full refund and a reduction as her customer chose to try on a deep red Doris Day-style tweed suit with boxy jacket and mink collar; the warm red hues set off her hair and the brown of the mink matched her eyes.

'Perfect.' She sighed looking in the mirror. 'That dress did me a favour,' she said, her gaze firmly fixed on her reflection. 'He was going on and on at me as I fidgeted, telling me to sit still, to leave the dress alone, and that if it felt so tight it was my fault for putting on weight and I hadn't!' She smoothed the waist of the tweed across her enviably flat stomach. 'But he kicked off when I asked him to take me home because he said it would inconvenience the others and the thought suddenly came to me – I'd liked the safari dress but not madly. It had been his choice. I had wanted this suit, but he said it was too staid, and then I thought: This is it. This is him. He cares more about somebody else being a little inconvenienced in a restaurant than he does about me being scratched to pieces. And it was as if I was on a fast-forward of our lives together and how it would always be the way he wanted things, how it already was only ever the way he wants things, how he never ever meets me halfway. He doesn't want the wallpaper I like on the wall, he doesn't like the way I look in photographs, I should go to the gym more, he doesn't like duvet covers with flowers on and I suddenly thought of Katie Holmes and the rumours of Cruise Control and that's when I decided no, this is not happening to me. So' – the girl turned away from the mirror to Rose with a big broad smile – 'We're over and I'm free.'

And, by way of an apology for injuries sustained whilst wearing Vintage, so was the tweed suit.

'So she's managed to break up and move on quickly, then?' Lily heard the whole thing, but the pointed comment went over Rose's head as she was talking about Carl again and, though she didn't want to admit it, was even beginning to bore herself. Lily seemed more than a little cranky today and wasn't in the mood to listen.

'He called me again, you know, about coming to see the shop – and me, of course. He said that he feels torn and conflicted and that he's not sure any more.'

'About what?'

'About him and Isabelle, of course.'

'He's a shit-bag.'

'Lily, it's not that straight forward for him; you know that.'

'Straight forward? Straight from behind with that dirty cow Isabelle! He's a lying, cheating shit-bag.'

'SShhh!! You don't want Leia to hear that language, do you?' Rose now raised her voice above the drilling coming from the back of the shop. 'And weddings, I've read, can make men panic about losing their freedom, so a last-minute fling – as Mimi said – is an evolutionary device.'

'So is eating your offspring in certain species of the animal kingdom. It doesn't make it right.' Lily was also shouting. In frustration. 'Rose, why are you bothering? Frankly speaking – and Mimi and I have tried to let you get over this in your own way – he's letting you down gently; although how having sex *in your bed with your friend* is meant to be "gently" I don't know.' She made little rabbit-ear/inverted comma marks with her fingers which, she knew, Rose found extremely irritating. 'You're behaving like a doormat. You're letting him – and her – make a fool out of you. But it's over. You should face facts and ask yourself if it's worth trying to have him back? Would you want him? Really?'

The sisters were in full-on sibling quarrel mode. Thankfully, there were no customers in the shop because nothing could stop them now. Had it gone on much longer there would have been hair pulling and nose flicking. Rose pulled out her trump card.

'We all make mistakes – which *you* are, incidentally – with that man in there.' She waved her arm in the direction of where hammering was now coming from the laundry. 'And up till now, *Mimi and I*' – said in a gesture of Ahaaa! – 'we've been talking about you too! Not so smug now, are we? Mimi and I' – said again to drive the point home – 'have kept our noses out of it, but who are you to preach about relationships? At least Carl and I haven't got a child together – yet – so what the hell are *you* thinking? You take a child away from her father for what? It's not like he's a monster. It's not like you don't get on, is it? You're best friends, for God's sake! So why cause so much pain? Some selfish whim that you can't even tell your own sister about? Because you think you deserve something even better than a happy relationship and gorgeous child? What could be better than that? The trouble with you is you were spoiled because you had everything when Mimi and Daddy had money. And as for Carl, you don't know him like *I* know him. We were together a long time. Those are lots of memories and you should know how hard it can be to let go when your lives are—'

'Mind your own business about my relationship! Keep your nose out! But your Carl's a cheat, he's a smarmy prat and you can't deny it! And you wanna know something. He tried to hit on me just after you announced the wedding. There, I said it. And I forgave that mistake because he'd had a bit to drink and I didn't want to upset you but is that what you want? Is it worth giving *that* another chance? The sort of man who hits on your own sister?'

Then a male voice that sounded just like it had rolled in from *Coronation Street* chimed in 'Corr! That's a bit of a dilemma, love. Give *him* another chance? Is he worth it? But then, on the other hand, maybe you'd like to take a chance on me! John' – he held his hand out, pure Gallagher Brothers wide boy – 'Rich's other 'alf. That introduction gets us into some trouble in certain night spots – know what I'm saying?'

Rose and Lily had been so busy arguing that they hadn't even heard Hands Solo Design, who had arrived to install the new system, enter the shop. Rich Clarke was standing there with his hands in his pockets looking a little embarrassed, whether at his tactless workmate or the argument overheard, Rose couldn't tell, but she could feel an anxiety rash beginning to flame across her chest and neck.

She didn't want Hands Solo Design to know all that about her. She wanted them to think of her as, well, a cool, level-headed businesswoman, not see her as . . . what? Sad and dumped? Pining for Carl? Loveless chump? Cheated, blind fool?

Lily wasn't embarrassed at the intrusion. No, not at all. A bit of Mancunian charm and she'd suddenly gone all booby and leggy, sucking her waist in, pulling herself taller and tossing her bob about as though it was still the mane of blond it once had been. She was out miming Mimi.

'So you're the second-hand clothes shop I've heard so much about,' John announced, pronouncing clothes as cloves and looking around in admiration.

'Vintage, yes, and . . . and retro.' Rose was feeling more than a little spiky and she put on her posh 'telephone' voice in an attempt to claim back her ground as cool level-headed businesswoman.

'Do you get any old Lacoste? I love that old-school look, know what I mean?' He seemed to end all his sentences checking whether people knew what he meant. Rose nodded in agreement; she certainly did. 'I used to think me old man and his mates were the dog's bollocks when they went down the football all geysered up and looking sharp. Old Pringle, I bet that still makes a pound or two, got any of that knocking around? You know, the old casual look fetches top dollar in London. All the city boys, the bankers and that, want to look like they were in *The Firm*. Where's your men's stuff? Upstairs? I'd love to have a look through.'

'I'm sorry. I don't stock men's clothes.' Rose was warming to him now. She loved talking shop and he obviously knew his stuff.

'Just as well,' Rich interjected. 'We'd never get any work done. I'm sorry that my partner is so in your face, that's why I never include him in first meetings. No offence, mate.'

'None taken!'

'Well, come on, never mind trying to talk your way into some free Fila vintage, we've got to unload the stuff from the car.' And he turned back to the door. John waited until he was gone then, full of confidence and swagger, said, 'Anyhow – these blokes that are giving you two the run-around – give them the heave-ho and come out with us tonight. I've got a feeling that Rich would like to get to know yous guys better.'

'Where have you got in mind?' Lily purred without any hesitation.

'Thanks, but we'll have to think about it,' clucked Rose, ushering Lily to the back of the shop where Matt, in a lull from his work in Rose's laundry, was sitting on the floor doing a wooden jigsaw with his daughter and, judging by his face, red-hot under his beard, and the way he avoided eye contact before making his excuses to leave, Rose and Lily's argument was not the only conversation overheard.

Rose couldn't sleep. Even with the hefty dose of brandy in her bedtime milk. She was just too anxious. Mooch wasn't in and she hadn't seen him all day. She'd stood on the back step rattling his tin of dried kittie nibbles into the alleyway at least fifteen times and even opened a tin of tuna and wafted it about because that was almost guaranteed to make him turn somersaults of delight. Nothing. He was nowhere to be seen.

Cynthia hadn't seen him and was rather obliging in checking her shop from top to bottom, including the window where he had been found once before when an American tourist had asked to purchase the taxidermied cat from the display. But there was no sign. The ladies of Ye Olde Coffee House hadn't seen him either and he was always there at closing time where he was fed any meat produce bordering 'best by' dates. This visit took rather a long time as the ladies listed all his favourite treats.

'Cheese. He likes a red Leicester.'

'No, no. He prefers Double Gloucester with chives.'

'But he likes his wafer-thin ham —'

'But you have to feed it to him in small portions, torn up.'

'He doesn't like it cut with scissors.'

'And he likes it fed by hand.'

And so it went on. Rose felt a small stab of jealousy then, thinking of how free he was with his affections when a titbit was on offer, and couldn't understand why she found herself thinking about Carl. Mrs Bridges and Mrs Waters even tentatively considered that he might have followed a 'visitor' down into the Old Dairy and Rose was invited to check along with them. She declined but there was no sign of him anyway, although the ladies revealed that he liked to come and look at each new tenant as they arrived. Rose hoped she'd masked her shudder.

The last she'd seen of Mooch, he'd been following Matt around as he worked. Sitting in his toolbox, climbing inside the very cupboard Matt was trying to fix to the wall, and always making sure that he was just out of Leia's reach. He had kept to Matt's heels like a builder's faithful Jack Russell terrier.

Matt's leaving had unsettled Rose too. It was no wonder she couldn't sleep. He'd made some excuse about taking Leia to the farm to see his folks but had left wearing his hurt on his sleeve like a heartbreak Brownie badge. She couldn't bear the look in his eyes and knew better than most, from first-hand experience, the pain and confusion he must feel. Rose felt helpless and guilty, even though it was not she who had inflicted the wounds.

By the time Lily had left, she and Rose were barely on speaking terms. Grunting terms, really, once Lily had finished flirting; leaning over to look at the computer whilst sticking her bottom in the air, laughing too much at every slight quip made by John, widening her eyes, putting a pen in her mouth suggestively, and doing all those other 'endearing' body language gestures that work like a charm on men but are so transparent to other women.

Then Mimi had turned up, adding herself to the mix with the comment of: 'My little granddaughter not here? Thank goodness! Now I won't have to think up another excuse to avoid playing tea parties!', which nobody believed for a moment judging by the crestfallen expression that had flitted, unimpeded by Botox, across her face before she corrected it. Hands Solo Design sparked a reunion of sorts for the Senior Citizens computer course.

'You remember us? That's John and I'm Rich.'

'Darling, I never forget anyone who's rich!'

And then there were reminiscences about the end-of-course party and a card game that, of course, Mimi had instigated and, of course, she had won because she was an expert in all parlour pastimes, especially those where money could be gained. Mah-jong, crib, poker; she was a master of them all and a very elegant drunk.

She was not one to be found with her skirt up around her waist, her tights ripped and make-up running down her cheeks *Ab-Fab* style. There was simply a point where Mimi would stand, albeit a little unsteadily, and announce that she would retire to bed. It didn't happen often but it had happened that night and she had left stripping the other pensioners and their teachers of every vestige of cash and taking with her more than a few IOUs.

But then a spiteful part of Rose, knowing how all daughters fear turning into their mothers – particularly her own sister – had felt delighted and smiled smugly when Rich had pointed out how Mimi and Lily were so alike. Lily shot Rose an angry look. But this was followed by: 'Well, Rose does follow her Daddy.' And Rose was stung with imagined slights about being so obviously shorter and rounder than her elder sibling, and worries that she had the facial hair of a Croatian lady shot-putter.

Her self-esteem had never quite recovered from Carl's choice of Isabelle over her. Isabelle who, if you were to strip away the clip-in platinum hair extensions, the false nails (including the disturbing French manicure toe ones she wore in summer), the spray tan in shades of Soap-Star through to Footballer's Mistress, was not actually that good-looking.

'But she knew how to make the best of herself. Men always fall for glamour,' Mimi had explained when Lily had raised the whole issue of Carl's visit and cheating ways in front of Hands Solo Design again. Rose had glared at her sister. But her family hadn't finished humiliating her yet.

Rich had asked for a tour of the shop and premises, explaining, 'You've got a basic site now but we like to get to know our customers' likes and dislikes in terms of design and to use that to inform our construction. It's important that the site reflects you and your business, not Hands Solo Design. I really want to get a feel of you.'

There had been a brief, awkward moment of silence before John, Mimi and Lily had roared with laughter.

'That's a bit of a Freudian slip, mate!' His work partner spluttered whilst Rich and Rose stood looking at the floor with reddening faces. Then, as they entered the newly fashioned laundry area, Lily gushed, 'Now this *is* Rose. Show her white goods and a well-organised utility area and she is practically stiff with excitement!'

That was bad enough, to be shown up as some housework-obsessed weirdo, and Rose could have brushed it under the carpet (with a leopard-print-handled broom with firm bristles, of course. There can still be beauty in utilitarian design!) because, after all, they were men who collected bobble-heads of Spider-man, so who were they to judge?, but for it to be followed by Mimi's pitying: 'Darling, you really need to get out more. Come with me to salsa on Tuesday, there are lots of eligible men there. Plenty of action.'

'I am not going on the pull with my mother!' Rose

had asserted but really wished she had not said it aloud in front of the web design duo. She loved her mother and her sister but today she had really wished, really wanted, for them to just . . . just – she was searching for the right words . . . piss off. That was it! There was no other way to describe it – and to leave her alone to run her shop.

But, now Rose recalled how Hands Solo Design had loved her choice of kitsch pinball machine and fifties cocktail bar in the shop and they had liked her whitewashed winter wonderland flat with the seventies fabric cushions on the sofa and sarees hanging as blinds at the window. And Rich had crouched at her charity-shop vinyl collection delighting in her finds of Tijuana Brass and hits-from-the-musicals soundtracks and wowed in awe at her Big-Eye picture gallery and swooned at her Pan book titles lining the shelves.

'I'm a bit of a hoarder!' she explained, shrugging her shoulders as Rich heaped praise on her taste for the mass-produced and now unloved items of the post-war years. Lily, Mimi and John had long since wandered off to guffaw – probably at Rose's expense – over coffee somewhere.

'This is how Red or Dead started!' he had enthused. 'Maybe you should think about sneaking in some of your own designs alongside the vintage-wear; you've obviously got the skills.' And he had said the sweetest things about her own work – the sketches and ceramics, the cushions and embroidered hangings that she had produced so long ago for a course that had absorbed her utterly. She had never found her way back there creatively, she found herself explaining to him, confessing thoughts she had barely admitted to herself in years. Funny how easy it was to talk to Rich about it all. How he understood. There hadn't been time or something. Something . . . she was never sure what; a stifling, a numbing of her artistic self.

What was it? She wondered now, looking anxiously out of the window, scouring the square for Mooch. Life, maybe? With its demands for bills to be paid, student debts to be cleared and pensions to be planned. Then a thought crept in, sneakily, through a not-often-used side door. Or was it Carl? He did have a sneering way of judging artists, actors and anyone who didn't do a 'proper job'. Didn't like the clutter and the chaos that came with the creative process. No, she didn't want to think that. She thrust the thought from her head. Carl had loved her. He had wanted to marry her. Once he had got that fling with Isabelle out of his system, once he'd come and seen for himself how the 'old' Rose was back and better than before, then it would all return to normal. And she tried to ignore the unsettling feeling of exactly what that might mean.

He would be here in forty-eight hours and she still hadn't decided what to wear. She had been exercising every day, dancing around in front of the telly to a celebrity exercise DVD that promised wonderful toning and weight loss (with no mention of the time spent with 'exhaustion' in a 'clinic' from where said celebrity had emerged looking suspiciously more svelte with a face stretched to a shine). Another week and her upper arms would have been so toned that she could have even gone sleeveless but now there was no time. And hair – should she find an old-lady salon to give her the sort of shampoo-and-set Rita Hayworth tumble of curls that he used to say he liked or go for two plaits to project a playful, puckish charm with just a hint of fetish sexy? Maybe team it with a fifties cow-girl vibe. Or were pigtails too much? Too straining to be Britney in a Hit-Me-Baby-One-More-Time-way that was not always becoming in a woman the other side of twenty-five? How old was too old for pigtails?

And she would ask Carl directly about that thing with Lily. It was sure to be some easily explained misunderstanding. Carl could be a little over-familiar with people at times – well, not men, just women, really, to be honest. They didn't always understand that he was just being friendly and, judging by the way Lily had angled for John to repeat his offer of a night out, her sister wasn't above flattering herself with male attention.

But it would all blow over, their sisterly rows always did; without them having to talk it through and achieve resolution like they were in an episode of *The Cosby Show*. Sometimes it was just best to ignore it ever happened in the first place and she didn't regret the things she'd said to Lily, not at all, why should she? Maybe it would make her think about what was right for her. And she did not see any irony in her thoughts at all, whatsoever.

Her body was so tired, aching for sleep, but her mind was buzzing and flitting from one thought to the next and always finding its way back to where on earth had Mooch got to? So Rose lay there worrying about fast cars and slow cats, hungry, predatory city foxes and old ladies luring away his affections with hand-shredded ham. She felt like a mother waiting anxiously to hear her drunken teenager fumbling to put a key in the lock. And she couldn't escape the dark memories and urban myths about travelling fairgrounds and all the cats going missing, reappearing in the next town as real-fur purse prizes.

Carl. Mooch. Lily. Matt. The thoughts whirled around in a wheel from one to the next and back again with occasional punctuations of Rich Clarke and his kind words. There are some people with whom it's possible to feel an instant, inexplicable connection. That a shared love of an obscure tatty paperback is enough to ignite a spark to spend more time with them, to find out more, to dig deeper for their thoughts, their laughs and pet hates. So long as their hates did not include pets. And Rose's thoughts were back with Mooch again, into the cycle of worry, before they moved on.

Maybe she and Lily should take Hands Solo Design up on their invitation to go out. No – she couldn't do that to Matt. She could not be party to adding to his burden of hurt. Not until she really understood what had gone on between them and where Lily really thought it was going. But then if she, Rose, was there, acting as chaperone, it couldn't hurt, could it? They would only be going out as business associates, after all; she would only be taking Lily as company. Best not to mention any plans to Mimi because then she'd want to tag along. And if she did, then who would babysit? Matt? That would be wrong and too complicated. Her thoughts tumbled around like dirty smalls in a washing-machine. Was that Mooch she could hear?

'**H**ideous!' Rose pulled a brown crepe swing-dress over her head and threw it on to the sofa, before clambering into a pencil-line day-dress of smart vertical stripes. She turned to the mirror.

'Uggh!' The dress was flung on to a growing pile of rejects. Rose rummaged through a cardboard box and pulled another frock from the depths and zipped herself up in it.

'Disgusting!' A beautiful Horrockes dress of grey and yellow bands trimmed with tiny, pink ditsy flowers was discarded on to the floor in a tangled heap. 'The glamour of cotton' dress was sublime. A potential museum piece and, ordinarily, Rose would have treated it with care and respect. Now it fell to the floor like a bad buy from Primark.

There was nothing wrong with the clothes. The clothes would all sell quickly and become pieces cherished by their new owners. Another time, Rose might have tried on any of these dresses and decided to keep them for herself. But today they did not fit. Today nothing about them was right. They were too long or too tight. The colours were too draining or the feel of the fabric made her skin crawl. Some were deemed too 'Sunday School', others too slutty. There were tops that made her feel what she called 'milk-maid' top heavy, bosoms spilling out over boning and the pencil line of cleavage ending somewhere under her chin. There were waistlines that should have been hourglass but ended at empire-line with Rose's modern figure and she stood in front of her mirror feeling dumpy, pudding-like and as shapely as Mrs Tiggywinkle. She was filled with self-loathing.

Today was not a good day to choose clothes. Especially when so much hinged on looking good. When the pressure was on for this special reunion with Carl and it was not enough to look 'nice'. She had to look perfect. As the saying goes, never shop for food when you're hungry, and to this should be added another maxim – never try on new clothes on a Fat Day. Fat Days are not real. Nobody is ever thin on Monday and grossly overweight by Tuesday. Fat Days are a product of the imagination linked more to fluctuating self-esteem than a changing dial on a set of scales.

But Fat Days feel real enough when clothes that once fitted perfectly seem stretched to capacity, zips, that usually glide into place, wedge and won't run home, and a skirt that made a walk a wiggle suddenly makes a waddle. If Rose Taylor was being honest with herself, it was not just a Fat Day – it was an Ugly Day. A day when

Rose almost felt too unattractive to be front of house in Vintage Magic. It was, in fact, full-on Body Dysmorphia Day – ankles had become cankles, Rose's muffin top had become a cottage loaf and her bum didn't just look big in this but threatened to obliterate the sun and cast the whole of the western hemisphere into darkness. There were times when Rose could be overly dramatic.

The courier driver of her new delivery hadn't helped. Half a dozen heavy cardboard cartons cram-packed with clothes all chosen with wowing Carl in mind. Not exactly a quick drop-off but in the whole transaction the twenty-something, baseball-cap wearer had not once acknowledged Rose's existence as a woman in any way. Not even an initial appraisal that Rose was aware of, not a flutter. OK, she wasn't exactly dressed to impress for an early morning delivery in carpenter jeans and turtleneck; plus, she wasn't really interested in having his attentions at all – he had a red acne rash flaring on his neck and a pointy Adam's apple that could take out an eye, but a look would have been nice. A little flicker of a flirt, at the very least, since it is almost mandatory, regardless of age gaps, between a male delivery driver and a female deliveree. But nothing. Only a mumble as he offered out the hand-held, electronic signy thingy then got back into his van, so that Rose – already starting the day feeling jaded from worrying about a still-missing Mooch and panicked that within twenty-four hours she would be seeing her ex, and had not yet met all her standards of

Operation Win Him Back – was left feeling unseen and invisible and assumed that she must also be deeply unattractive to all men on the planet.

What cognitive therapists call Magnification and Mimi would call 'making mountains out of molehills' was exactly what Rose was doing. She now had 128 different retro outfits chosen with her size in mind and in the last hour had eliminated 90 per cent of them and wasn't even sure about the rest.

For some people, the problem of what to wear is never a dilemma at all but then they lack any touch of the Carrie Bradshaw. Such folk might consider Rose was being superficial, pathetic even, considering all the good things she has going for her – glossy thick hair, nice straight teeth and strong legs.

'Excellent qualities in a horse,' she snorts derisively to herself. Rose has been known to cancel evenings out and to call in sick for work when such a dark mood has descended on her before and nothing in the wardrobe feels right, matches or fits.

She wanted to look stunning, she wanted to feel sensual and glamorous, for Carl's arrival but everything she puts on makes her feel dowdy, frumpy and about as sexual as a mum at the school gates in a pastel storm-cheater.

So now, Rose was making matters worse, wallowing more than a little in self-pity. Everyone has their personality faults but Rose was concentrating on her physical ones. She was looking at herself in the mirror, in a harsh early morning light in a not particularly flattering pair of greying, once-white pants and mismatching 'nude' sludgy, unsexy beige bra. A bra that was so old but actually so good at its job that she couldn't throw it away. One day it would need some sort of burial. With full military honours.

But standing staring at a reflected image in a cold-blue light with goose-bumped legs mottling in the chilly air, in an underwear set that wouldn't even do wonders if Kelly Brooks was filling it, is not the way to bolster shaky self-esteem. Rose had been hauling clothes on and off for the last hour saying the sort of things about her image that she would never say to a friend or even an enemy. Judgements that – even at her most savage – she would never even make in her head about another person. Rose had told herself repeatedly for sixty minutes that she was revolting, off-putting, grotesque, repulsive. She was doing the exact opposite of what shelves of self-help books advise. She was doing to herself what she would not allow her own customers to do to themselves in her earshot.

But Rose was tired, having slept so fitfully, dreaming vivid, disturbing, now inaccessible dreams that left her feeling irritated and unsettled. Not how she wanted to feel when Carl arrived.

Now clothes were strewn over chairs, the sofa and landing banisters. An opportunistic burglar would think at first glance that the flat had already been done over. Rose then tried a different, more casual, tack; high-waisted, forties-style jeans and knitted sweater but, instead of looking whimsical and cute, she looked in need of care in the community.

She tried a pencil skirt and ballet shoe combo but fell short of Sexy Librarian, landing somewhere near the homely, support hosiery end of the scale. Her self-abusive internal monologue was only stopped by a shrill ringing in her head.

'Great, and now I've got tinnitus,' she grumped.

Vintage was not working its magic right now. It had deserted her. How had all those pieces chosen individually over several visits to the warehouse wound up such duds? Carl would be coming tomorrow, she had to open the shop in less than an hour, there was no chance of being able to shop around for something else, and she really wanted to have a good scout for Mooch, too.

Rose decided to give it up as a bad job, making ridiculous proclamations in her head that she would never keep about sticking to water-and-vegetable soup diets, and began to pull on a trusty pair of turned-up jean pedal pushers, ancient fitted dinner shirt with unwashable stain and cardie, shaking her head to try and drive out the incessant bell ringing.

'Not only do I look like Quasimodo but all I can hear are bloody bells,' she muttered. She was just about to vow outlandishly to go for a three-mile run after she shut the shop that evening when she recalled a legendary quote. Somebody thin and famous had once said that the key to staying eternally a size ten was to ask if the extra biscuit was wanted more than wanting to be thin. Rose considered it carefully. It was a fair point. There was no contest. The ginger nut or custard cream would win every time. At last, she was back in reality.

The bell in her head was ringing in pulses this time and Rose's stomach gave a sudden adrenalised lurch of recognition. Her doorbell!

'Oh God! Rich!' She had been so self-absorbed and swamped with self-loathing that she'd completely forgotten he was coming to help her get to grips with the new system this morning. No matter how many times he had talked Rose through it yesterday, guiding her hand with the mouse to all the right buttons and folders, she just hadn't been able to concentrate. Probably because of Mimi and Lily being around, she thought.

'It's no good,' she'd admitted in defeat, 'I think you'll have to come back and run through this again some other time. I just can't seem to get it.'

'Don't want to get it, more like,' Lily had said sideways, thinking Rose couldn't hear and making Rich's partner John chuckle, although Rose wasn't sure exactly what Lily had meant by that remark.

The bell rang again.

'Shit, damn.' Rose started frantically throwing clothes into boxes. 'I'm coming!' she sing-songed from the upper-floor window, then hated herself for using that phrase that was so laden with double entendre and what if he really thought a bit of self-love and not loathing was why she hadn't answered the door? And it would all look worse because she was looking flustered. Rose opened the door, smiling and trying to look like the in-control, small-business owner image that she wanted to project when she noticed that the last two buttons of her blouse were undone and a dirty pair of knickers was hanging out of the leg of her pedal pushers.

She casually retrieved them as she beckoned him in and pushed them into her pocket. He hadn't appeared to have noticed. Rose was babbling now.

'I'm so sorry! I just didn't hear you and I've had my hands full with a big package. I mean a big package has just come. I mean arrived.' And then Rose was tongue-tied. Why, oh, why had porn stolen that perfectly innocent word meaning nothing more than to move, to be brought forwards? And why did it bother her so much to use it when he was around? And why didn't she just say 'delivery' instead of 'big package' like some sit-com randy housewife?

Rose left him downstairs as she scurried to make mugs of tea, relieved that Rich had been happy to stay and start up the 'pute and not see the carnage strewn around the upper floor.

This time she got it. She was navigating cyberspace and ringing up – or should that be bleeping up – sales on her flat screen monitor in no time at all. This time – with just nothing to concentrate on but Rich and his instructions, Rose got it in double time. She was more than happy with the temporary site and its art deco font and shabby-chic feel so that, in the absence of making any adjustments, they were soon exploring the games and gizmos also accessible through the new machine and then they were 'WWIL Fing', although Rose had no idea what they were doing at all until Rich explained.

'It's when you wander off track, clicking on links and new interesting searches until you have forgotten what you were Googling in the first place. What Was I Looking For? W.W.I.L.F? It's geek-speak. Get it?'

Rose got that too.

Their WWILFing took them away and then back to favourite websites with excited 'have you seens . . . ?' and 'I think you'd likes . . .' They were sharing funny, obscure theatre shows of sweary, muppet puppets (Him) and the Pop Surrealist art of Petrruci's Kick Ass Cuties (Her). They looked at Vintage Magic from Google Earth and Google Streetview. Then Rich showed Rose via 360 degree Peg-man technology where he'd once lived in a crowded, insanitary shared student house in Ladbroke Grove and how the bicycle he'd once owned was still chained to the house railings. Or at least the frame was – thieves having long since made off over a period of years with the seat, handlebars, tyres, wheels and gears.

Together they explored London with a virtual eye. The London where they'd both once lived. Their own individual Londons of favourite delis and bars, cafés and parks, and they realised that they had walked the same streets, possibly rubbed shoulders at key concerts of times past and bought from the same market stalls because how many exotic fruit vendors can there be with two thumbs on one hand?

They tested the water of likes (camping when it's dry) and dislikes (camping when it's wet), trading small secret interests to see if the spark of enthusiasm, the chemistry of commonalities, remained. The differences (he liked cricket, she did not. She was fond of marzipan, he couldn't bear the smell) were not so marked as to repel, to terminate the contact and seek exit as soon as possible, as Rose had once done when someone chatting in a bar – seemingly normal up to that point – had said, 'You know how it is when the details of a murder get you aroused.' For the record – no, Rose did not.

So in a verbal and multi-media exchange of all the info that Rose would have (he had already) posted on Facebook if she had got around to finishing her profile they were each able to piece the clues of the other together and to conclude that there was enough there to keep the conversation going. She felt instantly comfortable with him and was reminded of the sorts of boys she was friendly with before Carl and before Carl had filtered out her phonebook of friends deemed 'work-shy' – artists and musicians – or 'losers' – anyone who wasn't a lawyer. He'd make a great friend, Rose thought, unaware that, as she suggested Rich walk with her on her planned Mooch search, she had been messing her hair around, licking her lips and pulling fluff from his jumper. Unconscious signs of interest and liking. Signs of – if she was being honest and could see past the Carl-shaped barrier – attraction.

They crossed the square which was slowly waking to a working day, a few keen shoppers fortifying themselves with coffee in the windows of Ye Olde Coffee Shoppe, and Rose was so busy scouring for a big black cat that she tripped against a kerb and Rich caught her before she fell, pulling her instinctively against him in an act of protection. But as they sprang apart, too intimate a contact for too fledging a friendship, Mrs Bridges and Mrs Waters could clearly be seen looking from their windows. They waved 'Cooee!' and gave knowing winks and Rose felt like a teenager caught slow dancing at a youth club disco by her aunties.

Rich and Rose walked around the block, crossing roads and traversing alleyways. There were no cats to be seen anywhere and Mooch with his bulk would hardly be difficult to spot, but they talked and talked and talked. About pets (he'd lost a hamster and was still haunted by its demise) and music (Rose: Pink Martini – so odd but so right) and friends ('I think you'd really get on with . . .') and living in Bath (Rich: 'I just kind of came back, like a pigeon does. I'm not cool enough to be a Home Boy, more of a Homing Boy') and the shared experience of childhood holidays in stuffy, unchild-friendly hotels forced to sit statue-still in church-silence through three-course dinners.

And they talked about clothes, which Rose found odd because he was not exactly a 'snappy' dresser. There was no trace of the Peacock about Rich at all. Nor even of Peter Pan, which was what she and Lily called men who clung to edgy skate or hip-hop jean and T-shirt labels long after their hair ceases to cling to their foreheads. So to hear him say his fantasy wardrobe would be Paul Weller's with a touch of the tweedy suits of Vic Reeves almost shocked and certainly intrigued her and made her think that there were layers to this business associate (quickly becoming a friend) that had nothing to do with his risk-free middle-class uniform of shirt-under-pullover attire.

Then they were back, all too soon, at Vintage Magic and they stood in awkward poses unsure about what next. Rose realised that her mood had lifted – the Bad Hair, Bad Body, Bad Face Day had passed.

'Thanks for all your help this morning with the computer, I mean . . . I'm just so slow with it, but looking for Mooch, too. I've been so worried . . .' Rose had her hand on the key in the door and he was backing away, taking his leave, hands in his pockets, shrugging off her thanks.

'Don't worry. Any time. Call me if you have any more problems with the system. But then –' His face split into a wide grin, his eyes twinkling, and he was now at a distance across the Square which meant that the conversation (or retaliation) was becoming more impossible. He paraphrased: 'If the rain starts to pour, I'll be there for you 'cos I've been there before.'

And Rose nearly dropped her key, drenched in the

shock-cold horror that he had known all along that she was the boozed-up bint who had vomited on his shoes.

For what must have been the fifteenth time Rose got up because she thought she could hear Mooch. A second night without him and her nerves were stretched taut. But the low scratching wasn't paws skimming on the nasty but secure and well-insulated PVC back door, it was the white noise returning. The voices of Vintage Magic.

Like the humming of a theatre audience speaking in low tones before the lights dim and the curtain rises. A buzzing akin to happy bees in a well-stocked, sun-warmed hive. Like an ocean rolling over shaley shores, it rose and fell, and Rose tried to blot it out, substituting its sound with the noise of her own thoughts of Lily and Matt or Isabelle and Carl. Even the latter was preferable to this irritating, unsettling sound that could drive a person – like Mr Brown – quite literally mad.

She tried stamping on it with logic, recalling sciencey facts about the mechanical waves of sound travel. Working her way through her list of Fright Erasers, repeating to herself *There's no such thing as ghosts*. But tonight it was more persistent. Logic, brandy and exhaustion couldn't obliterate the sound. The voices came in dislocated snatches and she couldn't tell whether it was in her head or in the walls. Her heart raced and she told herself she was just tired and anxious and she wished that her big black cat was curled up asleep safely at the foot of her bed.

Carl was coming tomorrow so she had to get her sleep if she was going to look her best. Look her best? She still had nothing to wear. Not a single one of those pieces – which she'd finally cleared away as she'd cleaned the flat, wanting it to be perfect, from top to bottom – had felt right. But it had been a good day, mostly. Tiring. Busy. The new system was easier than the old electronic till, and she smiled to herself, first at some story Rich had recounted, then at his parting shot. If only Mooch would come back then she could relax . . . Dammit! That sound again! Would earplugs do the trick? Best get some from the chemist tomorrow.

Rose was physically tired but she couldn't turn her brain off. Couldn't stop the churning, whirring of all that she had to do tomorrow before Carl arrived, the programme of events from heavy layering of body lotion to the sketching on of perfectly arched eyebrows. But as she thought of Carl, her mood darkened again; the associations of feeling bad, hurt and heartbroken compounded with her fears for Mooch and that familiar feeling of loss. Then, uninvited, slithering from her repressed unconscious, came the vivid flashbulb memory of finding Carl and Isabelle in bed together.

She was fighting so hard to stop dark thoughts from rising from the depths of her imagination and the bleaker her thoughts, the louder the whispered tones and murmurings seemed to get. As Rose tried to edge towards sleep, thinking of things she could wear tomorrow, her thoughts jumped to a good girl in an emerald dress losing her reputation but who didn't seem to miss it.

But then the night-time wanderings of her imagination unfolded like a pop-up book of fairytales. Vintage Magic as a gingerbread house, booksellers in straitjackets, scratched stomachs that became bodies unpicked like old clothing at the seams. She thought of ghost stories and folklore, myths and *The Exorcist*. Inexplicable happenings and satellite TV stations with their real-life investigations of haunted suburban houses and night-vision filming. She thought about parapsychology and how it can explain everything as tricks of light or slips of the mind. And she thought about listed buildings of white walls and dark timbers and all the lives, happy and sad, productive and destructive, that had played out their acts in its four walls.

Then a thought. Cool and calm. It's coming from the cellar.

The cellar! Of course. Silly me. Rose actually chuckled aloud. Mooch was always going into the cellar. He must have got shut in there when Matt was going up and down fiddling with the electrics and so on. There must be something in the cellar that had been making that sound all along. Old electrics buzzing or something vibrating all through the fabric of the house and if Mooch was down there – which he was sure to be – then his scratching to get out or moving around was making it worse. Perhaps some of those old boxes had been left there on purpose to dampen the sound, to pin down old pipes to stop them moving around and that would explain why a noise barely noticeable at first had lately become so unbearable.

She sprang up, no longer cowering under the covers like a kid scared of the dark, remembering she'd been here before, scared stiff with silly stories, when Cynthia had found the door unlocked. Poor Mooch, he must be starving and thirsty. Simultaneously, she was slipping her feet into old Indian beaded slippers and reaching for her glasses from the night stand. She was locked, loaded and ready to go to release Mooch from his underground prison. Then she hesitated. The cellar. How predictable. And there was a full moon too. How naff – how like a Famous Five mystery, getting up in the night to go and follow a hunch in your pyjamas down into the basement. How like the setting of a cheap eighties American horror movie where one by one the kids go down into the cellar and fall to some horrible fate. Rose almost laughed aloud again – then she would have looked well and truly mad. Best take a torch whose batteries are about to run out, she thought with black humour. Shame there wasn't a nubile nineteen-year-old with a pert bosom she could send down – they are usually the ones to die first. Precisely the sort of script to make cinema-goers question the sanity of anyone who would go down into a cellar alone.

But her fears had gone, and she was jubilant at the thought that she had single-handedly solved *The*

Mystery of the Missing Mooch and Mysterious Murmurings. Maybe she was more Velma from *Scooby Doo* after all – she'd better get an orange polo-neck. She padded down the stairs (making sure she switched on every light as she went) a tartan-pyjamaed, bespectacled Nancy Drew. The cellar door was in her sights now, a rectangular halo of light emanating from the cracks around it, the beehive door knob within her grasp. Matt had left the cellar light on. Funny that she hadn't noticed it yesterday. The noise, so clearly, so obviously coming from the cellar, now came in pulsed breaths with the rushing of sharply exhaled air. The light flickered and played and what must have been Mooch's shadow appeared suddenly to be many figures moving behind the door and, for a moment, Rose's nerve faltered. Then she grasped the handle decisively, told herself to get real and, with all the confidence of scientific explanation and logical deduction, twisted, pulled and opened.

Mooch shot past as though catapulted. Every hair stood out stiffly from his body and he galloped up the stairs to sanctuary. Rose nearly toppled over in shock and, cursing him, she reached out and flicked the light switch, knowing now that bed and sleep would soon be in her grasp. She flicked the switch again and then did it again and again. Damn those electrics – the thing wouldn't turn off! And damn that noise! She'd never drop off with that bloody racket going on. With the sort of psychotic irritation that only comes with lack of sleep, she stamped down the cellar steps ready to wrench wires, plumbing or kick over the building's very supports – anything to get a decent night's sleep.

The light was glaring, like walking into the path of the rising sun and it took a second for Rose to orientate and realise that its source was not the energy-saving, tubular, compact fluorescent light swinging from its flex that even at best gave out what can only be described as a glow.

The back of the cellar – where she and Matt had

noticed plaster had crumbled from the walls, probably due to the damp – had entirely vanished. In its place a great, infinite vortex-filled hollow had opened out.

Rose stood still, frozen, in her tartan pyjamas, the whole scene reflected in her black-rimmed spectacles, unable to make sense of the panorama opening out in front of her. The light shimmered and swirled, gaseous clouds in all shades of gold from hot-white through to yellow metal and warm rose, threaded and weaved over one another. Rainbow hues, like oil marbled on puddled water, swam through the mix that was dotted occasionally with flashes of jewel; a glimmer of emerald, sapphire flares or a brief blaze of ruby. Rose had never been one with magpie tastes for diamonds and blingy stones but now she was drawn to the lustre like a moth to a camping lamp.

Rose felt small and insignificant, terrified and awe-struck, compelled to stand there and just observe whilst all the time wanting to reach out and touch. In trying to explain the sudden disintegration of her cellar into this spectacle, she sorted through her stored memories like a CD player on shuffle. She thought of all the sci-fi programmes she had ever seen and fallen asleep to and wished she'd paid more attention. She recalled helmet-permed RE teachers and their coffee-breath scripture tales of creation. She thought of acid-induced hippy-trippy album artwork. She thought of Hubble photographs of the solar system, galaxies and nebulae and their candy-floss whirls of orb-spotted gases. And then it made a kind of sense. If ever a shop basement becoming a portal to the heart of the universe and a holding place for the secret energies of the cosmos could make sense.

Now something else caught her eye. Moving within the swirls of colour and energy were feminine forms – the first Rose noticed were languishing as if in repose like the sultan's favourites on harem cushions. But there were others draped across one another, leaning on shoulders, heads lovingly cradled in laps or legs intertwined in poses of familiarity. Every possible female form was represented from a cherubic babe with a halo of curls to the small-budded breasts of maidens in first flower to the almost Neanderthal shapes of women, heavy breasted and rounded by middle age. Some had bellies swollen with childbearing. Others were muscled like prime-time athletes or withered and stooped with age, skin hanging in sagging folds. There were faces of erotic satisfaction, Buddha-like serenity or smiles of beatific mothers steeped in love. Lined skin, of a silver pallor softened with age, told stories of the necessary acceptance of life and all its unexpected joys and unavoidable sorrows.

Femme fatales displayed themselves in primal nudity. Others were draped with diaphanous cloths or silks with the intention to highlight and frame but not to conceal. At once primitive and futuristic, colours and form echoed of dynasties long past and yet to be. It was a kaleidoscope of shapes, of limbs, of eyes and blossoms budding, blooming and shedding skins of petal.

The scene, the whole sensuous feast, unfolded as one of opposing dichotomies. Rose's left and right brains struggled to merge the conflicting images into a common-sense whole. Sublime youth and beauty were present, intermingled, interwoven with the decrepit, almost repellent, ugliness of old age. It was like looking into the faces of Hollywood matrons – or, indeed, Mimi – all the boxes of youth ticked – taut flesh, full breasts and plump lips – and simultaneously seeing the advancing years, obvious in the almost indiscernible clues of age spots or slight creeping of skin.

What Rose could not possibly comprehend was that she was looking at a single slice through time; all of history, and histories not yet written, was visible in this tear through the temporal dimension. Past, present and future unfurled, rolling out in different directions like roped red-carpeted walkways.

Rose felt like an intrusive voyeur but also longed to become part of the tableaux. In fact, she found she was grief-stricken to be left out. At the same time she was suddenly, uncomfortably aware of her fleshy, earthly form and it felt a clumsy, lumpy and vulgar mass of sinew, adipose and bone in contrast to these ethereal beings that seemed to be made from web and air. She was aware then of what she later felt was a connection to her very core, timeless and ageless, and the very essence of her femininity struggling to be free.

The noise, the noise that had been almost

unnoticeable at first, all those months ago, was intense now. It was the collective sighs, laughs and gasps of women playing with children, gossiping in herds or lowing in childbirth combined with the death rattles and wheezing of the old. Together they formed an ashtanga yoga breath that emulated archaic sounds – the pulse of the tide against the shore and the rippling of a summer breeze through leaves. Like being immersed in the best surround sound system, it came from every-where, all compass points, and echoed her breathing, weaving through her chest wall. Underpinning it was an almost imperceptible, unheard before, deeper bass note. A vowel sound, a vibration reverberating from the centre and source of everything, engulfing all as it rolled, outwards and inwards, pulling and pushing an energy that ancient writings call prana, chi or spirit.

'Don't be afraid.' The voice was smooth like a lullaby underlined with a stand-to-attention threat like a mother calling out a naughty child's full name. Rose had to ask herself, was she afraid? And her answer came back – yes, in bucketloads. But she had been told to release that fear, to let go of her panic and cold dread and she did so without question.

One woman emerged, rising and growing from the mass to stand eye to eye with Rose Taylor. She was not a being of solid matter, nor was she a faint, flickering hologram, as Rose might have expected from a deity. She was fluid. She was liquid mercury, seeming sub-stance and aqueous all at once. She radiated empathic warmth but behind the rapturous smile was a warning of an anger and vengefulness that Rose did not want to rouse.

She was the personification of Helen Reddy's feminist anthem 'I am woman'. She was a mass of contradictions like Meredith Brook's 'Bitch' song. She was larval fire and watery vapours and she shimmered with all the bright tones and heavy mysticism of Byzantine art. It seemed impossible that in one face, so Marilyn-perfect, a woman in the flush of youth and a toothless, decaying old hag existed simultaneously. The whole spectacle had such an air of hallucinogenic unreality that it could have been a perfume advert.

'Do you know who I am?' she said simply, without the arrogance of a C-list celebrity trying to get a discount in Debenhams, and Rose shook her head mutely. 'I am Minerva. Sulis.'

It took a moment for Rose to recognise those names, so familiar and at home in Bath. Etched on temple walls and sacrificial offerings, on ancient artefacts that pleaded for wishes or curses to be answered, matches to be made or fertility granted. But as she dredged up memories of visits to the city's tourist highlights, the list of names rolled on. Athena. Brigit. Epona. Saravasti. Isis. Mary. Sul. Durga. This was not just one goddess, this was the embodiment of all.

And still the names came. Divinities familiar – Freya, Hu-Tu, Gaia – and unheard of – Hinakuluiau, Omoikani. From all the civilisations that ever were or will be, the goddess herself recited all her names, her many forms in a robotic, hypnotic chant joined by the multitude of handmaidens. Time may have sped past or stood still, Rose had no way of knowing but, with the list complete, the goddess spoke again.

'So we return to our sacred grounds. Once we were welcome here . . .' she faded off and did not elaborate, her gaze looking beyond Rose to another time, another place.

Then in a hawk movement, she locked her eyes on to Rose, who could not look away. The goddess's elliptical, insect-eyes watched, scanned and bored into Rose, who became lost in the black, fathomless deep of her gaze and fearful of what might be found.

'Your heart yearns,' was all that was said as the words pierced her hurt with laser precision and Rose cried out, the pain of her rejection, the witness of his infidelity splitting from her chest was raw, burning, but it was a blessed relief. Body-racking sobs like a baby torn from its mother's arms engulfed her, and when she was done and the crying was silenced and only the shudders remained, Rose found she was curled on the cellar floor. She had shared it all with the goddess without saying a word.

'How do you want it to be?' and the goddess's attendants – she had more than was needed on an average Mariah Carey tour – seemed to press forward to hear Rose's answer. It came without hesitation. A well-rehearsed mantra.

'I want him back. I want him to look at me and want me so badly that every nerve in his body aches. I want to look sexy, gorgeous, beautiful. I want the perfect dress to blow his mind.' The goddess nodded ascent. Not empathy, not sympathy, but an agreement that this was the way it would be. Her will would be done.

She raised her hand, palm facing Rose, and as she did so, lifted her chin upwards. A regal movement. Behind her the vortex swirled more quickly. All eyes were locked on Rose and in one symphony-conductor flick of her wrist it was all gone and the cellar had returned to normal, floor intact, creeping damp on peeling whitewashed walls and cartons of flyers and coat hangers. All normal, except for one goddess, now looking very much like ordinary flesh and blood, sitting on a cardboard box, swinging her legs, watching Rose with a mixture of fascination and affection as though she were a big tartan foal struggling to its feet for the first time.

'Phew! Those big introductions wear me out!' The goddess put her hand to her head dramatically. 'Good though, eh? Rituals, pomp, ceremony. You guys don't have enough of it on earth any more. Everything is casual, do what you like, let it all hang out. Well, what's wrong with dressing it all up a bit? Making a show once in a while. You've got to admit it was pretty impressive! And it's not the first time I've seen it done – know what I'm saying?' Her accent was indefinable, with just a touch of MTV in the way the end of her sentences raised at the end in question. She had smooth skin the colour of milky coffee flecked across the cheeks with just a few dark, becoming freckles, almond eyes and a mane of dark curly hair that was reminiscent of Diana Ross in her 'Chain Reaction' video. She wore a draped tunic that shimmered in a metallic bronze and clung to her impressive Wonder Woman figure in all the right places.

Rose's mouth had fallen open. She could hear her mother's voice in distant memory: 'Shut your mouth, Rose, unless you are catching flies!' and she instinctively corrected herself to shut it. She pushed her glasses up her nose and wondered what to say.

'Shouldn't you have gone with them?' was the best that she could do.

'They'll come back when I call.' The goddess waved the comment away as if it were a trifle. 'So you want to get him back, then?'

Rose nodded.

'Stick with me, honey, and it'll be easy. A piece of cake. I don't suppose you were listening when all my titles were read out – even my attention wanders towards the end – but you know what? It's your lucky day – not only am I Minerva, goddess of the waters here in Bath, Sulis as was, but let's not go through that list again . . .' The goddess was talking at what felt like a million miles an hour and Rose struggled to keep up. 'But I am also the – yes, that's right, *the* – the One and Only Fairy Godmother – fulfiller of dreams, changer of lives, etc. etc., and also, as well – not a lot of people know this – the famous granter of wishes, otherwise known today as Genie, and don't – *don't* – believe for one single minute that that Aladdin thing was all done by a blue man in that lamp – Puh-leeease! A man? A magic man? A god? Don't get me started! The trouble with folklore is it becomes Chinese whispers and then it gets all out of proportion and you wouldn't believe what people end up saying and how they get it wrong.

'So I am your goddess' – she jumped down from the box and bowed a low principal-boy bow – 'at your service. The goddess, like all the other names, Mother Nature, Earth Mother – yadda, yadda, yadda is – how can I put it so that you will understand – just a job title. A position of office. Kind of like James Bond – the job description stays the same – killing baddies, spying, getting into fights, making love to beautiful women – that's James Bond's job, not mine, of course! But the faces change. Are you with me? So this is My Time now. My time to be goddess and I earned it. I've been doing this for a few millennia and, you know, it's one of those things where you're always learning but we – that's the royal we, you British folk like that way of talking, don't you – we have not been here for such a long time . . .' Again there was the wistfulness before Minerva switched and became all goddess business again. 'But we're here now and ready to receive blessings – that's an important bit, don't forget that now! And to make all your dreams come true and, while I'm at it, deliver a few curses if the need is pressing. Curses – now they can be a lot of fun – only to the ones that have got it coming, of course! You can't go around cursing the innocents or you've got it coming back at you three times as strong. You know that, though, don't you? But to those that have wronged you – take that Isabelle, for example' – Minerva gave Rose an almost sly, sidelong look, testing the water, reading for clues but equally putting coals on the fire, as it were – 'she would be a prime candidate for a curse. A perfect specimen, you could say. Now when it comes to curses, I like to see a bit of imagination, know what I mean? Death and disease – way too easy – but we can have a lot of fun with, say, a constantly dripping nose – that's a good curse, very inconvenient and anti-social or, one of my personal favourites, shoes that are never comfortable. Beautiful in its simplicity! Doesn't sound like much, does it? But try living with it!' The goddess clapped her hands together and chuckled wickedly at the memory.

Rose spoke finally, coming out of her daze but wondering at the same time if Lily and Matt had maybe slipped something into her milk as a joke. She hadn't seen these kinds of visuals since the time they had drunk mushroom tea at Glastonbury festival. 'Why here? Why Vintage Magic? Why me?'

'Why not?' There was a sudden steel-sharp edge to the goddess. An underlying anger like a powder keg of PMT waiting to go off. She didn't like to be questioned. She admonished Rose now, scolded her for her glaring stupidity. 'You should rephrase it, you know? Of course Vintage Magic! Where else but Vintage Magic? Lucky for me, Vintage Magic!' Minerva sat back down on the box, crossing her arms gruffly and turning her back slightly on Rose. She jutted out her bottom lip. She looked like a nine-year-old girl in a sulk.

And just like Rose used to do with her sister, she ran over to make amends and to chivvy her back to happiness. And, in this case, to try to avoid the black rage that seemed to bubble under the surface.

'I didn't mean "Why me?" in a moany way, I meant "Why me?" in a "What have I done that's so special to deserve all this?" kind of way. I mean Vintage Magic is just a shop. It's not even like a real magic shop, is it? I just sell clothes. It's not like a temple or anything. I mean there's a temple – your temple – not far from here. Why not show up there?'

'Full of tourists.'

'OK,' Rose said slowly. That answer seemed to make sense.

'*And* nobody has asked us to show up there for a while.' Minerva was still petulant. 'Oh no – everyone is too busy taking photographs but then popping over to the cathedral for a spot of worship. They built that to take attention away from me, did you know that?' Minerva spat through gritted teeth. Rose nodded, fearing that she was making matters worse but then the goddess softened her tone and once more became smooth as silk. Rose was beginning to understand why men said women were so unpredictable. 'It would be easy to show up there. You know, channels have been forged for a very long time, but you need an invitation at the very least. You can't just show up without being asked and the security guards would throw somebody out on their ear if they so much as lit a candle as an offering to me. I like offerings.' The goddess sounded like a spoiled child on her birthday. 'Not dead goats. I don't like that sort of messy business. Something with a bit of thought behind it. Something where somebody's taken the time to really get to know what I like. Do you know what I mean?

'Anyway, if I do something for you to win over this man of yours – you're going to owe me now, do you understand? You're going to owe me Big Time!' Rose nodded eagerly, willingly. 'I'm going to want to see some blessings – know what I'm saying, and I can't stand those generic offerings – the bottle-of-wine thing, the box-of-sweet stuff or same-old flowers. So why Vintage Magic, you want to know? Somebody's been practising Goddess Magic here for a while now. And all that feminine energy coming in and out every day. You, your mother, your sister, your niece and then all your customers. Like it or not Vintage Magic *is* a place of worship. Have you not heard the way the women coo over the clothes – is it not to celebrate being women? Being goddesses in their own right? Are they not seeking to find their dreams? Do they not stand in the changing room and look in the mirror asking for divine help from the fabric they're trying on to fulfil their needs?'

Rose didn't answer, she had fixated on one point. 'Who's been practising Goddess Magic?'

'Aaaahhh! That's for me to know!' Minerva tapped the side of her nose. Rose didn't dare press her further on that point. 'And anyway, I couldn't possibly try to explain to *you* the metaphysics of goddess manifestation. You're simply not intelligent enough to understand. It's a combination of very precise elements, a delicate balancing of points over which someone like you could not have any conscious control whatsoever.'

Rose was crushed, put firmly in her mortal place, but she had to ask. Had to because she felt some sort of moral obligation. They were her customers after all – not quite the same sort of responsibility as being a teacher *in loco parentis*, but even so. So she asked even if it meant she risked the hair-blowing, face-blasting, spit-washing rage that seemed likely to follow.

'Have you somehow done something to the clothes here?'

'Me?' Minerva was all innocence. 'What do you think?' she added darkly. 'I mean the changing room is right above our heads, right? It's not exactly difficult to listen in to people's thoughts, hopes and fears, is it? For some of them they may as well have shouted three wishes down the stairs, it was coming so loud and clear.'

'But that woman, the mousy one, the one with the green dress, you turned her into a vamp and the other one . . . the one with the scratches all around her stomach . . . that was . . . that was barbaric!'

Minerva looked unmoved. 'She wasn't listening hard enough! We had to do something to get her attention! And what she thought she wanted was actually very different to what, deep down, she actually wanted. And it all turned out for the good, didn't it? So what's the problem? It's a good job you don't know what happened to the others, that's all I can say!'

'What others?'

'Oh, you know . . .' And then there was a swift change of tack. 'Anyway, the effects seldom last for ever. Look, it makes my job easy when the women who have had the clothes before leave a trace of themselves. It's in the weave, kind of Essence of Woman, if you will. The stronger the personality of the woman, the stronger the memories left in the dress – put a new receptive soul in it and . . . kaboom! I just kind of . . . ramped it up a little, know what I'm saying? The green dress lady, the owner, she was All Woman and the one who bought it – she was ready to relieve herself of – well, keen to discover carnal delights, shall we say? And the owner of the dress that scratched up your customer's stomach? How was I to know she was a vengeful old crone? Sometimes the way I intend a message to come out – well, it can get a little lost in translation. I'm still quite new at this goddess thing, you know! And I'm only trying to do my best!' Minerva's voice was getting higher by the octave, straining, on the edge of angry, misunderstood tears. Rose prepared herself for blast-off. 'And it's not all my fault. Let's just say people should be careful what they wish for! Anyway, enough of all this technical talk.' She waved her regal hand again. That part of the conversation was now deemed o-v-e-r. 'It bores me. Let's get back to talking about that dog of yours!'

'He's a cat.'

'Not that mangy, own-bottom-licking thing!' Rose felt a surge of protectiveness at that insult aimed at Mooch. 'That man of yours! The dog that ran off with your friend. We can get him back, crawling on his knees begging forgiveness and all it's going to take is a little bit of old-school glamour . . .'

'Glamour?'

'That's what I said, isn't it?' Minerva was excited, keen, and as animated as a teenager telling her best pals about her best snog ever. 'Come over here, honey.' She rearranged herself to sit cross-legged on the cardboard box. A box that Rose would have crushed to paper flatness had she plonked her backside on it, but she sat on the cold stone floor at her goddess's feet instead, before opting to drag a *Sunday Times* from a pile of recycling as a barrier between her and the cold, recalling old wives' tales about piles.

Sitting now like a nursery teacher and class at story time, Rose listened to all of the goddess's instructions. Glamour, it seemed, had lost its way or, at least, the meaning of the word had. Glamour was not, as is commonly interpreted, lipstick, powder and paint ploys of catching a man's attention – although it could be part of it. Nor was it 'Glamour' in the sense of 'modelling' –

the bare-all approach – which could make you very popular for a time at least whilst the front end held up. And Rose was relieved to hear it was nothing to do with being a size eight bulimic lollipop-head, or even her mother's preferred route once she'd over-shot forty – plastic surgery. Mimi had even traded in the last of the family shares for labiaplasty, shouting over her daughters' screams that you wouldn't keep sagging curtains up at a window. They wished she'd chosen a better analogy because it was an image they couldn't clear from their heads for quite some time.

No – Glamour was artifice of another kind. Glamour was allure, captivation and charm in the old sense of the word or *glammer* that had far more to do with magic, enchantment, sorcery and witchcraft. It was, in Scotch Gaelic, the learning of occult ways, the means of casting spells of deception and altering reality – the latter as true a definition of Mimi's labiaplasty as there ever could be.

The vortex had returned almost unnoticed by Rose until she realised she was surrounded by its warm, orangey glow as comforting as an open fire. She was at one with it, felt herself absorbed, swallowed up whole by it, and she gave herself over until she felt like she was floating on some warm, buoyant pool as cool hands stroked her forehead and limbs, washing away doubts and sorrows, and she felt herself filled with a purity of being that had nothing to do with being a good girl and everything to do with just being herself. Purely herself, undiluted, and Minerva's words washed over her – secret, ancient and laden with magical meaning connecting her to the goddess world without and her own feminine goddess power within, and a new energy ran through her veins like the quicksilver of anaesthetics.

There had not been any doubt about what she was doing. Rose had sat willingly to learn all the arcane tricks, the magic of the ancients. She wanted to captivate, to charm. She wanted to be beautiful, but her own kind of beautiful not a centrefold facsimile. She wanted to know how to use what she had got and then some. She had listened attentively as she once had to her lecturers of metallurgy for jewellery class but never had in biology. She had opened her mind fully to the possibility of winning her way back to Carl's heart and she had drunk sweet, cold liquids in goblets pressed to her mouth. She had inhaled incense as its smoke burned her eyes and allowed herself to be bathed in a shower of glittering minerals, and all the time her mind had been filled with the songs and intonations of Minerva's attendants.

But she could not remember a single word or, at least, she could not vocalise it. The spells hummed around her head just out of reach from conscious recall, slipping like a fish into the shadows as she reached towards them. But she could remember Minerva's last words, shouted as the shrinking vortex had disappeared into a pinprick of nothing, and Rose had woken to find herself stretched out on the dusty cellar floor devoid of her pyjamas.

'We'll get him back, sweetheart, we can't fail! Just leave it me. Leave it to me!'

As Rose trod wearily towards the cellar stairs, she tripped. A small box was at her feet, half filled with forgotten, unsorted clothes, and she tucked it under her arm, carrying it with her up the two flights of stairs, back up to her bedroom, clutching her unbuttoned tartan jacket around her for warmth. A grey light was stealing over the moss-speckled slate roof tops of Bath. Her mind swam, weighed down with troubling thoughts of divine beings and Bath's long history and fears that somehow she had wandered into Dorian Gray territory and had traded part of her soul. And there was one particular hectoring anxiety that would not go away, a quote from English lessons in Rose's dim past, she could not recall its origin, exactly. Something about gods using us for their sport, and Rose wondered grimly, as she slid into the cool cotton of her duvet and surrendered herself finally to the sleep that she had craved, if it also applied to goddesses.

12

She would not normally be seen dead venturing into a shop like this. It was too . . . too – she groped for a word – civilian. A place where normal people went. The ones who had to work for a living and could not afford anti-ageing pharmaceuticals. Not people like her, Tamara, who had worked harder to get ahead in ways these dull people with their non-waiting list, high-street handbags could ever imagine.

For a start, she had had to alter her birth name to project the right image. Tracey would not have opened as many doors but Tammy (as she shortened her new moniker to her men friends, they liked it – cutsie and kinda *Playboy*, conjuring images of cheerleaders) had been very successful in helping her to choose the right marriage partner.

Horrid little shop with its homemade labels and bare wood floor! Where were the reassuring adverts of named designers, the little cardboard stands of model-perfect men and impossible flawless women clearly sporting their Ds and Gs, Ls and Vs and double CCs?

But she had to have one piece of vintage for this arty-farty ball tonight. It was rumoured that it would be populated with the London set, media types, and she knew from all the magazines that vintage was the thing. That to say it was 'up-cycled' and that you'd found it slung on a market barrow held a peculiar kind of kudos with that crowd and that crowd was where she belonged.

Tamara wanted more parties like this one promised to be, ones where photographers lurked behind the potted palms and you were seen later in a glossy magazine clutching a champagne glass in the pages just before the expensive estate agent spreads. Only, this time, she did not want to be wedged between some ex-county cricketer with the bloated red face of a wino and the Lord Mayor, who had allowed his hand to casually drop and skim her bottom. Not that she could blame him. Her buttocks had been sculpted to perfection between her lunges and liposuction. Something that rather pear-shaped shop girl standing at that tacky bar-style counter could do with. Old Fat Arse over there wasn't fooling anyone with the flared skirt/wide belt hide-the-hips combo.

More parties, that's what she needed. Parties where she could meet people. People who would be good for a career. A career that she hadn't quite decided on yet – clothes, fashion, being famous – something like that. Proper people who lived in London – God! She missed living inside the M25 – people who understood about PR and power lunches and she was great at the meet-and-greet thing. The air kisses, the Ooh! You look fabulous, darlings. She knew how to give the right amount of eye contact to the Piers, the Lars and the Xanders – just enough to keep them thinking they might stand a chance – and how to expertly play their wives with flattery and talk about beauticians and cleaners – ya I agree, so unreliable and lazy, terrible when they can't understand your instructions, well, they should learn English if they want to stay here.

But she was bored with it in Bath. It had been nice at first, decorating the house – well, organising the interior decorator. What a pity he'd turned out to be gay, it could have been so much more fun.

Greg had always dreamed of retiring to the country and now that he wasn't having to pay all that wretched child maintenance to his first wife and her kids had grown up and buggered off, there was a bit more cash to splash around and, since he paid the bills, she could hardly say no. But even a heated indoor swimming pool gets boring after a while and especially the view on to nothing-but-green fields. She wished he'd always dreamed of retiring to Marbella instead.

But the London lot? Now this could be interesting. A handful of indie rockstars – not her thing, but who knew whom they knew? There are always people in publishing popping up and down between city and country and wasn't Jeremy Clarkson just a V8 turbo drive away?

She should have been in television. She would be so great doing all the photo spreads in *Hello!*

But it was annoying that Greg was around all the time now that he had left the business to run itself. So glad there was a golf course he could while away some time on. She never complained about being a golf widow; in fact, being a widow full-stop might have its advantages . . .

Of course you can judge someone by their clothes. You can judge what they can afford, for a start, and their taste. Did they know how to pick the right designers? Did they understand what was in or out? She never could understand the Kate Moss/Alexa Chung look. Dressing down? Wearing what looked like your mother's old cast-offs? Why did *Vogue* insist that they had style? It must be an Emperor's New Clothes thing because she couldn't see it. She'd never seen either of them in a shearling gilet and neither had a French manicure. And if, as it was rumoured, Kate Moss did have hair extensions, it certainly didn't look like it. Tamara fluffed her own to big effect, pouting as she did so. She knew it was a good look.

She pushed her glasses up Alice-band-style. It wasn't exactly sunny outside but those rays might penetrate the cloud cover and cause a crow's foot or two if she wasn't vigilant. She was obligated to never age. Greg may as well have put that in the pre-nup. 'Remember,' his first wife had told her, full of bitterness and fine lines from lying under a sun-bed for too long, 'there will always be someone prettier and younger than you snapping at your heels for your place in the bedroom and their share of the bank balance.' Tamara had laughed it off but it was worrying now that Greg had discovered Viagra. And it required more acting on her behalf.

She looked around the little shop. Striking a pose that she hoped projected Confident, Wealthy Shopper. Her Mulberry weighed heavily in the crook of her elbow but, with her hand cocked outwards at an angle, just so, she knew that she painted a pretty picture in her dark, slimming Chloe boot-cuts, unlike the art on these walls. Naff gypsy prints and oh, no, surely not, a Green Goddess! Had she somehow stumbled into a charity shop?

And, like art, when it came to clothes, Tamara knew what she wanted and that was something that she'd seen in a magazine and had a firm approval from somebody else. That was the good thing about labels – you knew where you were with DKNY and what she liked to know was that what she wore could not be worn by someone else with less than an income of one hundred thou' a year.

She flicked at a few rails, her diamond rings catching the light with more carats than a grocer's. Who cares how they are mined? If it wasn't for people like her buying diamonds, those men wouldn't have any work at all! They should think themselves lucky. Oh God! Where was she supposed to start in this fleapit? Surely the whole pleasure of shopping was buying something new?

*

Mooch strolled in from the back room giving the cellar door a slightly wider berth than normal and Rose's customer backed towards the door in panic and revulsion.

'You've got a cat in here.' It was a statement of fact hissed at Rose.

'Yes, he's the shop cat, Mooch. He's got to know a lot of my regulars. I'll put him out the back if you don't like him.'

'Do it quickly.' There was no thanks or please or sorry, or I have an allergy/phobia. Poor Mooch – disliked by customers and goddesses alike. Rose wanted to retort: 'I don't like your tone, young lady', but put her unaccountable irritation down to tiredness and spending most of the night naked in the cellar. Some people would pay good money to do that. Some MPs and racing car bosses for example. Her brain had not even had time to assimilate last night's events; she'd just thrown down two hefty cups of coffee and opened up as usual, slapping on a bit more concealer over the dark shadows (of her eyes, not her upper lip).

As Rose stooped to pick up Mooch, putting all her back into the effort, she wanted to slap the superior sneer right off her customer's face. Probably not the best way to improve sales, but if she saw her handle one of Peggy's garments like that again – touching with just finger and thumb as if she was about to catch something – then a slappin' might just be in order.

The customer followed Rose with her line of sight, her eyes narrowed into cat-slits as Rose removed Mooch, who stared right back without blinking.

'Actually,' she said, as if Mooch had just given her a splendid idea, 'do you have any fur?'

As it happened, Rose did. Not that she wanted to show this woman, but a sale was a sale. Rose wasn't quite sure where she stood on fur. Not literally, of course; she knew when she was literally standing on fur. In fact, she could recall a certain bearded flute teacher who had insisted she play standing barefoot on a sheepskin rug during his lessons and claimed it could enhance her technique. The more she thought about it, the more it seemed like the wrong sort of advice to give to a fourteen-year-old. Very wrong. More than wrong. Creepy. Almost an arrestable offence.

But the ethics of fur . . . it was a hot debate and she still burned with shame when she remembered her only brush with the law and it was all about fur because as a student, though she was short on cash, she had been big on principles. Along with other stripey-tights, army-surplus and Doc Marten-boot wearers Rose had assembled at the designated demo point to take orders from their much-pierced leader of ARS, or the animal rights society. Their morals were laudable and highly developed but their understanding of acronyms could have been described, at best, as naïve.

At the time, a local casino had been identified as the epicentre of fur-wearing ladies; mainly because it employed high-cheek-boned ladies of Eastern European origin who were not aware of the cultural taboo that was fur. The plan had been to yell: 'Fur is murder!' and fling blood-red nail varnish at the coats as the women entered before legging it in the opposite direction as quickly as possible. Rose had thought it would be a brilliant piece of artistic expression and intended to use the press cuttings of their daring protest as part of her art thesis on 'E-vulva-lution: changing women's history through art'.

But Rose had never really fully understood the brief. That is, that the lid should come off the nail polish in order to leave its red spatters on the white furs. So Rose had flung a firmly sealed glass bottle at a poor woman with limited English skills but no need for facial highlighter. It had glanced off the woman's shoulder, causing quite a bruise, and resulted in Rose being hauled to the police station and sobbing her way through a caution for her foray into protest through expressive art. Even now the sound of police sirens could make her feel guiltier than Harold Shipman.

The fur trade still seemed to Rose as horrible and cruel and exploitative as squashing sows into narrow pens where they could neither turn nor integrate with their young before slaughtering them for bacon. Even eating meat jarred with her love of four-legged fluffy things, but she did; striving to buy free range and looking for labels that promised 'happy pigs'. Although she wondered what that said about her. Would a cannibal only want to eat non-depressed people? 'This one had agorophobia and lived in a council flat? No, I'm not touching it. I only eat those who have regularly holidayed in Cornwall and worn Boden.'

And fur – how different is it to leather really? she would ask herself, and then remember all those late-night cider-fuelled student discussions, the parrying of words and argument as they passed around spliffs that were not filled with cannabis as they thought but, as it turned out, were bags of Schwartz's basil. They should have known, really, by the smell.

Charity shops wouldn't take fur these days but several of the original *I'd Rather go Naked than Wear Fur* supermodels had reversed their opinion. When Vintage Magic first opened there had been an endless parade of young girls coming through the door asking for fur on a regular basis. Rose hadn't turned them away with a lecture about ethical issues, just said her usual 'Not at the moment, but if you'd care to look around . . .'

But Rose had begun to feel that vintage furs were an expression of their time, in the same way that a CC41 label might tell of war-time rationing. Clothes as living social history, giving away clues about norms, attitudes and expectations of class. So, a little collection of furs had grown, which Rose kept hidden away lest she caused offence, but what Rose was coming around to seeing more and more, something that even the bizarre experience from the night before had strengthened, was that vintage clothes had a story to tell and some of that might not be pretty.

'Furs? Certainly, step this way.' Reluctantly, Rose unlocked an old whitewashed wardrobe framed in fairy lights, revealing the inner walls plastered in a sort of decoupage of images of old black-and-white movie stills. Movie stars known and obscure, famous for swimming – Esther Williams – or playing Tarzan – Johnnie Weissmuller. Her customer was unmoved by the artistic decoration. The woman snatched at this fur and that, throwing them into Rose's arms, expecting her to hold them, used to being served by an army of minions. She tried them on, pouting into the mirror, fluffing her fake hair, trying them with sunglasses, without sunglasses, posing this way, that way, with her handbag, without her handbag. Waiting expectantly, Rose believed, for praise. It didn't come.

The shop bell went and another customer came in who quickly needed a sale causing much harrumphing and shooting of daggers at the little student who was buying a brooch for her grandmother. Rose wished she could apologise out loud. When the bell went again, jangling loudly as the door opened, the scowling became an audible growl until it was silenced by some very crisp English vowels. The sort that made Mimi want to weep and sing 'God Save the Queen'. The sort that, to Mimi's eternal disappointment, her daughters had never quite mastered.

India Mannerley was one of those British actresses

of international acclaim who, despite appearing in every glossy and gossip magazine and being nominated annually for Oscars and Baftas, still managed to dress down and slop around the streets of her home-town in her actress uniform of large man's shirt, vest, woolly hat and Uggs unhindered.

Immediately, Rose saw the scowl of the Fur Bitch drop and become a jaw-dropping, veneer-gleaming display of warmth. Except for the eyes. It was like seeing a shark smile. Her customer flung the fur she was trying on unceremoniously over the wardrobe door.

'Hi.' She was all warmth, hand out ready to shake. 'I'm Tamara. Pleased to meet you.' She pumped away at the reciprocated hand before rubbing at the celebrity's outer shoulder in an over-familiar gesture that would be more suited to giving the bereaved condolences.

'Oh, are you the owner? I just wanted to have a look around.'

'Ehmmm . . . no, I'm the owner,' said Rose as she tried to peer around Tamara who was blocking her view. A goddess in the basement and a screen goddess in her shop. What next? Robert Pattinson, R-Patz himself, scrubbed, naked and waiting in her bed?

She wanted India to browse freely, to feel like any ordinary customer walking in off the street, which all her interviews and her persona suggested she appreciated but every step she took, Tamara was a step behind her. If she pulled an item off the rack, Tamara felt compelled to pass some toadying comment.

'Oh ya . . . beautiful. That is so you . . . I love vintage, yeah? I can't get enough of it.'

Rose had to do something.

'Hey . . . ehh . . . Tamara . . . would you like to try on this thirties silver fox cape? I think it would really go with your eyes.' Rose didn't add 'because it's grey and dead like yours', but she thought it and prayed that India Mannerley would not think that Rose and Tamara were somehow buddies.

Whilst Tamara posed with the cape around her shoulders, Rose explained how beautiful it would look with a floor-length bias-cut gown and when India nodded agreement, Tamara had her AmEx out faster than a paparazzi's camera, saying loudly: 'I hope it goes down well at the Bath Arts Fest Ball' as a purposeful event-dropper barometer to gauge whether the 'local' international celeb would also be attending.

What a connection that would be! A proper celebrity and not somebody who was once in The Wurzels! Not that Tamara had ever rated India Mannerley's performances. The off-beat scripts and roles were one thing that she struggled to understand but India's very famous, very flat chest was another. Why if you had all that money would you not fix it? Maybe she could drop her surgeon's name into the conversation later over the canapés. She could have a feel, too, if she liked. What Greg crudely called Tammy's half-melons were actually very realistic to touch.

'Yes, maybe, I'll see you there later.' India was

famously polite to all. 'I'll just pop into the changing room with these – oh look, there's a cat at the door' – and a celebrated animal lover – 'he wants to come in . . . oh he's huge but so sweet – there you are, come on in, you handsome thing . . .'

'Don't mind if I do!' It was Rich Clarke from Hands Solo Design following on Mooch's heels and he was almost flattened as Tamara made a hasty exit. Just for old times' sake, Rose had the urge to throw a sealed bottle of nail varnish at the back of her retreating head.

13

There is a goddess in my basement. It's the sort of line that's almost guaranteed to empty seats on the bus and to get people to move away faster than halitosis. So Rose simply shut it in a box in her brain to review later, didn't mention it to Lily or Mimi who had both turned up in the morning commenting on how tired she looked and tried to forget it had happened for the time being. Not that she entirely hoped it – or rather she, Minerva, Sulis, etc. etc. – would go away, but there was a certain unpredictability about what would happen next and Rose certainly didn't know what to do about the situation. But the thoughts kept climbing out of their box all day.

Like this morning when the acned delivery driver appeared with a box of imports from an American supplier. Rose hadn't even time to put her contact lenses in when she heard his familiar banging like a heavy-metal drum solo on the back door first thing. So, with specs on, a moth-eaten boyfriend cardigan and a pair of sagging yoga trousers (another exercise fad, but it had lasted longer than Armyrobics which had involved an ex-marine shouting at her to 'Keep jogging, you 'orrible, lazy slug!' around the park), she'd opened the back door without any expectations of attention of any kind.

'Hey there! Lovely morning, eh?' Rose had nodded, a little taken aback at his sudden foray into conversation but then almost dropped his electronic signature pad in surprise when he added 'Almost as lovely as you!' He was leaning up against the door jamb at this point, apparently trying to parrot a pose of sexy male soap-star photo spread in a Sunday supplement before taking off back to his van parked in the alley from where he gave her a big saucy wink. Rose flushed and found herself giggling girlishly before waving him off with waggly toodle-oo fingers.

'What was that about?' she asked herself moments later, staring at her early morning reflection. With really bad bed hair, zero make-up and four-eyes, if she was in a girl band right now she'd be nicknamed Really Fucking Scary Spice. Delivery Boy had flirted with her! Flirted with her at her worst! And, what was more, he'd acted like she was the most desirable woman on the planet! Was this glamour? Had she cast a spell on him? Was it in her aura now or something? Could this really be goddess magic at work?

And who could she tell about it? To tell would be to expose herself to ridicule, accusations of madness like the poor bookseller Mr Brown. And frankly, mad was exactly how she was feeling. Mad, stark raving, loony, frothing-at-the-mouth barmy.

So she had locked the cellar because she didn't want Matt stumbling down there and ending up as some love slave of Minerva's nymphets – although it might have cheered him up a bit and had probably figured as a sexual fantasy at some point in his life. And she tucked the key into her bra. A dramatic gesture that she had seen in an episode of *Murder, She Wrote*.

There were so many questions and not enough answers. Who was dabbling in Goddess Magic down there? Mimi? Lily? Matt had been the only one going down into the cellar. Could it be him? Why would it be him? She watched her sister and mother as they came into the shop but neither of them so much as glanced in the direction of the cellar, although Lily did say, 'Whatchu staring at?' in her inimitable, warm, sisterly fashion.

And if the goddess could read the thoughts, wishes and innermost dreams of her customers – if she knew all about her family – was there nothing Rose could hide? Just how omnipotent was she? On the other hand, maybe she could find out about what Lily really wanted after all? Find out what had really gone on with Lily and Matt. And then fix it.

The day seemed to pass more quickly than ever. It was a busier than usual Saturday, but each time Rose folded up the jewellery, the clothes or the hats into their tissue paper packaging she thought about the goddess's comment: 'It's a good job you don't know what happened to the others' and she found herself quizzing her poor customers about why they chose the piece, where they were going to wear it and were they hoping to have a good time.

'Rose, you're going to put people off with the twenty questions thing!' Lily warned. 'You are selling them vintage clothes, not re-homing an abandoned puppy!'

A Peggy Mountford dress going to a married woman who would be dining out with her husband didn't worry her, but when a mother said she was buying her daughter another of Peggy's va-va-voom dresses for her sixteenth birthday, Rose couldn't let go of the carrier bag. There was a tussle, a slight wrestle and the bag was ripped and the dress had to be rewrapped as a result.

'Tell her to be careful!' Rose had yelled as the mother left the shop quickly, casting nervous glances over her shoulder, and Mimi had drawled before she left: 'Would it make you feel better if you supplied free condoms with it?'

More than anything Rose wanted to curl up in front of the television in a Slanket and get some perspective on things, think it all through, but after an almost sleepless night and the busiest morning in her retail history, there was now a screen siren trying on item after item in the changing room, Rich Clarke fiddling around with her system (yet again! She'd gone and lost some much-needed stock information and no matter how she tried she just couldn't retrieve it. Anyone would think she was doing it on purpose!) and Carl arriving at any moment. Oh God! Carl! She had almost forgotten he was coming. How could she forget he was coming? She had been building up to this moment for months and here she was feeling deranged and looking drug-user pasty in her favourite but frumpy period-and-plump-days ensemble. This wasn't the way it was supposed to be, surely? Wasn't she meant to look screen-siren gorgeous? And that thing with Delivery Boy must have been a one-off, probably a piss-take, because Rich, staring so intently at the screen there, hadn't exactly gone beserk like a kitten on cat nip in her presence. So much for goddess magic!

Not that she wanted him to; she told herself that would ruin things. But to cap it all off, Rose was dying for a wee. A trifling inconvenience on the scale of things but she was beginning to do the little-girl-dancing-on-the-toes thing and did not want to cough, laugh or sneeze for fear of what might happen. There was nothing else for it; desperate bladders called for desperate measures.

'Rich, would you just look after things for a minute?' she whispered. 'I just need to pop upstairs.'

'I thought so,' he whispered back. 'Most people don't jog from foot to foot just from excitement about their new website going live.'

There was something nice about the intimacy of their heads close together and his joking about toilet functions.

'And don't let India Mannerley leave before I come back. Keep her talking or something.'

'OK,' he mouthed, giving her a conspiratorial wink then bellowing at the top of his lungs: 'Oi! Manly Mannerley! Don't go anywhere till Rose comes back from the loo! And just for the record, I've got a bigger chest than you have.'

Rose's mouth opened wider and wider in horror. 'What the hell?' she mimed, her hands windmilling all over the place.

'She's my cousin.' He shrugged, laughing. 'I told her about this place, told her she'd love it, and, judging by the clothes mountain building in there, I'd say I was right. But you're the posh end of the family, isn't that right, Manfred?' He yelled the family nickname back in the direction of the changing room.

A string of four-letter expletives was volleyed back at Rich; they were obviously very relaxed in each other's company.

Rose scampered off, sprinting up the stairs two at a time and leaping on to the loo for a pee that she thought would never stop. If she was quick she could scout through that box from the cellar – the baseball jackets, prom dresses and Jackie O suits she'd seen on first rifle. There might be a dress in there worth wearing, fluff up the bed-hair, slap on a bit of red lipstick – always guaranteed to turn attention away from tired eyes – and then, when Carl did arrive, she would at least look something like an approximation of what she'd hoped would blow his mind.

You know when it's the Right One, thought Rose, fiddling with a hook and eye fastening at her neck as she made her way down the stairs, not thinking about husbands-to-be but a good Vintage find.

'Wow,' India let out a low whistle, 'that's some dress.'

'Oh this?' This *is* the Right One, Rose grinned inwardly but was playing it down. 'Well, I've got a friend arriving today and I wanted to look nice. I had a bit of a late night, and—'

'Nice?' India laughed. 'You don't look *nice* – you look illegal. Look at my cousin's face!'

Rich, looking a little reddened, mumbled something about how it was a very nice dress indeed and turned his attention back to tapping away at the keyboard.

Rose caught sight of herself in the shop mirror then and was very pleased with what she saw. The linen-mix wiggle dress was an oatmeal colour that normally Rose would have worried would add pounds, but it was trimmed by a dark brown velvet shawl collar and thick hem that narrowed the silhouette and just emphasised her curves in the right places. Plus, as a bonus, it had sleeves ending at the elbow with a broad velvet cuff masking any concerns of upper-arm wobble. It had zipped up like a second skin evoking that delightful feeling that comes with a dress that feels as if it were made to measure. The warm autumn colours heightened the smooth whiteness of her skin and her eyes seemed bigger, wider and were well and truly channelling Sophia Loren with the hastily applied kohl and eyeliner flicks. Her fluffed hair made her look fresh from a roll in the sack.

Everything felt right. Everything looked right. The dress was sublime. There was no waistband digging in or fear of Visible Panty Line due to a lining as well made as its exterior. Seams ran the length of her body and ended in pointy darts at the tip of her bust; both supporting, slimming and accentuating the hourglass of her figure. Some invisible boning added a corsetry effect that made her stand tall but did not dig in or cause back bulge or fat wings at the rear. She wanted to wear dresses like this for ever. For the first time in a long time she felt gorgeous, sexy and feminine. If it were possible, she would say that the dress didn't just suit her it *was* her. The mix of linen and velvet was like the practical and the sensuous parts of her personality. The fit was figure-hugging but she was covered. There was no barmaidy cleavage hanging out. It was sexy but subtle, not Isabelle-slutty – something Rose could not do, could not be. And at first the dress seemed nice enough but, looking closer, exposed attention to detail, secret touches, wonderful crafting and expert seamstress skills. That was her entirely. Maybe not much on first impressions but the rewards of digging deeper for someone who loved her would reveal her thoughtfulness and her hidden talents.

She wanted to linger in front of the mirror and succumb to vanity. Instead she said, trying not to appear too smug, 'It's all right, isn't it? I'd not tried it on before but I think I'll keep it.' *And get it copied in every colour and fabric imaginable*, she made a mental note.

Was this Goddess Glamour? The way she filled every inch of the dress fluidly as though poured into it? How she sat on the bar stool at her shop counter, with her tummy in and bottom out instead of slumping and feeling like an old Buddha? The silky lining moved over her body in sensuous rhythm, making nerve endings tingle, mimicking arousal. Was this Minerva's doing? Had she placed the dress there for Rose to find? Had she worked magic on the fit and the form? Was this the dress that would change the order of things?

And was she imagining the eyes of her web designer roving over her more than necessary? The smile playing at the side of Rich's mouth as if she amused him? As if he was delighting in this new side of her? How he seemed to be beaming with pride and pleasure as she laughed and gossiped with his famous cousin?

It was over two hours later and quite dark outside when India Mannerley started to take her leave, aided by Rich, who was carrying the bulk of the many packages of hats, gloves, handbags and more. The time had passed as quickly and as easily as sitting around with Lily and Matt chatting about nothing, like deciding who they were most like in *Sex and the City* before deciding they had more in common with the cast of Leia's favourite CBeebies show *Balamory*.

They had chatted easily about Mooch, about India's

London, about India's new film and then Rich recommended that Rose give her a tour of her flat and though she resisted at first, she blushed as Rich led the tour, pointing out the paper-thin bowls of white china cast by Rose herself and the framed abstract artwork hung in groups on the white walls. He seemed to take a pride in these small achievements that Carl had always dismissed as 'Rose's pottery class pieces'.

One picture caught India's eye: 'It's so fresh, the colours are so vibrant so . . . like the embodiment of spring – it would look great in my New York rental – would you sell it?'

Rose shifted uncomfortably from foot to foot, prompting Rich to ask if she needed the toilet again and Rose had to confess: 'Actually, my niece painted that one.' And it was such a relief to hear an actress reportedly earning over three million pounds per movie roar with laughter at themselves, although she made Rose promise to ask if Leia would paint another.

'And every time I look at it, it will remind me to stop getting above myself and remember that I'm just a girl who made good from Bath!'

Then Rich had volunteered for a teacake-and-toast run to the ladies next door who had then delivered their bounty themselves, wanting to look at the home-grown international star that their spies had seen entering. They just so happened to have a camera on their person.

'We'll get this developed.'

'To put in our window.'

'You can be next to Timmy Mallett.'

They beamed and India laughed and said, 'I can rely on Bath for a "grounding"!'

Quite a few of the Peggy Mountford stage costumes had found a home.

'Perfect for when I'm in LA,' India explained, tossing the capital letters down as easily as if she was saying M&S. Then she chose two Biba pieces that a famous ex-groupie who now bred show dogs nearby had brought in.

'Those dresses have partied with the Stones,' Rose explained.

'So have I!' laughed India, 'isn't it mad?'

But as they packed away the pieces Rose had to say something. Her memories of last night drenching her happy mood like a pee-filled pop bottle thrown at a festival mosh-put. She couldn't expose this beautiful young woman to who-knows-what from the goddess-influenced clothes. She had no idea what India's wishes or dreams might be and Minerva's admission that things might get 'lost in translation' (a film, Rose had learned, India had auditioned for but had not got) was not reassuring. Even if she risked the goddess's wrath, something had to be said. But it was not easy finding the words.

'India, I called the shop Vintage Magic for a reason.' She struggled for what to say next. 'You see, I believe that where the clothes have a strong backstory I think that, well . . . this will make me sound mad . . . but I think sometimes the clothes weren't quite ready to be put into storage, if you understand what I mean . . . they wanted to go on. I mean some of the previous owners, like Peggy, for instance, were quite feisty ladies, strong-minded, unique individuals and sometimes the effect owning those clothes has on the wearer is stronger than you might imagine . . . I don't think I've made myself very clear—'

'I know exactly what you mean!' said India, her eyes shining. 'A couple of years ago I bought at auction – at great expense—'

'More than I pay all of my staff monthly, as I recall!' butted in Rich.

'OK, OK, but it was a piece of history! I bought an original Valentina suit as worn by Katherine Hepburn herself and when I wear it and I do, a lot, perhaps more than I should—' India broke off then, talking girl-talk with Rose about how she had combined the jacket with jeans and brogues and how she had worn the trousers to a red-carpet event with a very feminine blouse, until Rich intervened.

'Get to the point, woman!' Rich snapped and India punched him on the arm.

'Anyway, as I was saying' – and she glared at her cousin – 'when I wear them, I feel as though she's right with me, standing at my shoulder, whispering in my ear in those gravelly Connecticut vowels, giving me confidence, telling me to break a rule here and there. How can I describe it? I almost become her and I know

I'm an actress and it's my job to play pretend, but the whole thing is more subtle than acting. It's a morphing of myself with her—' and she broke off, shaking her head. 'There you go. That's a press scoop for you! India Mannerley is as barmy as a box of frogs!'

'No,' said Rose, her eyes almost welling with relief. The fact that someone might have even the slightest, remotest understanding of what was going on in Vintage Magic was overwhelming. 'It doesn't sound crazy at all. You and Peggy's clothes are going to get on just fine.' And Rose flung a spontaneous embrace around the tiny frame of India Mannerley.

'Listen – I can't leave yet until I've shown you how to access the stock records!' Rich started, dropping the packages and carrier bags. It seemed very obvious that he was stalling for time. He started to lean around Rose who was standing in front of her shop monitor and he was trying to click at the keyboard awkwardly with his remaining armful of packages and there was a jostling, a losing of balance on behalf of one or the other, so that they fell awkwardly hip to hip, chest to chest, face to face, Rose pinned slightly under Rich's weight against the counter. India sniggered and Rich and Rose went scarlet and all three jumped as Carl burst through the door dragging his case on wheels behind him and chuckling at the sight of what he thought was their surprise as Rich and Rose jumped apart like repelling magnets.

Rose was suddenly fuming about his bumbling

entrance which was not how she expected to feel at the first sight of the man she had loved – still loved, she reminded herself to phrase it in the present tense – so desperately after so many months apart.

'Carl, you scared us half to death!'

'Rose – wow – Rose, you look amazing, I mean really stunning – wow.' And he was forcing a kiss on to her and she was surprised to find herself offering both cheeks as if they were friends, not as if she had been waiting, praying for him to take her in his arms. 'Your faces – it was so funny – you were so shocked!'

Yes – we were, you bloody great ape, thought Rose, but she made introductions swiftly, watching his eyes boggle as she glossed over the Golden Globe, thrice-nominated-for-Oscars, Academy Award-winning actress, introducing her only as India.

'How are you?' India asked politely, offering her hand to shake.

'Not three bad,' Carl guffawed – using yet another of his irritating quips, planting kisses on the back of her hand and adding oodles of unnecessary eye contact.

Rose winced, trying to divert his attention. 'This is one of the website designers from Hands Solo Design whom I told you about.'

'Hi, I'm Rich.'

'So am I – mate! I'm a lawyer.' Carl snorted with the sort of arrogance only commonly heard at the suited long lunches of the Square Mile. It was enough to provoke anyone to yell: 'Class War!' and to man the barricades with petrol bombs.

Rich extended his hand in a display of good manners and Carl took it in one of those firm grips intended to unnerve the other in a display of alpha-maleness.

'Carl,' he introduced himself, then added superfluously: 'I used to live with Rosie.' A crass comment and crude display of territory like a dog cocking a leg to mark its scent. The use of 'Rosie' implying intimacy and ownership but all the time the tone, neutral and polite. Maybe he had seen their accidental collision after all.

'Oh yes! I know who you are.' Rich recalled an overheard conversation, cementing his dislike of this man, and reciprocated the handshake squeeze with additional force so that the two were locked in eye-to-eye greeting combat. Their faces were going a bit red, their civilised smiles turning into grimaces, and their knees buckling just a little as each squeezed the blood from the palm of the other.

'Tea, Carl? Cake? Sugar?' Rose's voice was as high as a nervous school-teacher at an Inner City comp and had become suddenly, ridiculously, Joyce Grenfell-posh, but it broke the deadlock and they both dropped their grips, rubbing at sweaty, reddened palms as they did so.

'Serpently! Don't mind if I do!' Carl laughed again directing his joke to India, whom he clearly thought would be impressed, and took the weakly warm cup. Rose cringed – why not just say 'certainly' like every other normal person? Should she tell him that it was not funny? Just downright irritating? Did he not notice that nobody else laughed?

Carl's arrival was the cue for Rich and India to leave, although a part of Rose had felt that India would have preferred to cry off the Artsfest ball that night and stay put, swopping stories at the counter of Vintage Magic, had it not been for the arrogant entrance of her ex-husband to be.

Moments later, when Rich returned to retrieve India's mobile phone left carelessly behind on the bar counter, he was to hear Carl braying:

'Woof! Woof! That India Mannerley is a bit of top tottie, isn't she?'

'I'll be sure to tell my cousin,' he said, and smiled, revelling in Carl's embarrassment. 'She'll be delighted to know how you feel.'

Then to Rose he said, 'See you around, Rose. Email or text if you have any more problems. I don't think I'll have to come in again, unless you need me to.'

See you around? Was that a goodbye? A line drawn to signify where the friendship had ended and the business relationship began? Almost an 'It's over' and she instantly wanted to look at her new website and email to get back that connection he seemed to be shutting off.

'So where're the other two witches of the coven, then?' asked Carl, taking in Vintage Magic for the first time and looking in semi-interest at the racks.

He couldn't imagine Isabelle in any of these old get-ups.

Rose ignored the derogatory comment that once she might have thought of as a term of endearment or affection. He had lost his right to talk about them in this way. 'They were here earlier. Lily will be getting Leia to bed and I expect Mimi is avoiding babysitting by taking off to some cheese-and-wine drawing-room event in one of the homes of the great and the good.'

She didn't add that both of them had said they wouldn't set foot in here whilst you are likely to be around. 'They'll probably pop by your hotel tomorrow to say hi if there's time.'

'You look great, Rose. I mean I don't think you've ever looked better. Have you changed your hair? I can't figure it out, but you look different . . . in a good way . . . better. All I can think of is *La Dolce Vita*. Really, I mean, gorgeous—' He checked himself, aware that his compliments were beginning to sound over the top and, though he wasn't quite sure when he should tell Rose, he was newly engaged to be married.

So, for the second time that day, Rose gave a tour of the business and living quarters of Vintage Magic, not once mentioning the cellar. She felt like she should be giving out audio-guides in seven different languages. Carl nodded and 'mmmed' and made little noises about 'great period features' and spent more time eyeing up Rose's bodily soft-furnishings than the ones she'd stitched together for windows and sofas. She was mesmerising in that dress; it clung to her shape and curved under her full bottom, which seemed to be crying out, 'Bite me, I'm a peach!', and the way it lifted her bosom up and outwards in a gravity-defying display, he wanted to push his face right into the centre of them and suffocate. What a way to go!

But it wasn't just the dress, although it gave a certain something to her walk even when she was padding around the flat in bare feet. Was it confidence? Rose had always been in someone's shadow – her sister or his own or Isabelle's. Isabelle was much more of a match for him, especially with that fiery temper that seemed to come out more and more. Whatever it was that was new about Rose, it was damn sexy and he'd never really got her out of his system. Tonight she was witty and sparkling, and he realised how much he'd missed her company and how good it felt to make her laugh. He wouldn't mention Isabelle unless she did. Best leave talk about the engagement until tomorrow. Isabelle had given him the ultimatum – 'Tell Rose or we're finished'. She could be really hard at times. That's why he'd come to break the news in person. Part of being fair, being friends. Doing things the right way, the respectful way.

Should he have done it by email or over the phone? Because, looking at her now, eagerly scooping dip into her mouth with a Kettle chip (the type of snacks no longer allowed in the house by exercise-obsessed Isabelle) and laughing as she wiped a drip from her chin, he didn't want to break her heart all over again.

Had he made the right choice? He must have wanted to see her or he wouldn't have come at all.

Now they were choosing where to go, where to eat, wondering whether to open a bottle of wine. He didn't want to do Chinese, though Rose could eat it until the cows came home. There was a comedy show or dancing, a nightclub with entertainment and a bit of a burlesque theme. He leaned over Rose's shoulder as they surfed the web, looking at the options, wondering about taking in a film, breathing in her scent, feeling, as her hair brushed his cheek, as though an electric shock had passed through him.

'Shall I just leave my case here and pick it up after we've eaten? I can check in any time.' And she had nodded assent and, all the while, he calculated that he might not have to check into a hotel at all. There was still that spark between them. He could feel it. Just once more, perhaps? If that's what Rose wanted. As friends only, of course. Nothing more. They would be clear about it from the offset. That wouldn't be wrong would it?

So he had asked to shower in Vintage Magic before they went out, though he could think of another word for the 'quirky' water system and, when he came into the bedroom and Rose was sitting at her dressing table, surrounded by her bottles and potions, putting on her lipstick, he had said, 'It's just like old times, isn't it?' and held her gaze in the mirror as a romantic hero in a film might do and hoped that she could read his expression which said: 'I miss you, I want you, this love triangle is all so desperately confusing.' And he let his towel drop just a little from his waist. Not enough to be like the main man in *The Loin King*, one of the films he and Isabelle watched to enhance their lovemaking, but just enough, maybe, to jog Rose's memory a little. Remind her of what she must be missing, because there couldn't possibly be anything going on with that nerdy bloke who'd been here earlier and she'd always been fairly game in bed.

He didn't check in. They didn't eat out. But they worked up an appetite. It was a good job that Rose knew by heart the numbers of all the Chinese takeaways that would deliver.

14

'We shouldn't have done it. It was a mistake.'

Heavy words for such a beautiful morning. Rose needed to take the full meaning of the words in. She moved to the window, looking out into the square where the trees were budding into life and would soon be laden with blossom. She felt heavy with sorrow as those words were spoken. All those months of planning towards this event and this was how it ended? It really was over. The birdcage outside squeaked out its little rusty song and, despite Carl's complaints about it last night, that he would never sleep, she realised that she liked it, was even comforted by it, especially now. Cynthia was crossing the Square to her shop and they waved a greeting to each other. They would both be opening this Sunday as warmer weather brought out the shoppers.

Rose had never thought it would be her who would say those words to Carl, but it was.

The goddess had not let her down. Whatever subliminal instruction Minerva had given to her about feminine wiles and courtesan arts had worked like a charm. In fact, it had been ridiculously easy and she found herself swept along with the tide of her seduction when all the time a voice in her head – not from her walls – had told her that she didn't want this, didn't want him. Visions had flashed into her head of Carl bloated and pompous at forty-five, quaffing wine and dallying with his secretary and now – now she felt a kind of revulsion creeping over her. A sickening, that she had lowered herself to playing the games that he had.

But Carl had been awake since the dawn, baring his soul like he was in confession, admitting all his wrongs, begging for forgiveness, whispering words of love and promised faithfulness that he could never keep. And Rose listened, out of habit, interest, morbid fascination, she wasn't sure which – agog at his arrogance and stunned at his lack of sensitivity.

'You've got it all sorted and I've screwed it all up. You look great, the flat looks great – except for those creepy big-eye pictures, of course. You've got your own business, state-of-the-art on-line shop, film star clients.

'You know, I'm the victim in this, don't you? And it's not just the money, the moving house – there was a big emotional cost for me too. It's Isabelle, she's a manipulator. She's done all this. She's created all this havoc in our lives and I never wanted to hurt you – you know that, don't you? I think Isabelle orchestrated it all along, that you would find us like that in bed together. She must have known you would come home.

'Isabelle wanted me to tell you that we were engaged but I need you to know it was not my doing. *She* asked *me*. In fact, there was no ask about it. She told me. I can't believe how I've been made into a trained monkey by that woman. You've no idea how controlling she can be and the hang-ups? CDs in alphabetical order – I get that – but the food tins in the cupboard, the jars in the fridge? The products in the bathroom cabinet? I don't know whether she wants the Tampax put under T or filed under S for sanitary wear!

'And her cleanliness obsession – always dusting, bleaching, knocking on the bathroom door when I'm "dropping the kids off at the pool" in the morning and reminding me to use wet wipes first, dry wipes second.

'But now – now she's said can't I wait until I get to work to do it? Can't I even take a dump in my own home?

'Frankly, if the sex wasn't so good I doubt if I'd be there at all, but she overplays the whole being-like-a-porn-star-thing. I mean, it was great at first, but the page three poses in the bedroom all the time – it all feels a bit fake and she's not exactly airbrushed up close, if you know what I mean. But here with you now, I like that you're natural, you don't mind that your stomach sticks out a bit and that you look a bit rough in the morning with your glasses on before the old contact lenses go in; whereas she gets up before me and puts on her make-up. Frosted lipstick at six in the morning!

'But that shag last night – Rose, you were amazing.

I was putty in your hands – well, putty that had gone rock hard! GRRRR! I feel things are definitely coming up Rose's – wink! wink! It was right up there with that Thai girl I met on my gap year, you know, the one I told you about. The one who was very pretty but for her square jaw and big rough hands. I haven't told Isabelle about that – she gets very jealous, even about my past. She doesn't trust me at all. I don't know why.

'She wouldn't have let me come here on my own except I promised her that I would tell you how things are, with the wedding and everything, and that would be that. You might have gone a bit Bridezilla on me, but you should see Isabelle in wedding mode. She's Bride Kong, Bridenstein and Count Bride-ula in one. It's as if she's worried I'll change my mind and wants to snare me before the potion wears off. And my mum and dad aren't happy about it at all because Mother always said I shouldn't marry the glamorous type because they are too flighty and self-centred and I think she's right.

'You're the sort of girl Mother wanted me to marry. Dependable, homely. I knew it then and I know it now, and we can get our old place back and you can sell on this little clothes shop here and we'll find premises in London and you can invite that India Mannerley and her show-biz friends along. Or you could just do the whole thing on-line—'

And that's the point at which Rose spoke and she did not hold back. She told him that to hear that all was no longer peachy for him and Isabelle on the home front felt like divine intervention, justice being served, a bit of John Lennon's Instant Karma. She'd kept her counsel as he spoke with such staggering self-centredness and once would have taken his criticisms to heart, waking in the night to worry about being 'homely' or 'a bit rough in the morning', but Carl sitting there, running his hands through his Richard Madeley hair, and with the first signs of moobs – how dare he – how dare he judge her – and Isabelle, come to that, like they were in some sort of livestock contest.

No, there would be no selling of Vintage Magic. No return to London. She was extremely proud of this business that she had developed and the impact that it had on people's lives. Clothes are not just fripperies, she explained to Carl, and then realised he would never have the insight to see it. They are armour, crutches, disguise – yes, bait, even. They shape us, nurture our hopes, feed our psyche. They are as vital to our sense of well-being as good food and a warm bed. They define us.

And Vintage Magic is not just a shop, she added. It's a meeting place for like-minded women. A 'field of dreams' more important than any football stadium. It's a place of worship for the expression of our female selves. It is a place where broken hearts can start to mend and a new life can be forged from the ashes of an old one.

'All because of a dress?' he sneered.

'Yes, all because of a dress. Thank the goddess within

us for that,' she added, wondering silently what the goddess in her basement would really like as a gift of thanks – a book of Carol Ann Duffy poetry? A vintage brooch, perhaps? An original Rose Taylor ceramic?

As if he could read her thoughts, Carl looked at her as if she were quite mad and asked her: 'Have you become a feminist or something?'

And Rose shook her head in pity at all the different levels of his ignorance. She hadn't finished. There were more truths to be told. If he had observed Isabelle properly, Rose lectured, really properly, beyond watching her bend over in a skirt too short and heels too high at any point prior to bedding her and moving in with her, then he would have seen that she was a mess of neuroses, strange eating disorders that had not yet made *Psychiatry Today* and obsessions with hoovering the computer keyboard, but he should love her anyway and give her the support to get past all that.

And as for last night – Rose was sorry if she had misled him, made him think it was more than it was – but it was just about sex. Nothing else.

It was a need she had been denying but with him it was easy, because it was safe, if not a little samey. 'No, Carl – you might think it's about knowing how to play a familiar tune on an old piano – which is not a flattering analogy – but it's actually . . . boring.' There, she'd said it. 'And another thing – all those things you've just said about Isabelle's performance, have you considered for one moment that she's trying everything, everything she can, to get you to respond to her as though she's a real woman and not one from *Men Only*?'

And she hadn't put that dress on on purpose – well, she had, and she was sorry that she had seduced him – those were his words! – sorry that she had misled him about her intentions – all right, Carl, you were powerless; I used you.

She looked at the dress discarded now on a heap of other unwashed clothes on an old paint-peeling ottoman. She'd waited months for last night, slimmed and gymed, planned and waited for him to come here and come round to see what he'd lost. She'd scoured the net for months searching for something that was just-so and it had just turned up all of its own accord in a box of random oddments sent from another continent. There was a seam fraying slightly, what looked like a cigarette burn, she noticed now, in the fabric of the hem, and a hook had divorced itself from its eye as she had hurriedly undressed last night. Last night it had seemed perfect – just like the idea of getting back with Carl – but now in the cool blue light of the morning she saw it was imperfect, torn and in need of repair – how like our lives, thought Rose, how like ourselves.

A dress that Rose would never know had been made for a mistress somewhere around 1962. A woman who finally decided she no longer wanted someone else's husband but one of her own. Who had walked away from wealth and a paid-for apartment to shack up with a sun-bleached tousle-haired surfer on the west coast.

Who saw out the sixties with flowers in her hair and their children playing in the sand at her feet.

And Rose had finished her speech with: 'We shouldn't have done it. It was a mistake.' She watched the city pigeons take flight and swoop in a big circle before settling back to their window ledges and the breadcrumbs being scattered by the ladies of Ye Olde Coffee House and she was filled with a lightness of being as though she were floating on the most warm, buoyant, caressing ocean, coloured with all the sky shades of a rising sun and dotted with brilliant jewels.

'I had to come back before I went. I'm leaving for London in an hour but there were a couple of other Peggy outfits that I couldn't get out of my mind and I wanted to make sure nobody else got them.' India Mannerley had been banging on the door before Rose had had a chance to open up.

'I'm going to show them to my wardrobe assistant in this movie I'm doing now. They'll be perfect for the role of the rich, bored, Vegas – in the Rat Pack years – housewife I'm playing. How excited would Peggy be to know that she was going to Hollywood? Plus I want to take some flyers for my friends.'

India was already pulling costumes off the racks and piling them on the counter before rifling through a box of evening gloves and pulling them on to her slim fingers.

'How was the ball?' Rose wondered if it had been as dull as India feared.

'Oh my God! Oh my God! I can't believe I nearly didn't tell you!' India, no longer preoccupied, was jumping up and down on the spot and waving her arms around. 'The woman in the silver fox cape – what was her name? That friend of yours? Tamsin?'

'Tamara – not a friend, just a first-time customer.'

'I've got to tell you – it's the oddest thing! The ball itself was nothing out of the ordinary. Food very same-old, same-old and the usual troupe of dignitaries you see in Bath's society pages, and I presented the main prize, but skip all that. Let me get on to the good bit.

'To her credit, Tamara – is that her name? – did look very beautiful in a Desperate Stepford Real Housewives of Atlanta kind of way. The cape looked fab but the dress was a bit of a polyester fire hazard, if you know what I mean. Although I think she must have left here to go and have one of those Botox facials that does an extra temporary freeze because there was no way the woman could emote. I did say, "Hi, remember me?" And I honestly couldn't tell if she was pleased to see me or livid that I was wearing the mocha twenties silk crepe that I picked up here that she seemed to have her eye on –

'Anyway, I saw her later; she was causing quite a stir because she stood at the buffet scoffing – I mean stuffing it down – and that's a woman who looks like she only chews then spits out! There was food falling from her mouth, down her cleavage, all over the fur as if she'd been starving, and this was the first food to touch her lips. Her husband was trying to move her away and she seemed to savage him verbally but I was too far away to hear what was said. And then she started, grabbing it from people's plates as if she were worried someone else would eat all the food first.

'She was snarling and spitting and the food was flying from her teeth and she put out her hand when her husband tried to chivvy her along and scratched him all down his face, drawing blood. Well, by then security were asking them to leave and she yowled, screamed like a banshee, as they tried to get her away from the buffet and her husband was saying she was tired and stressed and that maybe she'd had a bad reaction to some medication. Then it all happened so quickly – she broke free from the security guards and lunged for this woman who was wearing another fur stole and you've heard the expression that the "fur was flying"? Well, it was – quite literally. She was tearing and biting chunks out of this woman's clothes and I couldn't help laughing out loud because all I could think of was Rod Hull and Emu – remember that comedian with the glove puppet? It took four security guards to carry her out and they say that before she left, she squatted down in the foyer and peed a little. I overheard a security guard say it had a kick to it that could make your eyes water!'

Rose was gasping along with India but inside she was squirming, worrying about silver fox fur capes that seemingly come back to life when, completely from nowhere, India said, He's a good guy, my cousin.' The comment could have been lost, not heard, it was so casually, softly spoken, almost as an aside, but for India's pitch-perfect accent which would be enough to make Mimi worry that her eggs had been stolen to spawn a super race of English actresses.

'Yes, he really knows his stuff and the site he's designed is like a work of art—'

'And he's a good guy,' she repeated. Then she added, 'It's a pity that he's single. I've never understood why he's not been snapped up.' The message was loud and clear as was, now, the reason for her visit, when a text, email or visit to the website could have easily sealed the deal.

The silence that followed was, to say the least, stilted, but there was a step-thump-bump crashing that made Rose start, as if a man with a wooden leg pushing a handcart was trying to come down the stairs, but it was just Carl dragging his case behind him.

He threw the cellar key dismissively on to the shop counter between Rose and India with a hang-dog look and his tail firmly clamped between his legs.

'Here – I found that in your bra last night,' he grumped, before slamming off through the shop door. Rose tried not to meet India's gaze. Carl's timing was really, badly, off. And not, it seemed, only in the bedroom.

15

Leia was crying. Crying as though her heart was breaking. Her shoulders shaking at the tragedy of it all. Little diamond droplet tears were rolling down her cheeks and plopping to the floor.

'Foxy gone! Foxy gone!' was all she could say to explain the dreadful calamity that had caused such distress.

Coming through the shop door behind her daughter, Lily rolled her eyes.

'They moved the road-kill from outside the flat. Leia loved it. She liked to poke it with a stick on the way to and from nursery and now some over-zealous council cleaner has gone and shovelled it up. And nothing will console her. No toys. No sweeties. Nothing.'

Rose darted off, opening up the cellar, where she made silent promises to the goddess that she would be back, back with a non-generic, totally unique offering, if only she could think what, and emerged with a fox stole, minus an eye, suffering from alopecia and, gruesomely, with only one of its two front legs attached.

Leia was in love. She embraced the long-dead pelt, cooing and stroking and wiffling away as she arranged it on the floor in a remembered replica of the corpse fox's prone position. She found a pencil. She started to poke it. She was happy.

'I'll keep it here for her to play with – it's too tatty to sell. Just don't let her wear it, OK?' The hairs rose on her arms at the thought of what might happen.

'Don't worry, I won't!' asserted Lily, wrinkling her nose in revulsion.

The door crashed open and a streak of spray-tan in leggings and layered jersey draping made a beeline for Rose.

'Isabelle!' Rose gasped.

'Don't you Isabelle me!' came the nonsensical response.

Rose was confused. 'But that's your name . . . ?'

'Don't get smart!' An orange palm was raised upwards in a talk-to-the-hand pose. Isabelle hadn't followed the cardinal rule of washing her hands well after application. 'Where is he? Where's my fiancé?'

'He's just left for the station.'

'So he stayed the night, then? I knew it!' Isabelle's favourite soap was *Eastenders* and it showed. She was in character, channelling for an Albert Square Roxy-vs-Ronnie-style showdown. 'He's been ignoring my texts and my calls and the Premier Inn had never heard of him. I've driven like the clappers to get here to catch him at it. You're nothing but a man-stealing slut.'

The atmosphere of Vintage Magic suddenly switched to Dodge City. It was a Mexican stand-off and Rose could have supplied the ponchos. Two customers made a hasty exit, the bell on the door swinging an alarm. Two others took shelter behind a clothes rail, pretending to be absorbed in choosing eighties batwing sweaters but their eyes were firmly fixed on the scene in front of it. Lily ushered Leia to the laundry room along with fox skin and pencil, shedding fur as they made a retreat that became a kind of metaphorical tumbleweed as it rolled across the space between Rose and Isabelle.

'Isabelle.' Rose spoke slowly, narrowing her eyes, moving (in the absence of a cigar) the Murray Mint given to her earlier by Mrs Waters from one side of her mouth to the other. She could almost hear the flute and ocarina coyote call theme music of a spaghetti western. She drew herself up to her full not-very-tall height. Her fingers twitched like they were flexing for a quick draw but she was actually fighting the desire to stick a finger in each of Isabelle's nostrils and pull. Instead, she took a deep yoga breath. 'I think that's a bit rich, coming from you. I was going to marry him first, remember.'

'Yeah, well,' Isabelle snarled, curling her lip, 'I'm marrying him now, so you'd better get over it and move on.' Her finger was wagging and waving in Rose's face. 'It's been months already. Get a life, Rose. He's not coming back, whatever you do. It's over. O-V-E-R. *Capiche?*'

Wrong movie, thought Rose, frowning. That's *The*

Godfather, not *The Good*, (me) *The Bad* (Isabelle) *and The Ugly* (Carl), but she agreed.

'It *is* over, Isabelle.' Lily's face, just out of sight, became a picture of joy: 'Yes!' she mouthed, punching the air in triumph. 'I won't be coming back to London,' Rose continued, her voice soft and low. 'I won't be emailing, texting, calling – whatever. I've no interest *whatsoever* in Carl, trust me – he's all yours, if you want him. But the biggest betrayal for me was you. My friend. Or so I thought you were.' There was no anger but Rose's voice cracked a little and her eyes filled. 'I consoled you when your love affair went wrong, invited you into my home, listened to all your problems, and you responded by jumping into my bed with my husband-to-be? How could you do it? How could you do it to me?'

Isabelle's mouth, previously set into a hard-face-bottom-jaw-jutting-out invitation to a fight, softened a little and her lips, coated in extra-booster collagen volumising serum and boosting balm enhancer for a longer-lasting shine, wobbled just a little. Her eyes dropped from their Paddington stare and she mumbled something almost like an apology.

Rose continued, 'It's up to him to tell you about last night, but if you are going to cause a scene, please leave my shop. We can talk about this somewhere, any-where else, if you want, or another time, if you'd rather, but if you go now you may just catch him at the station.'

Rose's cool, calm, detached tones had an instant deflating effect on Isabelle's born-within-the-sound-of-

Bow-Bells wrath. Plus, she wanted Carl in her sights more than she wanted to argue with Rose, and what more was there to say anyway?

Isabelle continued to scowl, just a little, but Rose realised it was not ill-feeling, just the natural resting place for her face. Then Isabelle turned on her heel (platform, purple suede, metal-spiked tips – very OTT for a Sunday morning) and stalked off, pausing at the door to say, quite genuinely, as if they were still the buddies they once were: 'Nice shop, Rose, and, you know, you look good. Have you spruced yourself up a bit?'

'Yeah. Thanks.' Rose nodded then the door banged shut as Isabelle left, followed shortly by the two customers, *sans* batwings, who were clearly very disappointed that it had not turned into a hair-pullin', eye-gougin', heel-kickin', bitch-slappin' fight.

'Is that it?' Lily emerged from the back of the shop. 'No hairspray sprayed in the face? Not even a "Don't go there, girlfriend!"?' And she mimicked a Jerry Springer/Sally Jesse Raphael/Geraldo Rivera finger-waving talk-show guest.

'Oh yeah, there was lots of that.' And Rose waggled her finger and wobbled her head. 'But I guess that's it.' And Rose looked perplexed and shell-shocked, marvelling to Lily at how easy it had been to rid herself of the huge baggage of hurt she had carried around with her for a year.

'No, you dated him for three!' quipped her sister.

All the pain, the lack of self-worth, the emptiness and

the If Onlys . . . gone. Evaporating into the air like soap bubbles blown through a penny-sized hoop. It hadn't required some cataclysmic event, some revelation earned whilst canoeing the Amazon or some seismic shift in thinking from mind-body healing mediations. Just somewhere, somehow, the scales had fallen from her eyes. Maybe time is a healer. Maybe things really do happen for a reason. Maybe wearing the right dress can really change your life. Maybe goddesses have the power to know what's best for you after all.

Rose and Lily were hugging as Matt arrived. He joined in, putting his arms around them both.

'Yay! Yeah! Whoo!' he cheered enthusiastically, the awkward moodiness between him and Lily temporarily forgotten. He was jumping up and down along with them on the spot and doing the hugging hard to one side and then the next and, in the same high-pitched voice of celebration, he asked, 'Why are we doing this?'

'Rose is over Carl, even though she slept with him last night, I think, and Isabelle came here for a fight but Rose just kind of used her Jedi powers to deflect her anger and she's just gone chasing Carl to the station. Isabelle, not Rose, of course, and oh, Leia was really upset about the dead fox being moved but Rose found her an old fur wrap thing out the back and now she's playing with it, but it's so mangy, don't let her put it on.' Matt's head bounced along with each newsflash delivered by Lily but before he had time to comment, the back door opened.

It was Mrs Bridges and Mrs Waters.

They did not look happy. There was none of the usual beaming smiles, plate of biscuits and 'Do you want to finish off these macaroons?'

Mrs Bridges spoke first. 'Is this your idea of a joke, Rose?'

Followed by Mrs Waters.

'Only we're not very happy about it.'

'We may be old –'

'But we haven't lost our sense of humour and—'

'We've tried to see the funny side, but—'

'It's very demeaning.'

'Very disrespectful of our visitors in the dairy.'

Rose cut in. 'What is? What's happened? Who's been in the dairy?'

'You'd better come and see.'

Rose was about to resist but, after seeing off Isabelle, seeing a corpse couldn't be so hard, could it?

She left Matt and Lily to watch the shop and followed the two ladies out into the shared yard, steeling herself with a deep breath as she followed the ladies down the stone steps into the cold gloom of the temporary resting place for the deceased.

'It's the time of year,' said Mrs Waters.

'The flu,' elaborated Mrs Bridges. 'The Old Man's Friend, as they say.' She didn't say who exactly.

'It carries them off.'

'That and the NHS –'

'There are some wards that if they admit you—'

'You know that you're never coming back.'

'So there's a backlog –'

'Which is why we have two guests at the moment.' And they snapped on the lights.

Rose had expected to see cold stone mortuary slabs and bare feet sticking from white shrouds with brown tickets attached to toes but the dairy was – although not somewhere she would choose to go from choice – quite welcoming. Peaceful. Relaxing, even. Its whitewashed walls were softened by curtains in neutral colour prints of abstract leaves that hung at the entrances of inner rooms that created private spaces for the deceased. The natural stone of the walls had been exposed here and there and the original slate floor, polished and sealed, was covered in jute matting that gave off the subtle earthy scent of mown hay.

There were stripped pine seats and wicker baskets of sticks and dried fruit on wire. There was hand-wrought black ironwork holding up large fresh-flower arrangements, beeswax candles and peace lilies. Soft lighting warmed the interior, old beams had been stripped and waxed to a warm honey colour, Egyptian cotton sheets topped the resting places of the visitors.

The whole look was modern-rustic spa. All it needed was pan-pipes playing from the speakers recessed into the wall and Rose would have lain down on a gurney and asked for a facial.

'Well, you didn't think it would still look like a dairy, did you?' said one of the ladies when they saw Rose's face.

'We told you that we like to look after our guests!' said the other.

It was a beautiful, dignified, tranquil place to be, somewhat spoiled by the fact that one of the elderly deceased in an open casket was wearing a 1940s fascinator of wax cherries, ruby-red glitter *Wizard of Oz* sixties ballroom dancing shoes and a floaty pink chiffon evening dress worthy of Barbara Cartland. It didn't really suit him.

Mrs Bridges swept back another curtain to reveal his lady companion arranged in a sort of 'I'm a Little Teapot' stance on her berth, wearing a wide-collared, bri-nylon canary-yellow shirt and huge chequered flares. The look was accessorised with a huge pair of seventies round spectacles and suede tasselled bag. It was a Dead-go-Pimp look.

Where the first corpse had sunken cheeks and a puckered mouth as though disapproving of the whole caper, this one had a big, wide, toothy smile which was almost a grimace.

'I think somebody's swapped their false teeth around.' Mrs Waters shook her head sadly and Mrs Bridges tut-tutted.

'I can assure you,' began Rose, 'I would never . . . I couldn't, I wouldn't . . . I don't know how this has happened –'

Suddenly from across their shared yard they could hear shouting, screams, swearing and the sounds of a very definite struggle. Without a word passing between them, the three took flight up the dairy stairs, following the sounds of banging and smashing. Practised in the art of shop defence, Mrs Bridges and Mrs Waters took up arms instinctively. A broom was swept up by Mrs Bridges and a clothes prop hooked by Mrs Waters as they tore into the back of Vintage Magic.

Lily was leaning sobbing over Matt, who was sort of slumped on the floor. Blood was pouring from a gash above his eye and Lily gestured weakly to the side where Rose's computerised till and screen were smashed to smithereens. The open till that had more than a week's takings which Rose, lazily, hadn't bothered to sort out, was empty but for loose change.

The shop bell rang and Mimi stepped in from the square, fresh and fragrant from church that was less about worship and more like a morning meeting of the Conservative Club.

'A very rude man just barged—' she began, smoothing down her Jacques Vert suit and then her Disgusted from Somerset expression morphed – despite the injectables, fillers and muscle relaxants – into a look of horror.

She saw Matt bleeding, Lily crying, the two ladies from next door trying to help, dabbing at Matt's wound with one monogrammed embroidered handkerchief and mopping Lily's tears with another, and Rose staring at the smashed remains of her expensive system. The loss of the money did not really register or matter to Rose, but the violence of the attack on Vintage Magic and

Matt was represented appallingly in the tangle of wires, plastic shards, and broken circuits.

Mimi's eyes scanned the shop again. And then again, and when she spoke, she was already moving with purpose, with primary aim, motivated with concern, but her voice was loud, strong and more than a little desperate to get all of their attention.

She took off her gloves. She was a leader of the Empire now. She was one of the privileged few raised with the principle of the greater good, service to one's country, and to not mind getting hands dirty if it was for this Green and Pleasant land. She had a voice that could command armies to small islands off the coasts of Argentina. She was an angry headmistress with a band of sorry smokers, heads hanging in shame, lined up against the wall outside her office. She was a matron with a ward of wounded to nurse back to health with routine and regime and strict adherence to visiting times. And she raised her voice louder, repeating herself because they were all in such shock and not thinking clearly and somebody had to take control of the situation.

She knew how to make her voice heard. She knew how to publicly speak. She knew how to enunciate every vowel so that it was clear and singular and distinct. And she said it again, for the third time, because they were all looking at her – irritatingly – with blank faces and dead eyes.

'Answer me, will you?' she ordered, only this time,

her stomach lurched and she was already running, not really sure where, and her words were wild, strangled and thick with elemental fear.

'Where's Leia?'

16

Children get lost all the time. They wander off in supermarkets. They run to see a fifty-pence-a-go mechanical elephant ride and the crowd goes one way and their mother, the other. They hide under shop displays and don't emerge even when their frantic parents' voices become louder, high pitched and tremble on the edge of hysteria.

All it takes is the split second to address a shop assistant or to turn to look into a bag for a purse or ragged tissue to wipe an unsightly nose, and they are gone.

The heart-stopping fear. Like an ice-cold hand has been plunged into the chest and has wrapped around the most vital of organs. There is no room for logic — they can't be far, they must be here somewhere, the street is clear, they can't have vanished into thin air.

Instead, thoughts are replaced with images of bogeymen, grainy CCTV footage of three boys walking seemingly innocently hand-in-hand in a Merseyside shopping centre or unmarked white transit vans.

In a split second, the mind is filled with headlines of the past. The Hindleys and Bradys. The Huntleys, the Blacks. Cold faces lock eyes from press-released police photographs and are a stark reminder of how quickly hell can unfold right here on earth.

All the clichés apply. My Worst Nightmare. I Have Never Been So Terrified. You Never Think it Will Happen to You. Then it's over. A cry or a giggle, a small hand reaching for comfort. Or a face appears – a kindly stranger is asking, 'Have you lost a little girl/a little boy?' And then the relief. A tidal wave arching and then crashing down, washing the adrenalin through blood vessels already swamped, becoming an irrational anger and the telling-off follows. Thirty or forty years earlier, a smack to the leg would have been a reminder never to wander out of sight. Now (and then) ridiculous threats are made. 'I'll ground you for life if you ever disappear again.' Then it's forgotten.

But what if it is not immediately over? If desperate adults are racing up and down stairs calling ever more frantically? Opening cupboards, looking under beds? Running almost blindly without organisation in circles and irregular zig-zags? If their calling in the street brings female shoppers to start their own search and workmen – fathers themselves – hurrying from their roadworks and traffic cones, feeling sick as they check down open manhole covers and exposed drains. But for the parents, the aunties, the doting neighbours, all the time the Fear. Lodged like the splinter of the Snow

Queen's mirror in Kai's heart, spreading its cold infection from the core.

And then there are promises and plea bargains made to gods who don't get spoken to very often. Attempts are made to broker deals, to beg forgiveness for unknown or forgotten sins, to ask Why? What have we done wrong?

But there is no answer from the heavens, only sirens moving closer. Was there a man? Yes, but he left with only money in his arms, nearly knocking Mimi to the floor in the process. Was there an accomplice? Too chilling, too horrific to think about for too long but no, how could there be? The back entrance had been locked until Rose went to the dairy and then Mrs Bridges had remained in the doorway – *nobody* could have got past without being seen. And then a tatty fox stole is found, dropped or discarded, lying prone on carelessly left-unlocked cellar stairs, and Rose stares down into the dark void, the weight of responsibility clamping around her like an iron maiden and she knows, she knows where little Leia has gone and who has taken her.

But the search is given over to The Law with their dogs and their heat-seeking equipment and their scanning and road cameras and their knowledge of every movement of the local nonces and then endless questions – How long? Who was there? Where was she? This man who smashed up the till – did you know him? And the creeping realisation that everyone – the ones with tear-streaked faces, the mother with the heart breaking, weeping, ageing in front of their eyes, held up by her ex-partner whose own eyes are staring, unseeing, who wants to be the man, to be as strong and wise as the father of the Waltons, but is crumbling, disintegrating – no one is above suspicion.

Not even Rose, with blood rushing through her ears and skin prickling with the surges of adrenalin. Rose, who is struck almost mute, mumbling her way through questions. Who can she tell? How can she tell? What can she do?

But Rose is not the only one with knowledge of Leia's whereabouts. There is someone else, very nearby with a full understanding of goddess magic. Someone better placed to make the authorities understand that this is not an act of human evil but celestial fun and games.

Questions are followed by noisy, uniformed visits to the dairy, no resting in peace to be had there and no comment is made about the deceaseds' attire and inquiries are extended and the ladies are opening locked doors to Ye Olde Coffee House and fists are banging on the door of Birdcage Antiques sending vibrations up through walls and rattling its namesake which is now swinging on its hinges.

Cynthia is slow to get to the door, making her way from one of the far reaches of her cluttered shop, and time spent undoing all the chains and bolts and the turning of keys passes with irritating slowness and she sees the uniforms and the anxious faces and she is already mouthing something at them through the glass that they can't quite make out. But when the door is open and they hear her, what she says throws the young rookies, who never thought they would hear it said in their lifetime, thought it was a myth or even an in-police joke. But the older ones spring into action, leap for the radio to get the wheels in motion because they know that every second counts; now, more than ever, and they think of the parents and wonder what is worse – this or some other, more earthy scenario of shallow graves or Interpol tracking across borders. They can't tell them yet. They have to be sure and then usually when they have to sit the loved ones down and send a WPC to make a cup of tea. Usually, then, it's too late to do anything at all.

A few little words and everything changes. Before the trench coats and suits arrive from head office, before an archive that can only be accessed via a biometric scanner is opened by the few in the know, and the Top Brass is paged and fetched from semi-retirement, it will be up to Cynthia to try to reach the little girl and save her as she was trying to do and now, now, they have wasted her time, interrupted her flow and this situation is a Code OWL and don't they understand how time is against them?

'Don't be so ridiculous!' Mimi had to be restrained from assaulting a police officer. 'I've never heard such nonsense! You expect me, us, my daughter, who is absolutely distraught – look at her! – to believe that Leia has been kidnapped by a supernatural being from a mythological world? What is the name of your superior? I shall take this to the top! And I shall write to *The Times*! This is ludicrous! Insane! And you are wasting time when little Leia, our darling Leia, is out there, God knows where, frightened, alone . . .' Mimi's voice wavered.

The Top Brass had arrived and when he did, they were led to comfortable chairs whilst a capable-looking WPC was sent to make the tea. This did not seem to bode well and they clutched at each other for support. Unlike the others, he was not in uniform, just a plain shirt and a loose tie along with the almost universal police regulation à la *Colombo* beige mac. He was chewing gum, solemn, hard-faced with thinning hair, looking like he knew a thing or two about life and its seedy underbelly. He had coughed to get their attention, explaining in plain and police terms the very serious nature of the situation, the need for complete cooperation and when he spoke his voice was full of backstreet gravel and pre-smoking-ban pubs.

'I appreciate how this might sound, Mrs Taylor, but we can only go on facts. The dogs, the CCTV footage of the square, the evidence provided by Miss Wootten from the antique shop—'

'Oh yes! Cynthia! The old warlock from next door!' Mimi spat. 'Our resident Wiccan, now we learn! The local pagan with a cellar full of altars, goats' heads and a broomstick at her back door, no doubt! I hope that you're investigating her thoroughly! She kept that side of her hobbies well hidden, didn't she? Do you not think that our local constabulary could have given us some warning that we had a witch in our midst? You'd better have men crawling all over that place. *That* type are always involved in horrible goings-on and she's trying to create a smokescreen, can't you see that? It doesn't take police training to figure out what her game is—'

'Mrs Taylor.' His words were carefully chosen in Estuary English. 'I don't think you have listened carefully enough to everything I've told you!' And even Mimi shrank back in her seat when the policeman's finger jabbed in her direction and his tone – once only reserved for dockland gangsters and inner-city murderers – was concrete-hard. 'My unit take a Code OWL – Other World Leak – very seriously. These cracks have a habit of appearing now and then, with far-reaching consequences – Leia going missing is one such example and you do not – I repeat – *do not* want to know some of the things I've seen.' His face left Mimi in no doubt that she didn't.

'There are not many who even know that such a code word exists, but Miss Wootten has worked very closely with us for a number of years and is considered to be one of the elite in terms of what she knows and what she can do. Because of the fault line here and all the residual energy hanging around in these old streets, she's taken up residence in Bath to control and monitor Other

World activity and she's been able to prevent anything like this happening before more times than we can mention. We, as a Special Unit and as a nation, are very grateful to her and her guardianship of the Gateway. If what she did wasn't so confidential, then she – Miss Wootten – would have a string of honours after her name. She does a more than full-time, very dangerous job purely as a volunteer and, like it or not, Mrs Taylor, there are things that go on that the police forces, military and Government just cannot explain. That is, until they get my Unit in. Rose –'

Rose jumped as soon as he said her name. She had, up to now, sat there in absolute silence trying to be invisible. Her stomach was wound into a tight knot of fear and guilt. Leia disappearing was all Rose's fault. She had left the cellar unlocked. She had not warned her loved ones of what wonders and dangers lay in the basement for fear of being judged and found wanting of rational thought. She had been so caught up in the earthly demands that she had entirely ignored celestial needs. She alone knew what was there and had still, carelessly, left the door open *and* handed Leia a fox stole crawling with charms and inexplicable magic. How could she ever look her sister in the eye again?

And it all made an odd and twisted kind of sense. Cynthia had been the one practising magic all along – not to summon the goddess, but to guard against her unpredictable appearance. At some point in the madness of the morning, Leia had wandered down into the hitherto forbidden territory of the cellar, probably delighted at finding it unlocked and being able to explore without the inconvenience of health-and-safety-fearing parents, probably following Mooch, who was last seen scooting past the sniffer dogs from the cellar as soon as a canine paw was on the first stair.

'Rose,' he began again, and his swimming-pool blue eyes fixed on her like a gun sight. 'I think you can help. I think that there's a lot more you can tell me about the situation we have here.' His voice was calm but controlled, as if he was about to explode into a frenzy of 'Sorry, M'Lud, she just slipped down the stairs as we were escorting her from the premises.' What can you tell me about the goings on here at Vintage Magic?'

Rose stuttered, 'Emm . . . I . . . well, it's difficult, really.' All eyes of her family were on her now. Lily with a face of pure WTF disbelief and rage.

'Think!' he ordered and his snarl said, 'You'll be a victim of police brutality when I've finished with you.' It was amazing how it helped her to focus her thoughts and Rose began with the voices and the odd stories gleaned from customers, such as how a pair of sandals had walked in a direction the wearer really didn't want to go, taking off like the shoes of Snow White's wicked stepmother, which danced until she dropped dead. But, like all fairy tales, it had actually ended happily because the shoes had walked her into the man she was now going to marry. And Rose talked of Peggy Mountford, of safari-suit damage to flesh where no pins could be found and, all the while, the Top Brass was nagging at his aides.

'Have you got that?' Did you get that down? What do HQ think? Does it correlate with what they've got?' And his minions sat typing into laptops, talking into headsets and cross-checking data, graphs, charts and monitor readings from computers being set up all over the lounge and in every other room, they would learn later.

'Go on, Rose. Call me Chief,' he encouraged softly as though he were some kindly priest letting she, the sinner, unburden her sins. He was Good Cop now and Rose talked. He was her friend in all this. He, alone, could understand how she felt in this odd, the oddest of odd, situations. She told all; of fur coats returned to the wild and spells of glamour to captivate men. Of swirling, luminescent vortexes that stretched out into an infinite beyond. And of cadavers in fancy cross-dress. Of a customer who claimed that, every time she put on a Vintage Magic-bought Bianca Jagger-broad-brimmed wedding-style hat, she had visions. The buyer had thought that maybe it had been a little too tight and constricted the blood flow to her head, but her description of smoke-filled parties, psychedelic wall art and iconic rock stars sounded a lot like the memories of the groupie-turned-dog breeder who had sold it to Rose in the first place . . .

'All this and you still kept selling the goods?' The Top Brass changed his tone to one of disgust. He wasn't her friend, he was Bad Cop just doing his job, trying to jigsaw the picture together on this case and now she, Rose, irresponsible and (he made her feel) morally corrupt, was guilty as charged. 'Did you not wonder for one single second how this might end?' He slammed his hand down on to the arm of the sofa and they all jumped in fear. Lily curled into a ball, overcome with exhaustion and the effort of trying to understand. Matt's arms wrapped around her and, tight-lipped, his inscrutable gaze did not waver from looking at Rose. Mimi was chain-smoking herself into a stupor.

'Goddess Magic. I should have known. I could have stopped this.' The Chief was pacing the floor. Slamming one fist into the other and scanning over the shoulders of his co-workers and their multiple laptops. He was talking aloud to himself, cracking the gum in his mouth then chewing even harder the skin around his finger-nails. 'I need to talk to Cynthia. I need to talk to the Top. Goddesses – shit, damn! This is bigger than I thought. They don't play by the rules. Not any rules we understand, anyway.' A field telephone had been brought to him. There was talk of leave being cancelled, of scaling up the alert. The Pentagon was mentioned – an interesting choice of words for a building that, Rose now learned, held the international archive on magical worlds. White houses and black presidents were notified and bushy eye-browed ministers of defence were called.

'Mimi,' the Chief suddenly snapped. She stood to attention, ignoring his familiar address. 'I'm going to need a cigarette.'

'Will it help with the goddess magic?' Rose ventured.

'No, but it will help me. I haven't had a fag in five years but, God knows, I need one now.' And he disappeared with a team of followers to Birdcage Antiques, shouting orders about sealing off the square and had Thames House been in touch? And could they get those twittery old dears from next door to bring round some cakes?

Rose turned in panic to the distraught parents. 'Lily, Matt – I'm sorry. I didn't mean for this to happen. I couldn't understand what was going on. Who could I talk to about it? I thought it was strange coincidences or me, my imaginings . . .' Nobody answered, nobody knew what to say.

Rose's life seemed to be unravelling like the plot of *Lost*. Each passing minute seemed to disclose yet another layer to events or another challenge to her understanding of metaphysics and, like with the plot of *Lost*, Rose could not keep track.

But it was Lily, wretchedly pale and only half alive, it seemed, who spoke first.

'Matt, Mum' – a term of endearment Mimi – this time – accepted – 'will you just give Rose and me a moment alone?'

Standing, nodding assent, they left without question, Matt circling his arms around a Mimi who suddenly, despite her glamour and surgical lifts, looked frail and very, very old.

Rose was already pulling her sister into an embrace,

saying she was sorry over and over again.

'Don't blame yourself, Rose – this is why I wanted to talk to you. This isn't your fault. It's all mine.' Lily broke into shoulder shaking gulps.

'How can you blame yourself, Lily? It's me whose been meddling with the goddess, practically selling my soul to get back that stupid goon Carl. And there was so much going on, too much to keep track of everything, and the cellar – well, what can I say? I left it unlocked and I can never, ever forgive myself for doing this to you.'

'But *I* should have been watching her! I'm her mum and I let Leia down. Not just today.' Lily pulled away and sank into a chair. 'This is a punishment. Karma. Payback for what I did.'

'Lily, I can't imagine that there is anything that you've done, especially not to the daughter you adore, that would deserve *this* as a punishment. There isn't a god I would believe in who would punish a mother by taking away her child. And I really don't think punishing you is Minerva's motive here—'

Lily cut in.

'It's because of me – because I was unfaithful to Matt. I have to tell you. I have to tell you everything because this must all be my fault.'

Rose was speechless. Her world rocked – and not for the first time that day. Now Matt and Lily breaking up all made sense. Lily was seeing someone else. Lily's words tumbled out as she unburdened herself.

'That's why I left. I couldn't live with myself. I

couldn't live a lie pretending that everything between Matt and me was normal, that we were a normal family. And I couldn't tell him either. It would crush him. Kill him. And I couldn't tell you. With all that you'd gone through with Carl and Isabelle, to hear that I was no better than them, cut from the same cloth . . . I couldn't bear you to look at me with that same disappointment, Rose. It happened when I was at the farm.'

An image of the elderly cowhand, missing three fingers, the only single man for five surrounding miles, flashed into Rose's mind. Lily, almost able to read her sister's thoughts, managed a weak kind of smile.

'No, not Ernie! I met someone on Friends Reunited. An old school friend—'

'But we went to an all-girls school . . . oh!' Rose's eyes became very wide in shock.

'No! Wrong again! If you let me finish . . . it was Abbie's brother. Do you remember them? I went and stayed with her in the holidays a couple of times, their parents had a place on the coast. I went to Abbie's wedding – ages ago before Leia was born. Anyway, it went from chatting on-line to texting and emails. All very innocent at first, but then there was a bit of flirting and I was flattered. Matt and I had got so . . . I don't know, like brother and sister and living at the farm a room away from his parents wasn't exactly great for our sex life. I was bored and missing all the things I used to do in London and jealous that you were there living the high life—'

'Hardly! Working in a building society and living with Carl?'

'Yeah, but you had all the shops and theatres on your doorstep and I felt that I had become just a boring old mum at the nursery gate. And then here was this man – wealthy, successful, a photographer, and I was just swept away by it all. I couldn't believe that somebody like him would spend time chatting to me. So it went on, only on-line, at this point, and Matt never suspected—'

'Because he wouldn't. Because he trusted you,' Rose hissed. They'd both lowered their voices to a whisper.

'I know, don't you think I know? Don't make me feel any worse, Rose. I couldn't feel any worse than I do now . . .' Her voice wavered but now that she had started she had to go on. 'So, he – Abbie's brother came to Bath. I said I was meeting friends in town for lunch and Matt didn't even ask who.' Lily buried her head in her hands.

'So you had lunch and then what?' Rose prompted.

'It was all so ridiculously sexually charged. I hadn't felt that way for years. I felt so desirable, so alive, and I thought I was in love with him. I fooled myself into thinking it, although I never stopped loving Matt. I still love him . . . and then, when the meal ended, he kissed me and I kissed him back.' Lily was crying now, wiping already swollen eyes on her sleeve.

'And?' Rose wanted to hear it all. Lily had kept this bottled up for so long and it had poisoned their closeness, made Rose feel shut out of her sister's life.

'That's it. I've told you everything.'

'So, you didn't sleep with him?'

'No. How could you think that I would go that far?'

'Is that a "No" in the Bill Clinton/Monica Lewinsky sense of a no? In the manner of sending a naked text of oneself is not perceived as an unfaithful act? In a "Oh – I just happen to be humping your best friend in your bed but I'm not cheating on you really"-type of unfaithful?' Rose felt herself getting angry.

'No! No! Nothing like any of that. Just what I've told you.'

Now Rose was confused. 'Let me get this right. You left Matt who – as you've just said – you love still, and took Leia away from the only home she'd ever known and her besotted grandparents and her doting father because you kissed a man in a car park, OK, admittedly with tongues. And now you think that Leia's going missing is somehow punishment for that? Just that? So are you still seeing him?'

'No. I never replied to a text, email or anything again. I blocked contacts and wiped details. But don't you understand? Don't you get it? Leia has been taken because I'm being punished for going the same way as our parents – "The gods visit the sins of the fathers on their children" and all that? I don't want a marriage like Mimi and Daddy!'

Rose grabbed Lily by the shoulders and managed to stop short of shaking her.

'Stop with all the medieval church punishments rubbish! I can't believe you were actually listening to all that nonsense in school assembly! It's just myths, stories, ways of controlling the populace or, at the very least, the hormonal surges of teenage girls in a single-sex boarding school!

'Leia is missing and what you have done is peanuts, a cosmic inconsequence compared to things that other folk do every day and live normal, happy, unblemished, unpunished lives. I don't know why this has happened but I think the Chief will get to the bottom of it and you-blaming yourself, wasting all that energy, isn't going to change anything and will just make you feel worse. And, lastly – what on earth makes you think that you and Matt would end up like Mimi and Daddy?'

'Look at me.' She pointed to her hair, managing that tired smile. 'You think I don't realise that I'm a carbon copy of her? And I was unfaithful to Matt over and over in my head so I'm made in the same pattern! It's in our blood, for God's sake!'

'Environment!' Rose countered. 'You say nature, I say nurture. Mimi and Daddy were a product of their time! Like LSD or . . . or the moon landings, Mary Quant, or . . . I don't know, the Cuban Missile crisis. They married too young and never had time to sow their wild oats.'

'Maybe, or maybe it's a failing. The genetic equivalent of the Pennyquick fault that caused the springs around here?' Rose was completely side-tracked and gob-smacked by her sister's geographical prowess. 'Well, I did get a GCSE in Geology – yes, with extra time for my dyslexia. Even though Mimi said I was just being slow deliberately.'

Rose suddenly missed her father very much. A big bear of a man, he would have taken charge now; talked on equal terms with everyone involved in the operation, pulled all the strings of his connections and then, when it was over, hosted a banquet of Georgian indulgence with all of his new friends.

'But when you think about it, Mimi and Daddy had a great marriage really. OK, so their after-dinner entertainment was a little unusual, but they were in love, crazy about each other right until the very end. I used to think that there wasn't room for you and I, they were so . . .' Rose groped for the right word – 'consumed by one another. And all Mimi's dalliances since – well, that's just an outlet for her grief. She's not been the same since Daddy went.' Then suddenly she said, 'Everyone is unfaithful in their heads, Lily. It is perfectly OK to think about it. Everyone does. But you have to tell Matt *everything*.'

'How could I ever tell him? It would break his heart.'

'And you think leaving him, taking away his daughter, breaking up his family, was better? I don't get your logic. What do you want from here?'

'I want to make like Cher.' A sisterly short-cut way of explanation.

'And turn back time? To when?'

'Before. Before all of this. I want Leia back. God –' The pain of her loss almost caused Lily to double over.

'And I want Matt. But I think it's too late. I think he's moved on. That day you had the computer installed. I know I was flirting like mad with that chap from Hands Solo Design. John, is it? But I was only doing that because Matt had said he'd been asked on a date. I don't know who by; somebody, a friend of a friend. He asked me if I thought he should go. He obviously wants to move on.'

'He wanted *you* to say he *shouldn't* go! It's bloody obvious! You have to go and tell him now. Tell him everything and just start again.'

But now wasn't the time. Now, worries over a kiss in a municipal Pay and Display seemed wholly irrelevant.

17

Cynthia, exhausted from her naked rituals at her cellar altar and wearing a kimono for decency's sake, was now perched on a bar stool front-of-shop in Vintage Magic. She was dabbing at her face with a towel, looking like an old stripper after a long night-shift of stag parties.

'We're losing our touch,' she said to the Chief. 'When did it get so hard?' He laid a hand on her shoulder; it was obvious that they were old friends. There was none of her usual prickliness but still Rose's cellar remained a damp, dark storage place and not a crossing place, a worm hole between worlds.

It was an enormously serious and laughably ridiculous situation. It was being Punk'd. It was a bad dream or a dodgy film plot. If only it didn't involve Leia. But Rose had seen it all now – if 'it all' included seeing your middle-aged lady neighbour kneeling naked, prostrate in a circle of salt. The Chief was making Rose and Cynthia go over events for perhaps the hundredth time.

'Full moon, missing cats, corpses in the dairy. Come on, people!' he was shouting, already working his way through his fourth cigarette in five years and cracking his gum (nicotine) even louder than before. His team were clicking away on their computers in communication with witches, warlocks and neo-pagans across the world. 'There must be something we're missing here. Somebody must have something, some key for us to unlock this door!'

But there was nothing. Years spent practising spells of protection and yet, with all of Cynthia's frantic back-pedalling, she could not open it. She had known when the portal opened, felt something shift in the air, and when she heard the voices, frightened and frantic searching for Leia . . . call it intuition or second sight, she had known instantly what must be done, then found it could not be undone.

The Chief was pacing the floor going back over the events of the evening when Rose had stumbled down into the cellar and found that it was a crossing place between worlds. 'Let me get this straight, Cynthia. You closed up the shop, you did your protection spell, and you went home.'

'Like I told you. Shut the shop, did the spell, finished off my game on the computer, locked up and went home.'

The Chief ran his hands through his hair, repeating words over and over to himself in between deep draws on his cigarette. 'Shut the shop, spell, shut down the computer, went home. Shop, spell, computer, home.'

He kept mumbling away whilst Cynthia rubbed Rose's hand.

'We'll do our best.' Rose was unnerved. It was as though Cynthia had had some sort of personality transplant made all the more unnerving because the kimono was beginning to gape a little.

'And what about this morning? What were you both doing this morning when Leia went missing?'

Rose went back over Carl leaving, India arriving, Isabelle ranting, Mrs Waters and Mrs Bridges rebuking, armed robbery, Matt bleeding, Lily crying, Mimi panicking and Leia missing. Cynthia added:

'I opened up the shop, did some knitting, checked for any Internet sales and played my game.' She shrugged. The Chief was still pacing the floor, chewing on his fingernails.

'That's it! That's it!' He was clicking his fingers wildly now, stuttering in his haste to get his words out. 'Cynthia. The computer . . . the game . . . What were you playing?'

'Planet Universe. A role-playing game. Orcs, elves, goblins – that sort of thing. Why?'

The Chief was jubilant, ecstatic. 'You're right, Cynny – we are old timers losing our touch!' He slapped her on the back, nearly knocking her off the stool and causing the kimono to fly open and Cynthia's breasts to swing like a Newton's Cradle. 'The world has moved on since we were top of our game! But I think we've just found our way in!'

*

Rose had always believed computers worked by sorcery and now here was the proof. The Chief's new theory was that Cynthia's game had been the conduit for the goddess to pass from one world to the next. They argued between themselves about the possible theoretical mechanics of it all whilst Rose looked on, feeling the strong desire for a double brandy with a whiskey chaser. She was beginning to feel it was a hoax, one of those elaborate fantasist set-ups to con her out of her money with stories of belonging to the SAS or FBI conspiracies.

Too male an energy source, Cynthia argued, and Rose agreed, thinking about Gigs and Megs and Ram – all sounding ultra-masculine and like cock-rock heavy-metal bands. No, the Chief countered, think of our basic training, the rules – all things contradictory are in fact complimentary! All things are connected across the spectrum of creation. The universe without and all the worlds within – could it not also include the man-made worlds, the microcosms of Sim Cities, Worlds of Warcraft and Calls of Duty? Could passageways and time-slips cross real, mythical and cyber worlds?

He was winning Cynthia over, wooing her with his logic.

'But how does this connect with my cellar?' Rose lagged behind, finding it very tricky to keep up with the conversation. Suddenly, her world was one where digital machine code combined with spell book and candle.

'We've known for a long time that – for whatever reasons – this shop was a site for paranormal activity. That's why Cynny was posted here. To keep an eye on it all. I won't go into how it might have managed to align itself with Cynthia's computer but it has. There might be something in the geometric patterns of the—'

'Stop there!' Rose put her hand up. She was too wired about Leia to even bother to feign interest.

'Anyway, it's worth a shot. What have we got to lose?' the Top Brass concluded.

And Rose could not contain herself any more, bursting out hysterically with tears coursing down her cheeks. 'My niece! My niece! Leia! That's what we stand to lose!'

Tears were not the Chief's bag. Facts, practicalities and paranormal abductions were his thing. He left Cynthia to it and fled up the stairs to consult with his minions.

'No, Rose.' Cynthia was back in stoke-mode. This time it was the side of Rose's face and then she tried to wrestle Rose into a hug because Cynthia felt that is what the situation demanded, but it was not comfortable for either of them. 'The Chief is right. I really think this is the way we get her back.' Gently she quoted from *The Complete Idiot's Guide to Universal Metaphysics* and *Myths and Legends for Dummies*.

The greater the human grasp of science and reason, Cynthia explained, the more worlds and creatures beyond logical control have been fenced out of this world. Ancient scriptures talked of gods walking the earth once upon a time and faerie realms existing in harmony with our own and so there were, until knowledge of how to draw down the curtain of reality, had developed. Humans needed protection from these entities that were capable of great kindnesses but also horrific cruelties, who switched allegiances without plan or provocation as a whim took them.

'But the goddess seemed to have a game-plan – she seemed to know what was right for people,' Rose questioned.

'But then she dressed up the deceased next-door for her own amusement and took Leia. Look at all the pain that has caused. If the gods can't live by our rules, we can't have them here and that's what the Chief and I have worked nearly all our lives to stop. It's bad enough, all the crap humans cause, without adding celestial beings into the mix. There are too many variables, too many probabilities. And think of all the magic they bring with them – not all of it good. You said yourself that the goddess had reawakened energies, unpredictable energies in those old clothes, that caused events that even she could not anticipate—'

'Cynth! Get your machine on!' There was no more room for debate. The Chief, clattering down the stairs wanted action. 'Log into Planet Universe! There might be nothing there, but there just might be something, and if your machine is on, then we stand a chance of opening up that portal. I've no idea how or where it might have happened but we need to explore the top, bottom and middle of that Tolkeinesque earth.' He was already walking off, followed by a navy-suited assistant, scribbling notes on a spiral-bound reporter's pad. Cynthia's words caused him to stop sharply and the distracted follower to collide with the Chief's back.

'We can't. Or I should say I can't. Not alone, I mean. Planet Universe has more cyber square miles than Australia and I can't access all the different levels. I'm really only a very basic player. A newbie, they call me—'

The Chief cut her off. 'Who calls it you?'

'The guys at Hands Solo Design. They put it on my machine. They all play it. They're Elite players.'

'And they have access to all the different levels?'

'I think so.'

'Good. Then get them on the phone.'

The Geek shall inherit the earth. And then become the richest men on the planet. Computer nerds are the new messiahs. Keepers of knowledge and shamans of all the secrets that ensure the civilised world runs smoothly. They can find lost files, cure sick machines of crippling viruses, and navigate unexplored cyberspace. Within minutes, through communication on forums and social networking sites, they can have an army of trolls and elvish scouts searching virtual continents for glitches, anomalies and signs of mythological goddess passage in the temporal and spatial matrices of a fantasy role-playing game. And to them, weaned on *The Hobbit* and the complex world rules of *Star Trek*, it all made sense. They felt like they had been preparing their whole lives for this moment. Hours spent studying the philosophy of *The Matrix* or watching *Fringe* and *The X-Files* had not been wasted.

Hands Solo Design had given themselves over to the mission once they had rung home to tell their mothers that they wouldn't be home for tea and then rung for delivery pizza. Added to the tubes of Pringles, packets of Quavers and the trainers kicked off, the whole office had a musk of teenage-boy bedroom. Every computer was on and manned and laptops lay open on every available flat surface. With the wires trailing and the fervent typing, the shouting into headsets and the scanning of monitors, it was like Space Command Central with John at the helm, a Mancunian Buck Rogers, not from outer space but out of Salford.

Not that the team needed an excuse to be in the office and playing computer games on a Sunday. And anyway, Planet Universe was not just a game, it was a lifestyle. One of the many MMORPGs (that's Massively Multi-Player Online Role-Playing Games), it was an alternative world where people live, die, contract diseases, interact, work (shoeing horses or making swords), fall in love, marry, commit adultery and are then cited in real world divorce cases. Such was the pull, the draw to return, that a few – after obsessive marathons of play – had fallen at their machines in exhaustion. Now beyond getting to another level, collecting more gems or adding to battle powers with bow-staff skills, here, at last, was a real quest, a proper challenge, a genuine mission and word was spreading.

Nothing binds people together like a single goal and for the multi-species world of PU (an unfortunate acronym along with Wii that lead to many farcical conversations in the English language), a world as blighted with religious differences, territorial disputes, greed, evil and war as Planet Earth was, there was unusual cohesion. Orcs, elves, humans, dwarves were soon united behind identifying the point of infiltration into their virtual world. And they'd found it already.

One of the top rank players of the world in Tokyo had been exploiting a glitch that had allowed him to teleport from one location to another for the last week. He'd also been trying to defend its location from discovery and thought he'd succeeded until he saw an unidentified woman slip through, accompanied by a short female character – what he'd assumed was a dwarf. This was followed by a torrent of other feminine forms that he thought were Sexy Vampires from the Darkland forests. Now he was typing its location to Hands Solo Design, promising to report on any changes, vowing to intervene should the goddess pass that way and, because of the time difference, staying up way past his bedtime even though he had school tomorrow.

And in amongst the sheer hideousness, the surreal bizarreness and low-budget sci-fi series feel of it all, Rose had developed a crush.

Extreme circumstances strip personalities bare of all expected social norms and niceties. When everything is at stake there is no room for pretending to be cool or urbane or witty. All that is left is the core, the very essence of a person, and what was left of Rich Clarke from Hands Solo Design was basically a sound, nice person. As his cousin, famous movie star India Mannerley, had stated so boldly: A Good Guy.

The sort of guy who will appear on the doorstep with advice and equipment and a knowledge base derived in part from professional training and in portion from science fiction. The type of chap who won't ask too many questions but will just get stuck in, sleeves rolled up to administer help where it is needed and to co-ordinate Skype communications with his office. The kind of person who looks at a girl with a tear-streaked face and a niece in cyber-space and does not freak out and run the other way, but says, as if it was a regular sort of happening, 'Well, you know, things happen in Bath.'

Rose's crush was not the sort she had for Ellen DeGeneres. That was nothing to do with unrequited Sapphic longing, but was like how greasy-haired, bespectacled first-years (Rose had been one) might admire a cool sixth former. Nor was it like the one she'd had on Boyzone's Simon Gately, long after she was of an age where it was seemly to carry around his picture in her purse, and particularly since it was after his big Coming Out and there really was no point Yearning for a Turning. No, this crush had blossomed from a seed that was sown on their first meeting and was now germinating in her lady garden. And given the circumstances, her sister would kill her if she knew and kill her mother if she could see how Mimi kept casting glances at the Chief.

Never had the lyrics of Bonnie Tyler's 'Holding Out for a Hero' seemed so apt or profound. In a world of corrupt politicians and adulterous national-hero footballers, of prime ministers sending young men to be maimed in wars that cannot be won and breakfast television phone-line fraud, it does seem that the good guys and gods have deserted. But here was one – a good guy, at least – walking right into her shop, her life, and doing his best to find Leia.

Rich, Cynthia and the Chief were deep in conversation; their talk was of avatars – both the original meaning, the descent of a deity from heaven to earth, and its newest meaning, characters created on-line or in a game world, customised and idealised versions of the player's self. They were cut short when shouts and screams Skyped across the city interrupted their discussion.

John's face filled the box in the upper right-hand corner of Rose's computer screen. He had pizza paste smeared at the corner of his mouth, giving him a Jokerish grin and was yelling louder than if Manchester City had won at home.

'We've found her! We've found her! You can see her! Look! Look!' and he was holding a laptop screen in front of the web-cam, then Rich was frantically typing into Planet Universe to reach the location and Matt and Lily were running, jumping down the stairs, and Lily was trying to hug the screen where Leia – looking just like herself but for one of Rose's vintage tiaras – was not grieving, angst-ridden or desperate for home. Far from it, and why should she be?

Leia was splashing at the foot of a shampoo-ad-perfect azure waterfall in a shallow lagoon, edged with ferns. Unicorn foals waited patiently to play at the shore and mermaids leapt somersaults for her pleasure, tossing their hair over their shoulders, indulging their senses in a 'totally organic experience' style. A host of indulgent female carers, the goddess at the centre, languished on rocks, fawning and clapping at Leia's every move. Jewel-coloured butterflies fluttered by and silvery fish swam zig-zags through the water at her feet, nibbling at her toes. Who would miss home if every nursery was like this?

'Good news!' The Chief beamed, relieved that Leia was happy, unharmed and, furthermore, appeared to be having the time of her life. 'I'm pretty sure we can prevent Leia's passage out of the game. Getting her back here might be more tricky. Worst Case Scenario – she has to stay in Planet Universe until we can figure something out. But that's not too bad, is it?'

To be fair, the Chief was working from a point where it was his fear that Leia should simply disappear to an unreachable, mythical world for ever. He had seen such things happen but even this tough, street-wise cop took a step back when Lily turned, savagely snarling, from the screen.

'Not too bad? NOT TOO BAD? Do I have to spend my life looking after my daughter as if she's a Tamagotchi? A cyber-pet? You think that's not too bad, do you?'

Rich intervened. He had ideas, tactics, game strategies, he assured Lily, and he spoke with all of the self-assurance of a black-and-white movie RAF pilot. He was knowledgeable and confident and Lily was visibly calming as he spoke. He explained that, along with Cynthia's ritual magic, the Chief's knowledge of the arcane and his understanding of the gaming world, he was pretty sure that they had more than a good shot at getting Leia home.

Rose's heart swelled with relief and pride. No, he didn't know how to charm and smarm and stab others in the back to secure a law partnership, but he was pretty nifty with a cross-bow, using only the up, down and across arrows. He probably couldn't power-house his way through a spin class or hill-climb on a cross-trainer in a gym with a membership fee the size of an average mortgage but, he assured Cynthia and the Chief, he knew how to track silently through a forest in another reality and could talk to his virtual horse in coded Klingon commands. And he didn't say annoying things and think that they were funny, like 'Take a pew' or 'It's not rocket science.'

No, he was nothing like Carl at all. Thank goodness. And if they were in the playground now, Rose would kick Rich up the backside just to show how much she cared. And she hoped, a vague hope but way back in the queue behind the hope of getting Leia back from a parallel universe, hoped that India had not said a word about Carl's leaving this morning.

Only that morning? Really? It seemed like a week ago. A world away.

18

There is nothing quite as dull for a non-player as watching somebody else play a computer game. It's about as thrilling as sitting in the doctor's waiting room with nothing to read but copies of *The People's Friend*. Especially when the player demands your complete attention to the screen. 'Look! Look how I can get a hole-in-one on Golf Pro 10!' they squeal and the player expects you to be impressed. Non-players wonder what's the point of playing golf on a screen, indoors with the curtains drawn on a sunny day? And non-players can't fathom how someone who can navigate their way around a virtual world is then unable to find the cups (cupboard above the kettle) when it's their turn to make the tea. (This is how Lily felt about Matt's game-playing.)

For observers who are also players, there is such an itch to be in charge of the controls that they must practically sit on their hands to stop themselves wrenching them from the other person. It is torture to observe the obvious idiocy of the person currently playing. (This is how Matt felt, watching Rich far too slowly – or so Matt believed – navigating Planet Universe.) Their inability, the pathetic attempts, to coordinate the jump, kick and swing that will ensure they complete the level is excruciating to watch. But as game-show hosts have long insisted, one has to understand the effects having an audience has on performance. 'It's very easy when you're at home, folks.' (But really, is there ever an excuse for using all of your *Who Wants to be a Millionaire?* lifelines in the first three questions?)

And for the playee there is the annoyance of being told seven different shouted ways of doing something by people invading your personal space, looming over your shoulder and obscuring your view of the screen when they've been told they should never, *never*, touch it.

That's why, with tensions running as high as they were, Rich asked that Mimi (who was breathing smoke over the screen and being very negative about this being the right course of action), Matt (who was yelling 'Up! Up! Right a bit!' and other helpful instructions) and Lily (putting Rich off with her constant worry that Leia might get hurt by a unicorn) be banished to the upper floors of Vintage Magic to observe events on a distant monitor. Far more was at stake than just having to start the game from the beginning again. That's why John's Skype connection would also soon be turned off from Rich's laptop because he was the worst of keyboard bullies, known once to have pushed Rich out of the way to get his hands on the controls of Mario Cart.

Only Rose had been allowed to stay as Rich set up his pimped-up laptop on her shop counter. Rose, who would observe events from her own monitor, relay information from her headset connecting her to Hands Solo Design and the Chief's team above. Rose, who protested that she had never once played a computer game in her life, that she'd only ever seen the *Tomb Raider* movie and that she knew nothing about *Spyro* or *Assassin's Creed* and couldn't really be trusted with a task of this magnitude.

'But *I* trust you, Rose,' Rich insisted and he grabbed her hand, giving it a squeeze, and Rose memorised the weight of his fingers wrapped around her own.

Then, in getting down to business, preparing for the challenge ahead, Rich had pulled the pullover from his head and in doing so, his regulation shirt had ridden up, just a little, exposing dark hair flecking across surprising abs. Abs that could not have been won from sitting at a computer monitor and Rose found herself swooning and needed to steady herself at a bar stool. She decided it could only be the stress of the situation and nothing to do with the inappropriate timing of a rush of sudden lust. The flat stomach hinting at an unknown exercise regime, indicating more hidden layers to the man with a mouse in his hand, and she found herself watching with admiration at the determined line of his mouth as he frowned, tapping at the keys in front of him and adjusting his headset.

Knights in shining armour come in funny disguises

in this modern age. Rose knew someone who had fallen in love with their AA man. Another friend had married the policeman who had charged her for being drunk and disorderly. Now Rose's knight had arrived and Rich, already sweating like a menopausal lady in a centrally heated room, had cast off his M&S Blue Harbour V-neck and materialised in *PU*, on screen, as a long-haired, six-packed Fabio model-alike complete with billowy white shirt open to the waist, leather gauntlets and pirate boots. Despite the high camp, *Pleasure Emporium* book-jacket look of Rich's avatar, it really looked like him. Or at least a highly muscled, glossy, fantasy-barbarian version of him right down to the slight – that's why mums say don't run at the side of the swimming pool – scar on his forehead. And if Rose was honest, it wasn't a bad look. A Jack Sparrow/highwayman/dragon-slayer had entered her night-time thoughts more than once. Along with tattooed bikers. Oh, and being a sexily hypnotised love-slave of Paul McKenna. But then, doesn't everyone?

'Yeah, I know,' Rich said without even looking at her, as if waiting for the piss-take of his avatar character to begin. 'It's all very Boris Vallejo meets Jon Bon Jovi, but, you know, you should see the pictures of me with long hair.' And had the time been appropriate and the need to reach Leia not quite so pressing, then it would have been an opener to another conversation, but Rose tucked the thought away, promising inwardly to share with him her own photos of dubious rock-chick bubble perms and forays into being blonde that just had not worked.

On the surface it seemed an easy enough brief for all the assembled players of Planet Universe. Find the goddess, get Leia, reach the portal. Bob's your uncle. Easy, that is, if they ignored the little life hanging in the balance and the somewhat mercurial goddess.

John had organised trolls, orcs and elves to set up a covert watch at each of the disclosed portals with instructions not to let the goddess leave the game. Only one was unmanned – the one nearest to her. Troops of characters were defending mountain borders and the Tokyo schoolboy player was teleporting across the glitch, keeping watch for any unanticipated movement by the celestial entourage. Whether all of the players beyond the Hands Solo Design team realised that this was a paranormal emergency or whether they thought it was just another quest thrown up by the game, it didn't matter. It was a simple case of whoever could reach Leia and get her to the portal first was the winner. Quite how the three-year-old would feel if it turned out to be a cyclopean ogre or warty-skinned troll that got her there was unknown.

'But,' the Chief warned the gamers on-line, 'should you approach her, the goddess is an unpredictable entity.'

'I know,' John began hesitantly, his grainy Skype image looking sheepish. 'I've met her in the game before. I just thought she was another character . . .' His voice was guilty-sounding and embarrassed.

'Oh God, you too! I mean' – Rich seemed to be doing some frantic back-pedalling, directing his comments to no one in particular – 'it's just a PU thing. You know how it is. A bit of on-line fun . . .' Something about the way Rich cast down his eyes, didn't elaborate and scudded his toe against the floor made Rose feel like punching him on the arm. And Rich and John weren't the only ones. Other male voices were soon muttering about the goddess. She had made many, many casual on-line acquaintances, it seemed.

And so it was Game On.

More dull than watching others tap away at an on-line game is hearing about it afterwards. Blow-by-blow accounts of pressing the x-button, successful chopping actions and combat skills are worse than listening to other people's dreams. But the steps taken, the battles fought and hardships endured by the players of Planet Universe to be the first to reach Leia have become legendary tales – some of them true – with whole Internet forums devoted to events on that day.

Everyone wants to be a hero. Every player from the top Tokyo player to an Australian orc wanted to be the one to bring Leia home. Rich, John – even Cynthia, with her limited access and basic skills – wanted to be the one to see the gratitude on Lily's face when they handed over the child. By the time they were through, PU players had lost their on-line lives, were spattered in cyber-enemy's blood or had been soaked (the lagoon), baked (the desert) and frozen (snowy wastelands) like some Linda McCartney pulse-based casserole. Ultimately, it was not an easy brief at all.

Leia was playing at a far-off waterfall in a region of Planet Universe accessible only by Elite players and, to reach this idyllic setting, players had to cross several hostile, malevolent dark points of the game. Exactly the reason why the goddess had chosen this as her resting place, her undisturbed haven between worlds. She needed no protection when the landscape of Planet Universe provided it for her.

From all sections of the game, players advanced towards the goddess's lagoon to win back Leia. But it was not easy. A whole platoon of orcs lost their lives in the forests, falling prey to the patrolling zombie army and the regular booby traps of snake pits, man-eating spiders and blood-sucking bats. Others – dwarves and trolls – were lost still, walking frustrating circles in desert landscapes. Elves fought black-hooded raiders as they tried to cross through hilltop passes, losing comrades to the raiders' slave-caravans – there would be daring rescues. The Hands Solo Design team had been snatched one by one by wraiths as they tried to cross the barren stone-dotted moors of the Lands of the Dead and Cynthia fell early, one of the first; ironically lacking necessary spells of protection in this animated magical world. Within fifteen minutes, only a handful of players were left in these, the most extreme portions of Planet Universe, but John had managed to get as far as crossing snowy mountains, ahead of all the other gamers, making his descent until he was caught unawares by the furry, clawed snow monster the wild-man man-bear that was the Migoi Meh-Teh.

And this was the route that Rich had also chosen to follow, traversing difficult climbs and having the occasional spat with a goblin. So far it had been slow, but not too taxing, and Rose had quickly become familiar with the way of 'cheats' scanning Internet sites that exposed shortcuts and gave hints to players that helped them traverse the trickier points of the game. She was able to relay John's advice and found that she and Rich had slipped into being quite a team.

There was none of the irritated responses that she was used to getting when giving Carl directions in the car. Rich didn't get annoyed when she didn't understand a technical term, he just patiently explained or apologised for assuming that she would. Most of all she loved how he would begin 'Hey, partner' when he asked for a slug of water. Rose was even beginning to see the interest of a game of this nature – riddles, combat, interaction, unpredictable landscapes – surely better than spending the evening just watching another reality TV show where people are asked to dress as babies for a week with life-changing results.

Rose even began to consider what her own avatar might look like. A Xena Warrior Princess crossed with a kittenish Betty Page would be nice, Rose thought. An outfit of leather, cheetah print, bottom-skimmingly short, accessorised with amulets snaking up her arms and completed with tight-fitting thigh-length leather boots. A sort of Amazonian-meets-dominatrix look. Something she would really like to wear if only she had the nerve.

And it was whilst Rose was in her reverie about the potential benefits of chamois leather over PVC on women's vaginal health, a case of bad timing in terms of inattentiveness, that Rich began crashing his fingers down on the keyboard, hammering the keys in staccato rhythm and stringing together expletives.

'Shitfuckbuggershitshitshit. Get John. Get John!'

And Rose, snapping back to awareness, saw Rich on screen slashing, hacking blindly, slicing, defending, but the sword just seemed to glance and bounce off a great white furry, claw-tipped creature's thick coat and there was such a confusion of fur and steel and long hair flying that it was impossible to tell who was coming out on top. And John was panicking: 'I don't know what to tell him' and Rose was yelling: 'Hang on, Rich, hang on', scanning sites for anything, anything that might help and, suddenly, painfully aware that there were fewer and fewer players and the chances of getting back Leia were diminishing by the second.

Even in the blizzard-white-out of the screen, the blood spatters and entrails across the ice could be clearly seen, but Rich was still standing, chopping at the falling snow long after the creature, the part-bear, part-ape thing, had fallen at his feet and the voices in Rose's headset were singing victory songs.

From the shadows of the virtual world, the real victor emerged. An ogre, blinking his one eye, bowed low in front of Rich's Soft-Metal avatar and laid a heavy cudgel on the ground. In the game, Rich was shaking his hand, pumping it furiously in a very British gesture of thanks and patting the ogre on the back, saying into his headset ludicrous-sounding things given the circumstances of a mountain blizzard, an ogre and a splattered, flattened snow monster.

'Well done! Thank you very much! That was splendid! I mean really splendid. First class.'

A casual listener might have thought that the ogre had just delivered a winning PowerPoint presentation in marketing strategies or played a Grade eight flute piece in a school assembly, not killed the unkillable Migoi Meh-Teh with a single blow of his club. Lucky for Rich (very lucky for Leia) that in Tokyo, a schoolboy's mother had finally stopped nagging and gone to bed herself so that he could start up the game again (with the sound turned down) and guide these hapless amateurs through the final part of the realm to reach the lagoon and reveal the final portal.

There was no point trying to approach the goddess by stealth. She had her look-outs, her scouts and the approach of the leather-trousered elf warrior that was Rich had already drawn the attention of some of the more libidinous members of the goddess's court. The ogre hanging back a little did not, sadly, have such a draw.

Minerva lay watching his approach on a rock, accessible only through the water. She was flanked by attendants who were peeling grapes for a still-paddling Leia. Rich set his course wading straight in, the graphics making the shirt cling to his chest like Colin Firth's Darcy. Immediately, mermaids were circling him like sharks in the water. They were seductive, supermodel-beautiful, rolling languorously through the water until he tried to bat them away and then they bared their needle-sharp, deep-water fish teeth.

'Oh those girls! They do like fresh meat!' The goddess chuckled indulgently, then focused with laser-sight eyes. 'Haven't we met?' A small smile played at the corner of her lips and Rose was in no doubt that Rich and Minerva had. Momentarily, wild with jealousy, Rose wondered again what the 'bit of on-line fun' was, exactly, and which keys were needed for up and down in those circumstances.

'I've come for the child.' Rich was hero-assertive, straight in with a kick-ass, no-messing approach. The goddess drew herself up until she was standing; her hands on her hips, staring disdainfully down her nose.

'She's mine. Rose Taylor gave her to me as an offering for services rendered and there is no going back. No refunds and *no* swapsies.' Leia lifted her head at hearing her aunt's name.

'Hey, Rich,' she said, giving a chubby-fisted wave. Leia never forgot anyone who gave her chocolate, recognising his animated form despite the hair and dandy highwayman attire.

'I did say – did I not, and you can remind her – that I liked offerings, gifts? Some sort of an acknowledge-ment for efforts undertaken. Ain't no such thing as a free lunch.' Minerva's voice had lost all taint of the sugar-sweetness that it could possess. 'I believe I talked extensively about tokens of appreciation of the non-generic kind and nobody could have been more pleased and surprised than I was to see that Rose's gift to me was the beautiful and entertaining Leia.' Minerva's voice raised an octave and all the heads of her cour-tesans turned to watch. Storm clouds were gathering – metaphorically and literally, as dark clouds clumped in the skies of Planet Universe, dimming the on-line screen brightness for all of the remote observers. 'And what's it got to do with you, anyhow? Has Rose sent you? All I ever ask for is a token, a trifle. Something even remotely resembling a goddam thank you for everything I do!' She was shouting now like a stressed-out working mum whose teenager and friends have eaten all the food in the house, raided the booze cabinet and not bothered to wash up. Lightning forked out of the once-blue virtual sky. An electrical surge that could not bode well.

'Get the Chief,' Rich called out to Rose next to him, needing help, back up, and his words echoed from the headset.

'Chief?' the goddess roared. 'The Chief? Do you

mean to say that Chief Brown has something to do with this?'

Then it all happened so quickly. The electrical storm in the skies of Planet Universe raged. The dark, thunderous, heavy clouds flashed with sheet lightning and sent forks down into the virtual earth, wiping out anything in its path.

Rich did not wait to find out what would happen next. The goddess, so purely woman, entirely unpredictable and at the mercy of emotional whims, meant that Rich felt negotiation was out of the question.

'*Highos*,' he yelled, and since nobody had any idea what he was saying nobody moved. Only overweight and slightly balding men in *Enterprise* T-shirts might know. Even goddesses don't bother to learn Klingon and so, out of nowhere, Rich's cyber-stallion, a 'combat guardian' hard won from weeks of game-playing, a one-off life-line to be used in only the most dire of circumstances (the PU equivalent of 'Phone a friend'), came galloping across the surrounding plain, skidding and splashing to a halt in the waters of the lagoon.

In a series of F, shift-key and Ctrl Alt movements and mouse clickings, Rich had grabbed Leia and swung up on to the horse in a single Parkour movement that he could never hope to repeat in the real world without causing himself a hernia. He kicked the horse into a gallop, following the lumbering Ogre to the waterfall and Leia, far from being disturbed by events, was laughing, shouting, 'Faster! Faster!' all the way.

Rose was completely absorbed. It was easy to forget that a real life was at stake and that the man standing next to her, banging down on the keyboard, was actually initiating the action on the screen. It was like watching the most thrilling action-adventure, a Sunday matinee of an *Indiana Jones* for all the family and the whole scene added fuel to another of Rose's romantic fantasies of riding along a sunset-lit sandy beach. She was to be disappointed if she thought it was going to happen with Rich. He'd never been on a horse in his life. But in the shop, in the very real world of Vintage Magic, he was shouting at her to get into the cellar. He was near to the portal now and the goddess and attendants were closing in with their unnaturally swift flight.

Another Klingon phrase and the horse stopped. Rich slid down with Leia clinging on his back, broke through the curtain of the waterfall and sped through a cave where rock dropped away, melting into the swirling marbled vortex. He was so close, Leia would be home soon. Minerva's eagle screams of rage pierced his ears, but he was running towards the vortex as fast as repeated pressings on the space bar would let him and ran straight into what felt like an invisible brick wall. They couldn't cross. Rich did it again for good measure, looking like a bird smashing into a clean window. It was just like reaching the border of a new realm that you don't possess the password to enter.

Here the two worlds met. The micro cyber-world of Planet Universe with all of its realistic graphics and complex battle rules and plain old Planet Earth, but the passage between the two, the door connecting the times and worlds, was closed. Firmly shut. Somebody had thrown up a barrier and, judging by the screams now faded into Disney-witch laughter, it was obvious who. Rich, perspiring at the keyboard, governed his character across it, feeling for gaps, looking to the observers like an eighties rock-star Marcel Marceau.

On one side, lay the welcoming committee – Rose and Lily, whose anguish was made worse by seeing Leia, so close and inaccessible. From the shop front, they could hear Rich, linked once more to John, shouting for help, for advice, for divine (but not goddess) intervention. And the Chief was screaming for information from his overpaid assistants and Cynthia was murmuring incantations about the coming together of ancient and future magic, trying again to unpick the goddess's charms – charms that had caused so many to fall under her spell.

'It's no good. I can't . . . I can't summon it . . . There's not enough . . .' Cynthia was throwing herb potions around the room and wafting beribboned feathers and the word burst from her – 'magic.' And then in a flash of inspiration, or call it a hunch, even a wild shot, Rose was running up the stairs undressing as she took them two at a time and by the time she reached the landing in front of all the Chief's men with their printing-off data and state-of-the-art electrical equipment she was down to her bra and knickers.

Rose Taylor, whose own body filled her with shame about weight and not being good enough, was semi-naked in front of an audience without any hint of embarrassment, she was now pulling her dress – *the* dress from the night before – over her head quicker than a catwalk model between runs. Mimi, fag in mouth, not really understanding why but just following her daughter's shouted instructions, was zipping her up and then Rose was running barefoot, jumping, falling, down into the cellar, pushing past Cynthia.

'Goddess magic,' she yelled by way of explanation, 'there might still be some on this dress.' She thought she was proved right as Cynthia's voice raised in renewed vigour a recitation of long-unpractised enchantments. It was like the first opening of the patio doors after a long winter, something palpably slid open and the damp cellar was filled with a rush of clean, fresh air and the nebula swirl of the portal spilled into the room, chasing shadows from the corners and growing outwards into infinity.

Rose would forever believe that the slightly worn, maybe still magical dress had changed the course of events. In fact, everyone believed that to be the case because no one had seen a four-legged animal that was more interested in tins of tuna sneak into the room. It was Mooch's padded foot on the stairwell that had caused a shift in the space-time continuum, opening the portal between the two worlds, a place he liked to bask in the warm lotus light whilst he waited to catch rodents. It was an action Mooch soon regretted as he recognised the delighted shrieks of a toddler spinning, rolling and jumping through the pillowy, swirling passage of time as if it was the greatest bouncy castle ride in the world ever.

Leia ran instinctively to her mother and Lily, guided by some primitive response, ran with her daughter clasped in her arms to the farthest reaches of the house and Rose, governed by the same unconscious, homing device, ran to Rich or at least the tousle-haired cyber-version of him, standing at the crossing place, the very edge of that world and this.

As for the real, earthy Rich Clarke standing alone at his laptop, front of shop, fingers sore from keeping them pressed on the forward key and shift arrow, hearing shouts and commotion, he had an almost out-of-body experience as he watched himself on screen kissing Rose Taylor.

It was a grand old-movie-style kiss. The hero pressing his mouth to the soft, yielding lips of the adoring heroine thrown back in his arms. He is a rescuer, protector – all-male to her all-feminine self – and she is accepting, running her hands through his hair in a grainy, none-too-clear corner of the screen and Rich starts to wonder when he'll get a piece of that action, when from Planet Universe there is an almighty white-hot flare of electric lightning and the screen fizzes, flashes and the picture in front of him dies.

All that remained were a few pieces of blue tape that had secured wires in place across Rose's white-painted floorboards and a draining board filled with washed-up cups. Out in the square, a single piece of yellow and black tape fluttered from iron railings in the breeze.

The streets were empty now. All of the police cars, dog vans, the unmarked cars and anonymous-looking transits were gone. The bobbies returned to their beat, relieved that because of the special nature of their case that none of the usual mountain of paperwork in triplicate would be required. Even the Chief's special crack team were gone with all their computers, scanning equipment, monitors and strange coded terms spoken into headsets. The remains of the smashed-up till had been cleared and Rose's flat looked like maybe there had been a party but order was now restored.

Rose sank into her favourite chair that for once did not have Mooch stretched out in it. After all the intrusions of earlier, he had rooted himself to the spot at the foot of the bed with a look that threatened murder if moved.

Rose was exhausted. She was starving. She had already started scanning down the brochure to her favourite takeaway, but her mind kept wandering from shredded pork and squid.

It all felt so unreal, like a Bobby Ewing stepping from the shower moment. So many things had happened.

Carl won around, hers for the taking, until Rose realised that he was the booby prize. India Mannerley dropping large hints that opened Rose's mind to small possibilities and then the face-off with Isabelle. No longer seeming like a glamorous siren; not now that Rose knew the real meaning of glamour: glamour isn't fashioning oneself into a centrefold fantasy of what you think men want that includes the strange biscuity odour of self-tan and the fashion sense of a pole dancer.

She wondered if the police would ever find Matt's assailant but pushed any thought of her missing takings from her mind. She wouldn't starve, the takings were gone but Leia was home and a family restored in more ways than one; that was all that mattered. Leia was home with her parents now, where she would sleep the night in her absolute favourite place to be – 'in the middle' – tucked between them in the double bed for safety and when, eventually, they would let sleep take them, Lily and Matt would lock their arms over her and around each other tightly. Nothing sharpens the senses to gratitude than the threat of all the good things being taken away. Soon, they would discuss things, but not now. Lily would then find herself absolved of all guilt and they would step bravely into their future together.

Mimi had gone home too, after sinking to her knees and weeping into the hair of her favourite – only, but, nonetheless, adored granddaughter. From then on, Leia would be allowed all sorts of liberties that Mimi would never have allowed her daughters. Unexpected liberties – such as ice cream for breakfast and sleepovers where face washes are not allowed.

Mimi had been escorted home by the Chief, who said in a loud voice that he would not be fulfilling his obligations if he did not ensure that Mrs Taylor was safely in her home. They shared a night cap. The Chief's driver glimpsed, through the curtains, a backgammon board and two cut-glass tumblers, four fingers-full of amber-coloured liquid, and his boss did not emerge until morning, minus his tie and unshaven and looking like he hadn't slept a wink.

Rose thought then of all the thousands of Planet Universe players who would be unable to trade gemstones and solve their quests this evening as servers had blown with the mysterious electrical power surges that were already being blamed on a 'virus', and she marvelled at a community of folk who didn't speak the same languages or walk the same streets but who came together to help when a distress call was given. Then another thought vied for attention – had the corpses in the dairy been thoroughly defrocked and deflared? And then she wondered how that, undoing Minerva's mischief, would look as a job on a to-do list.

The goddess's fury, Rose had learned, had nothing to do with Leia being returned to her mother. It had everything to do with the Chief – Chief Brown, as they now knew his name to be. Hell hath no fury like a woman scorned and when it comes to a goddess . . . treble it.

'Mr' Brown had not exactly been just a bookseller, he told them. The shop had been a 'front' to paranormal investigations that had identified Bath as the epicentre. And after using EMF and ion detection, Geiger counters and Tri-field meters – two empty shops were identified as sources of unexplained activity. It was the seventies, the Force and the Military had good budgets for such investigations and two young rookies – one from the dockland ganglands and the other from a rural force – had been put into place, studying mythology by day and using practical magic by night, following up any Missing Persons where the story didn't quite add up or unexplained sights or sounds.

And what a team he and Cynthia had been. No one had ever guessed that Birdcage Antiques and Brown's Books of Antiquities had been a front to an internationally funded investigation. But they had paved the way for this lot now with all their mouthpieces, flashy computers and bugging the room with microchips the size of pinheads. Groundbreaking things they discovered then. Stuff that looks like child's play now or at least like an episode from *Most Haunted*. Days when ICT meant a walkie-talkie the size of a dachsund and you could tune it to a pirate radio station on your days off. *Sapphire and Steel,* the team nicknamed them. A name based on a dodgy British sci-fi TV series starring Joanna Lumley, but it had more in common with what they did than they could ever let on.

But he made mistakes – well, one big mistake. He, as Cynthia had hinted, got carried away by it all or, to be correct, swept away and bowled over by the goddess. There were nocturnal visits to the cellar which had nothing to do with the moon rising . . .

But the Chief had breached a basic rule of policing – Don't Get Involved – and he had. He'd gone and well and truly overstepped the mark and, he added, as if to explain the thinning thatch and the paunch straining at his shirt buttons, he had been a looker then. 'Wasn't I, Cynny?' he asked for reassurance. 'Oh yes,' she'd replied with an inscrutable twinkle in her eye. 'We were all a bit in love with you then.'

So 'madness' was the reason given for Mr Brown's sudden removal from his post and a transfer to HQ with one proviso – he would never seek goddess contact again – and he kept his word. Cynthia had stayed, watching, monitoring and continuing the good work and the powers that be knew that things were safe whilst she still kept her hand in with a bit of moon magic.

But he hadn't been the only one breaking rules.

From time immemorial the rule has been in place that gods should not dally with mortals and when you have an entourage bigger than Puff Daddy's, not all of them can be trusted. So a nymph of a lower order had ratted and the goddess and her loyal friends had been cast from the mythological world for ever.

No wonder she was angry. Risking all for the man she loved, a so-called mate doing the dirty and he couldn't even be bothered to call and say he was sorry. The goddess might have shown up in Rose's cellar still pretending she held her term of office but all the privileges that went with that role had long since been removed, shamefully stripped away.

The goddess was doomed to wander the universe trying to find a place she could call home and Planet Universe was the closest she'd got. It hadn't just been a wormhole, it had been her bolt-hole. Little wonder she walked the knife edge between bountiful goddess and bunny-boiler. She'd lost her home and her job – a top job all for a faithless man. It was the mythological equivalent of being crowned Miss World only to have the sash ripped off and the orb removed because some ex-boyfriend has allowed a blurry topless photo to do the rounds.

The Chief – being a coward and typical when it comes to confrontation of the romantic kind – hadn't wanted to face the raging goddess in the cellar. Not at first. Not until total worldwide server meltdown was threatened and infection of the global network. For him it had all been so long ago, but for the immortal goddess, it seemed like yesterday. All that pain still raw. All that love unrequited.

That was until she saw him. Thankfully the goddess was nothing if not shallow and the sight of the only man who had failed to fall hook, line and sinker for her charms as a grey, balding man in his sixties, the man who had once looked like John Travolta, now looked, to the goddess, frankly speaking . . . revolting.

She had laughed till she'd cried. Lucky for him that goddesses have a twisted sense of humour. He was off the hook – well, not quite. She needed a home, a base. All this travelling was wearing her down – and a job, the Devil making work for idle hands and all that. Luckily the Chief could pull a few strings, could talk to people in the know. He owed her one. He owed her this much at least and a deal was struck.

The door bell rang. Oh God, what now? Rose thought. What is it? Then she remembered that's exactly what her father would yell every time the telephone rang. Lily might have feared turning into Mimi but Rose was definitely turning into her father – complete with moustache. She looked down into the square and saw Rich, weighed down with food-filled carrier bags, waving up at her.

Rich, not quite a knight in shining armour, but near as dammit if an elvish warrior with a white stallion counted. Rich, who had praised her, said he couldn't have saved Leia had it not been for Rose's quick thinking to change into her glamorous dress. Glamorous – that's what he called her as well as his rock, his support, his partner. Rich who loved her art work. Rich who admired her shop and had forgiven her for vomiting on his shoes. Rich who had introduced her to his cousin not because India was famous but because he knew that she and Rose would become friends. Rich who had immediately gone home, downloaded and loved the music of *Pink Martini* on Rose's recommendation. Rich who had once had hair like Kurt Cobain, but now wanted to look like the Modfather. Rich. The computer nerd. The geek.

Funny how you can snog a virtual-man in gauntlets and pirate boots and it can be all you've ever wanted and more. Rose wondered now what it would be like to kiss the real thing. The flesh and blood of this man and not his avatar. She'd soon find out. She threw down the keys and he let himself in.

There is a vintage clothes shop, in Bath, in the old part of the town, that provides more, much more, than just good service and an extensive collection of timeless, quality pieces from every decade of the last century – Biba or the odd Pucci – Ladies Pride, Byroter or Gunne Sax.

There's something for everyone, for all pockets. From the student-loved Bargain Barrels to the collection of couture handbags in glass display cases. It sells men's clothes too. Sixties zip-front polo shirts, seventies shirts with prints of sailboats or geese in migration formation. The owner had to bow to popular demand after a mancunian web-designer started a Facebook group of 1,356 friends wanting 'equal rights for men in Vintage Magic'. So Rose started a rail of 'casual' to keep John happy. As it was, she kind of owed him.

But for every woman (or man who likes to dress like one) there is a warm welcome whether they're looking for authentic seamed stockings or an outlandish Dolly Parton-inspired sequined denim number to wear for a fancy dress. Vintage lovers can find the very things they've been looking for – an embroidered peasant dress, a suede fringed jacket. They can find their heart's desire.

Because Vintage Magic does provide that little something extra. Not 'something for the weekend', that old-time barber shops would enquire of their gentlemen clients. Not the 'little extras' of certain 'health clubs' that are open through the night. But certainly something unexpected.

You see, there is life in the old clothes yet and is it that the buyer chooses the item or the hippy belt of jingly gold coins chooses them? And chooses them for a reason?

How else can the two births (one still impending – Leia's little brother Luke), several break-ups, numerous one-night stands, the gross of Mr Rights and the glut of Mr Wrongs (Mimi: 'but it was fun while it lasted,' she says about the Chief), the Oscars nominated (Best Actress: India Mannerley) and the winner of the Heroes of Country Fancy Dress be explained?

And what about the marriages? Even Rose Taylor was not immune from that one. Rich asked, she said yes, he moved his *Star Wars* Lego men into the bedroom and they never looked back. The wedding happened on a snowy January day on a boat on the frozen River Avon. The bride wore floor-length vintage velvet. It was nothing like she'd spent her life imagining her wedding would be at all. And she didn't mind one bit. Not even when the Hands Solo Design team formed an arch of light sabres as they took to the shore. Nerds. If you can't beat 'em, join 'em.

Some say that Vintage Magic was built on the crossing place of ley lines – hence the happy atmosphere and unique aura that seems to be attached to the shop, to every item of its stock and to every customer who leaves with their desired purchase. Hence the peculiar happenings. Others claim that the whole row of wonky timbered buildings is built on the lesser known, original source of the sacred spring and that all three shops are a little other-worldly. You only have to see the owners to know that. It's said that it was a conspiracy by the druids to con the Romans to build the site of their ostentatious 'day spa' on a diversion and the real place of worship has been kept hidden for thousands of years.

But these are just rumours and it's not wise to believe everything that's written, especially if the source of the material is the blog of someone who goes by the moniker of Astro-God-Nature-Boy-Lord-of-Wode, because they could be just ramblings of the deluded. It could be nothing out of the ordinary. Merely random occurences. Coincidence. Or an excommunicated Goddess finally finding a home in a swirling vortex in the basement. You never know.

But don't just believe the rumours. As the saying goes, 'Try before you buy', especially with the unpredictable sizes of vintage. There are changing rooms that are really worth a visit; roomy ones with pictures of cheesecake pin-up girls and kind lighting and suitably placed silver-freckled mirrors. And they have doors; partly to keep out an inquisitive cat (cat? Isn't that big thing a panther?), but also so that there is no claustrophobic tussle behind a curtain that could fly open and expose a bare arse or tatty pants in all their glory.

And it's in the changing room (and not the bedroom as MTV *Cribs* would have it) that the magic really happens. Because sometimes – just sometimes – a visitor to Vintage Magic, having disappeared to test out and try on a coat-hangered selection of Vintage Magic's Finest, reports a funny fleeting sensation, an impression so transient that they think it must have been their imagination (or the lunchtime snifter of a happy-hour cocktail or two).

A brief vision of a nightingale's song in Berkeley Square and arms linked with a pencil-moustached handsome officer. Or so Rose Taylor has been told. Or of being the belle of the hunt ball in a diaphanous bias-cut creation and a Marcel wave. Or of underground clubs and Waterloo Sunsets, sweat running down the walls, locomoting in a dolly dress, white tights and razor-sharp bob. Or of being Queen to a King of the Wild Frontier, face in eighties war paint, hair in plaits, feathers and ribbons.

A flight of fancy? They were tired, over-thinking or was it wishful thinking? Some share what they saw, felt, smelled, heard or tasted. They say it aloud, shake their heads in disbelief, and shake off the experience. Others might say nothing at all but Rose Taylor knows the look. The slightly dazed stumbling from the changing area, the scratching of the head, holding out the garment in question to be wrapped and bagged, barely saying a word. Because whether or not they tell, they usually buy. And they always come back.

Look into their eyes when Rose's customers are at their glorious vintage best. Sure, they are in the room, dancing, drinking and laughing along with everyone else, but somewhere a part of them is shaking that sequinned boob tube in Studio 54. Or listening to jazz in a smoky speakeasy, wearing that drop-waisted, sequinned tabard-style dress. Or taking off the rest of those Indian-cotton clothes at Woodstock. It's not just a fantasy life because they can see it in their mind, and every fibre of their being feels it and acts as though it is real.

Because in vintage, something indefinable happens. Something of the history, of places seen, of loves won and lost, seeps into the wearer's DNA. Something from the very stitching that holds the garment together infects them with a memory, a feeling, almost a déjà vu of the life it once led, of times had by those who wore it before. It connects the woman within to the woman from the past and even if they can't explain it, this is what vintage fans know. That classic old clothes are quality, a real find, something superior that simply cannot be matched by a new buy. That finding the right one, the very piece that you have been looking for, can change a life, shift a personality, cast a spell, create a feminine glamour, an allure to captivate, charm or seduce. It can make every woman feel like a goddess and this is Vintage Magic.

You can buy any of these other
Little Black Dress titles from your
bookshop or *direct from the publisher*.

FREE P&P AND UK DELIVERY
(Overseas and Ireland £3.50 per book)

TO ORDER SIMPLY CALL THIS NUMBER

01235 400 414

or visit our website: www.headline.co.uk

Prices and availability subject to change without notice.